She Loves Me, She Loves Me Not

Selected Titles by Lesléa Newman

Fiction

Every Woman's Dream
Good Enough to Eat
In Every Laugh a Tear
Just Like a Woman (audiobook)
A Letter to Harvey Milk
Secrets
Girls Will Be Girls

Poetry

Signs of Love
Still Life with Buddy

Humor

The Little Butch Book
Out of the Closet and Nothing to Wear

Anthologies

The Femme Mystique
My Lover Is a Woman: Contemporary Lesbian Love Poems
Pillow Talk: Lesbian Stories Between the Covers (Volumes 1 and 2)

Children's Books

Heather Has Two Mommies
Saturday Is Pattyday
Too Far Away to Touch
Cats, Cats, Cats!
Dogs, Dogs, Dogs!

For a complete list of titles, visit www.lesleanewman.com.

She Loves Me, She Loves Me Not

ROMANTIC FICTION BY

LESLÉA NEWMAN

alyson books
los angeles | new york

MANUFACTURED IN THE UNITED STATES OF AMERICA.

THIS TRADE PAPERBACK ORIGINAL IS PUBLISHED BY ALYSON PUBLICATIONS,
P.O. BOX 4371, LOS ANGELES, CALIFORNIA 90078-4371.
DISTRIBUTION IN THE UNITED KINGDOM BY
TURNAROUND PUBLISHER SERVICES LTD.,
UNIT 3, OLYMPIA TRADING ESTATE, COBURG ROAD, WOOD GREEN,
LONDON N22 6TZ ENGLAND.

FIRST EDITION: APRIL 2002

03 04 05 06 a 10 9 8 7 6 5 4 3 2

ISBN 1-55583-701-8

CREDITS

- "SHOW OFF," © 1998 BY LESLÉA NEWMAN, FIRST APPEARED AS "SHOWTIME" IN *PILLOW TALK: LESBIAN STORIES BETWEEN THE COVERS*, EDITED BY LESLÉA NEWMAN (ALYSON PUBLICATIONS, 1998).
- "A STONE'S THROW," © 2001 BY LESLÉA NEWMAN, FIRST APPEARED IN *SET IN STONE*, EDITED BY ANGELA BROWN (ALYSON PUBLICATIONS, 2001).
- "JUST LIKE A WOMAN" AND "KEEPING A BREAST," © 2001 BY LESLÉA NEWMAN. FIRST APPEARED ON THE AUDIOBOOK *JUST LIKE A WOMAN*, BY LESLÉA NEWMAN (FLUID WORDS, 2001).
- COVER DESIGN BY MATT SAMS.
- COVER PHOTOGRAPHY BY PHOTODISC.

for Mary Vazquez

she loves me

Acknowledgments

I am extremely grateful to:

The Money for Women/Barbara Deming Memorial Fund, Inc. for their generous support,

Angela Brown, Greg Constante, Scott Brassart, and Dan Cullinane, who make working with Alyson Publications an enormous pleasure,

my amazing agent, Elizabeth Harding of Curtis Brown, Ltd.,

Susan Kol Goodstein, for answering my endless medical questions,

Van Farrier, for lending me his two-ton nursing books,

Annakir, Annie, Babs, Cory, J. Yo, and Patio, the wise and witty women of my writer's group,

Tzivia Gover, who is absolutely the *best* best friend a girl could ever hope for,

and Mary Vazquez, for giving me the honor and privilege of being her unlawfully wedded wife.

Contents

Stranger Than Fiction

L.B. runs into the house breathlessly, her wavy red hair flying every which way as she flings her books, papers, scarf, and hat across the kitchen table. Harriet looks up over the top of her black-framed reading glasses with a bemused smile. *I married a hurricane,* she thinks, not for the first time.

"I had the most *amazing* class," L.B. pants, still all in motion. She yanks open the refrigerator door, pulls and pushes things around until she finds what she's looking for—the orange-peach-pineapple juice marked with her initials so Harriet won't gripe when she drinks straight out of the carton. Which she does right now.

"Your fiction workshop?" Harriet asks, putting down her crossword puzzle.

"No, my advanced journalism class? God, I *love* my professor. She is so smart and so *cool.*" When L.B. gets excited she talks like the undergrad she was not so long ago, all question marks and italics. Harriet is sometimes charmed by this and sometimes annoyed, depending on her mood. "She was teaching us about interviewing? And she said a teacher of *hers* once said that you know your subjects are really speaking from the heart when they stop talking in complete sentences? *And,*" L.B. interrupts herself to swipe the back of her mouth with her sleeve, "she told us two questions that are guaranteed to make that happen."

"And those two questions are?" Harriet asks.

"Thank you for coming in for your interview today, Ms. Jacobs." L.B. sits at the table, takes Harriet's hand, and kisses the inside of her palm. Then she picks up the pen Harriet has just put down—Harriet always does the crossword in purple ink to give her confidence—and speaks into it as though it were a microphone.

"The first question is—wait a minute, you don't mind if I tape this, do you?" L.B. pretends the cordless phone lying on the table is a tape recorder and mimics switching it on. "Testing, testing. All right. You have to tell the person you're interviewing that you're taping them and record their consent for your own protection."

"I know," Harriet says. L.B. has told her this before.

"So is it OK to tape you?"

"Yes, yes, tape away." Harriet plays along, waving at the phone.

"So," L.B. continues speaking into the pen, "the first question is, 'Can you please tell me what you know about the circumstances of your birth?' "

"My birth?" Harriet raises an eyebrow.

"Yes, your birth. You were there, weren't you?"

"Of course I was there." Harriet leans back in her chair, pulls off her glasses and shuts her eyes as if she could see the scene that occurred 50 years ago. "It was August 17th—you know that. My mother was cranky because I was late."

"As usual," L.B. points out.

"As usual," Harriet agrees. "One of my many bad habits that started in the womb. Anyway, it was hotter than hell that summer, one of the hottest Augusts on record according to my mother, and living in a fifth-floor Manhattan walk-up probably didn't help. I'm sure the window fans my parents had did nothing but blow the hot air around." Harriet waves her hand in front of her face as though it were August instead of December. "So there she was," she continues, "bigger than a barn with this baby who refused to come out. On top of that, she had my two-year-old brother to take care of. And my father, who never lifted a finger around the house—but that's another story."

"Go on." L.B. tilts her head and gazes at Harriet with those big emerald eyes that still startle Harriet with their stunning color and splendor.

"So," Harriet clears her throat, coming back to herself, "since I was obviously in no hurry to make my grand entrance, they decided to do a cesarean. And it's a good thing they did, because when they slit my mother open," Harriet pulls her fist across her midsection in an exaggerated motion, "there I was with the umbilical cord wrapped around my neck." Harriet's right hand flies up to her throat, and she gasps and bulges out her eyes, replaying the scene. "As a child, I never could stand to have anything pulled over my head. To this day, I can't wear a turtleneck. I can't even stand to wear a necklace or a scarf, though I probably should do something to cover up this turkey wattle I've got going here." Harriet's hand strokes the underside of her chin, which is only slightly less taut than it used to be.

L.B. frowns. "Harriet, you do not have a turkey wattle."

"You're too kind, my love." Harriet smiles in spite of herself and tries to think of more dramatic elements to add to the story. "When my mother saw I was a girl, she cried. She said it was because she was so happy, she always wanted a girl, but I think it was because she knew how much heartache I would cause her. Which I guess I did." Harriet lifts her shoulders in an "oh, well" shrug. "Oh, and—I almost forgot this part: When I was born I had long black hair that all the nurses took turns combing—they said they'd never seen so much hair—so thick and dark and long—on a newborn before. I left the hospital with a ponytail—or maybe two pigtails—no, a ponytail I think, anyway what difference does it make? The point is they gave me a poufy little hairdo and put ribbons—and not just any ribbons—pink ribbons, pink *satin* ribbons—in my hair, can you imagine? You know how I feel about pink. I looked like one of those, you know, those stupid whaddyacallits you win at the fair, you know—those stupid, goddamn kewpie dolls."

"Aha!" L.B. sticks one finger straight up in the air.

"Aha what?"

"Right there at the end you started speaking in incomplete sentences. Just like my professor said you would when you felt passionately about what you were saying."

"Of course I feel passionately about someone tying pink satin ribbons in my hair." Harriet is indignant. L.B. knows she'd rather stick needles in her eyes than ribbons of any color in her short-cropped hair, which over the years has turned from black to salt-and-pepper to a handsome silvery gray. "From the day I was born, people were trying to make me into someone I had no interest in being." Harriet lets out a disgruntled sigh. "So, Ms. Reporter, what's your second question?"

"My second question, Ms. Jacobs, is, 'Have you ever had a near-death experience?'"

"Yes, on the day I was born."

"On the day you were born?" L.B. stares at Harriet blankly.

"Remember? The umbilical cord?" Harriet repeats her choking act.

"Oh, right. That's interesting, don't you think? Both experiences on the same day?" L.B. pretends to write something down, then looks up at Harriet. "OK," she says brightly. "Your turn."

"My turn for what?" Harriet asks.

"Your turn to interview me. Here, take the microphone." L.B. holds out the pen. "Ask me about the circumstances of my birth."

"I don't have to, darling." Harriet takes the pen out of L.B.'s fingers and grasps her lover's freckled hand with both her own. "Didn't your mother ever tell you?" she asks softly. "I was there."

❀

"Harriet, put your hand here. No, lower. And press harder. Even harder. Yeah, yeah, that's it."

Harriet exhaled deeply and licked her upper lip, which was salty with sweat. She hoped Celia didn't know how badly she was shaking inside. Harriet had waited so long—her whole lifetime maybe—to hear Celia say those very words. She'd dreamed about touching her, skin-to-skin, for more nights than she dared to admit, not to mention the hours she spent wide awake, fantasizing about what it would be like to put her hands all over Celia's soft, freckled flesh. And now the moment had finally come, but not in the way Harriet had ever expected.

"Can you feel it? Wait a second." Celia pushed a few strands of coppery red hair behind her ears and shifted her massive weight around on the worn, plaid couch before putting her hand on top of Harriet's and pressing her palm even farther into her hard, round belly. "There! He just kicked. Did you feel that?"

"You're supposed to say 'he or she,' remember?" Harriet reminded Celia what they'd learned in the consciousness-raising group they attended in Cambridge once a week.

"Oh, right. He or she. So did you feel him—I mean him or her, or it—kick?"

Harriet pressed her hand into Celia's belly again. "Wow." She looked up at Celia, who was grinning madly, already proud of her genius of an offspring. "You've got a soccer player growing in there."

Celia laughed. "Do I ever! Or maybe he or she's just inherited my big, ugly feet. Which I used to be able to see." Celia spread her bare toes wide and tried to catch sight of them over her bulging stomach, but it was an impossible task.

"They're not ugly," Harriet said for the millionth time. She didn't understand what the big deal was with Celia's feet. Sure, they weren't the prettiest things in the world—whose were?—but they weren't uglier than most people's. True, they were flat as tires with all the air let out and she had practically no nail on the littlest toes, but so what? Who noticed feet anyway? And besides, weren't they supposed to love and accept all parts of their bodies unconditionally and not buy into the patriarchy's impossible standard of beauty, since less than two percent of the population looked like that anyway? At least that's what the leader of their consciousness-raising group had told them. Easy for her to say, Harriet often thought, since the tall, thin woman looked like a fashion model and fit into that two percent herself.

"They're probably uglier than ever, all swollen up from being pregnant." Celia curled her bottom lip under and made a face. "Thanks a lot, babycakes." She cupped both hands together in front of her mouth and bent her head, directing her words to the child she had growing inside.

"Let me massage them," Harriet said, sliding off the couch onto the shag carpet and pulling one of Celia's feet into her lap.

"Heaven." Celia leaned her head back and shut her eyes.

"We're supposed to do one nice thing every day for the part of our bodies we hate the most," Harriet said, reciting the homework from their group. The group leader was trying to get them to love and accept every part of themselves unconditionally. Especially Celia, who seemed to be her pet project. "How are you going to love the little boy or girl growing inside you if you can't love yourself?" the leader asked her over and over.

"Ummm." Celia relaxed into Harriet's hands as they kneaded the flesh between her heel and her instep. Harriet tried not to let Celia's moan of pleasure go straight to her groin, but it did anyway. She closed her eyes, resisting the urge to pick up Celia's foot and kiss the sweet center of her fallen arch. Harriet had recently realized that she was in love with Celia and probably had been ever since the day they first met. And she didn't know what in the world she was going to do about it. Telling the women in her C.R. group that the part of her body she hated the most was the fourteen coarse hairs that grew around her right nipple was a piece of cake compared to admitting that she was in love with Celia.

They'd met a few years earlier, on a Sunday at the Laundromat. Celia was putting up a sign advertising for a roommate, and Harriet was scanning the bulletin board looking for a place to live. They'd gone out for coffee and found they had a lot in common: They were both recent graduates with useless liberal arts degrees, Harriet's in English lit and Celia's in theater; both of them worked jobs they considered temporary, while they tried to figure out what to do with the rest of their lives: Celia was waiting tables and Harriet was driving a taxi. Celia had just rented a two-bedroom apartment in Somerville and needed someone to share the rent. They shook hands on the deal, and Harriet brought over her meager belongings that very afternoon.

Though they had a lot in common, there were differences too. Celia liked folk music—Joni Mitchell, Joan Baez, Buffy St. Marie—while Harriet preferred wilder women: Janis Joplin and Grace Slick. Celia decorated her room with Indian-print bedspreads and beaded curtains, while Harriet kept her room as sparse as a Buddhist's cell (in fact, she was deep into Jack Kerouac and all the Beat poets, though Celia thought they were a sorry, drunken lot). The biggest difference between them, however, was that Celia, though she was only twenty-two, was in a big rush to find Mr. Right, settle down, and have a family. Harriet was in no hurry to do the same. In fact, Harriet wasn't even sure she ever wanted to get married and have a baby.

"It's the seventies, Celia," Harriet said one night when they were baking a batch of chocolate chip cookies, having enjoyed a little "herbal refreshment" after dinner. Harriet perched herself on the kitchen counter, banging her bare feet against the cabinets while she wove her long black hair into an uneven braid and tried not to stare too hard at Celia's denim-covered behind as she bent over to open the oven. Even if she weren't stoned out of her mind, it would still have been the most delicious-looking thing she'd ever seen. "Women have a lot more options now." Harriet tried to concentrate on what she was saying. "We don't have to get married and have children. We can do anything. Even run for president."

"But President Jacobs, what if some of us just want to stay home and take care of babies?" Celia shut the squeaky oven door and handed Harriet a rubber spatula covered with cookie dough to lick.

Harriet pondered this as she ran her tongue up and down the spatula, shutting her eyes and giving in to the sensual experience of sucking the sweet batter off the pliant rubber. She almost swooned as she felt Celia's hand on her arm.

"President Jacobs? I asked you a question. And are you finished with that?"

"Oh, yeah." Harriet slapped the now-spotless utensil into Celia's upturned hand and picked up a half-empty bag of bitter-sweet chocolate chips, which she poured directly into her mouth. "I suppose if taking care of babies is what you really want to do," she said, and it was obvious by her tone of voice—even with her mouth full—that she couldn't imagine choosing this option. "But Celia, why settle for a life like our mothers'? We don't have to be tied to some guy, picking his socks off the floor, cooking his meals, washing his clothes... We can do something meaningful with our lives."

"I think raising a child would be meaningful." Celia ran a finger around the rim of the mixing bowl to collect a clump of batter, which she scraped against her teeth. "And besides," she pulled her finger out of her mouth with a loud, wet smack, "my husband is going to do fifty percent of the housework. At least."

Yeah, right, Harriet thought. Most of the guys Celia brought home—and there were many—wouldn't know what to do with a broom or mop if they tripped over one. Especially the last guy, whom Celia really seemed to be gaga over. Until Harriet told her that after he and Celia had made love (she'd heard them through the paper-thin walls) and Celia had fallen asleep, her date had come into Harriet's bedroom and asked her if *she* wanted some. And the way he'd said it, it was clear he thought he was doing Harriet an enormous favor.

"Get the hell out of here," Harriet had hissed, and he did, much to her relief. She hadn't been scared; grossed out was more like it. But the worst part was, a few minutes after he'd left her room, Harriet could hear him and Celia going at it again. And it made Harriet crazy to know that some jerk who clearly didn't give a flying fuck about Celia got to put his hands all over her, while Harriet, who would lay down her life for the woman, had to lie in bed all alone so close, yet so far away.

The next morning after Celia kissed her beau goodbye, she came into the kitchen, where Harriet was making a breakfast of scrambled tofu and whole-wheat toast. "Can I have some?" Celia asked, her green eyes wide and dreamy. "I'm starving." Celia stretched her arms lazily overhead and let out a deep, contented sigh. "Oh, my God, what a night I had. You know, Harriet, he could really be *the one.* I know you think I'm like the boy who cried wolf, but seriously, this one's really different than all the others. He's—"

"Celia..." Harriet hated to burst her bubble, but knew she had to. "He came into my room last night."

"What? What do you mean?" Celia asked and Harriet told her. And though Celia never saw him again, it turned out he was *the one* all right—the one who had fathered her child. Not that she ever saw him again. As soon as Celia told him over the phone that he was going to be a papa, Mr. Wonderful was history.

"Don't worry, Celia," Harriet said one morning after Celia had thrown up for the third time. "I'll take care of you." Harriet liked playing nursemaid to Celia, holding a cold washcloth to her forehead when she didn't feel well, accompanying her to the doctor's office, making sure she ate healthy meals and didn't lift heavy things. And Celia seemed to have had enough of men for the moment. She was done with cruising the bars and picking up guys for one-night stands she always hoped would last longer. She had to be responsible. She was going to be a mother, for God's sake. She even let Harriet drag her off to her women's liberation group, though that was more Harriet's thing than hers. But as she often told Harriet, Celia hated being alone in the evenings, when she felt scared and overwhelmed by what was happening inside her body. And the group did turn out to be pretty interesting. They adopted her, in their own way, buying her bottles of organic prenatal vitamins, loaning her books about natural childbirth, and offering to go to the doctor with her when Harriet had to work. Since Celia's parents were staunch Catholics, mortified that their only daughter was having a child out of wedlock, they offered no help at all. The women in the group were Celia's family now.

After the group had run its ten-week course, the women met one last time to throw Celia a surprise baby shower. Celia laughed with delight over all her presents: tiny T-shirts and booties in every color of the rainbow except blue and pink; a nonsexist toy chest that included both dolls and trucks; and storybooks that defied stereotypes: *William's Doll* by Charlotte Zolotow and *Girls Can Be Anything* by Norma Klein.

"You guys," Celia beamed at her friends, and for once their facilitator didn't go on a diatribe about the use of the word "guys" to describe a group of women. "If it's a girl, I'm naming her Libby, for women's liberation."

"Hear, hear!"

"And if it's a boy, she's naming him Liberace," Harriet joked and everybody laughed.

Two weeks later Celia went into labor. Harriet had gone to the store to get them a late-night snack: hot-fudge sundaes from the ice cream shop around the corner. "And don't forget, I want marshmallow topping *and* whipped cream on mine," Celia reminded Harriet, who thought that combination was totally disgusting. She chalked it up to the strange cravings expectant mothers were supposed to have, and did as she was told.

"I'm back with the goods," Harriet called as she let herself into the apartment. Celia, who had been sprawled on the couch when Harriet left, didn't reply. "I'll be right there," Harriet called again, heading into the kitchen for two big spoons. Utensils in hand, she brought their booty into the living room. "Here you go." Harriet held out the treat, but Celia hardly moved.

"Harriet," her voice was barely a whisper, "I think it's time."

"Time?" Harriet put Celia's ice cream down on the old camping trunk they used as a coffee table, pried open the lid of her own container, and dug in.

"Harriet, I think I'm in labor."

"Oh, my God." Harriet dropped her spoon. "OK, OK, don't panic. Everything's under control. Did your water break? Are you having contractions?"

"I…ooh…" Celia doubled over and clutched her belly.

"I'll take that as a yes. OK, OK, don't panic," Harriet said again.

"I think you're the one who's panicking." Celia sat up slowly as the contraction subsided. "Just call a taxi and get my suitcase, OK?"

"OK, OK. Taxi, suitcase, taxi, suitcase."

"Harriet, relax. You're a total wreck."

"Of course I'm a wreck. You're having a baby."

Harriet completed her tasks and helped Celia get to her feet. They walked down the hallway and waited outside until the taxi came. Celia remained strangely calm.

"Aren't you nervous?" Harriet paced up and down, pausing to lift one hand over her eyes as she scanned the street. "Where the hell's that goddamn taxi? I knew I should have taken my cab home so I could drive you myself."

"It'll get here," Celia said, and just as the words left her mouth, it did.

When they arrived at the hospital, Celia and Harriet were whisked into the softly lit birthing room. Celia's midwife arrived, and Harriet took her place at Celia's head, coaching her to breathe as they had practiced during their Lamaze class. Celia clutched Harriet's hand and panted rapidly. It was a fast labor and an easy delivery; Celia had often joked about her "child-bearing hips" and how she was built for breeding. The midwife caught the baby and laid the brand-new infant on top of Celia's stomach.

"Hello, you precious, perfect gift from God, my child who I love more than anyone else in the world." Celia whispered the words she had practiced over and over, wanting the first sentence her baby heard to be full of nothing but love. *Whom,* Harriet grimaced, having corrected Celia a dozen times to no avail. "You don't want to start the kid off illiterate," she'd said, bad grammar being one of her obsessions. But it would be cruel to point that out now to Celia, who looked exhausted but exhilarated as she stared at her bundle of joy.

"Look at that tiny tuft of red hair," Harriet marveled. "And all those freckles."

"Isn't he or she beautiful?" Celia whispered.

"Oh, my God, we haven't even looked," Harriet said, and Celia gently turned the baby.

"It's a girl," she said. "Oh, my precious, precious girl. My sweet daughter. My Libby," Celia crooned as tears rolled down her cheeks. "Oh, Harriet, I'm so happy. This is so perfect." She let out a little sigh. "Except…except…"

"Except what?" Harriet asked, not taking her eyes from Libby.

"Except," Celia sniffed, "I just wish my mother was here."

"Your mother?" Harriet was astonished. "After all the awful things she said about you getting pregnant and having a baby without being married?" Harriet couldn't bear to utter the word "illegitimate," the term Celia's mother had used, in front of Libby.

"I know." Celia wiped at her eyes with the back of her hand. "But you'll see when you're a mother." Celia drew Libby close. "Whatever you do, Libby, you can always come to Mama and tell me all about it. Whatever it is. I'll always be here for you, sweetheart. No matter what. Always."

"Me too," Harriet whispered, though she didn't know whether she was talking to Libby or Celia. Or both.

And they were a family, in an odd sort of way. Celia took care of the shopping, cooking, and cleaning, and Harriet doubled up on her taxi shifts so she could support them both. Celia had no interest in going back to work, as she was adamant about not putting Libby in day care.

"But you worked in a day care center," Harriet pointed out one day when she came home early in the morning exhausted from driving most of the night.

"I know, that's why I'll never put Libby in one," Celia said, dipping a tiny spoon into a jar of organic baby food. "Children should be with their mothers the first few years of their lives. I mean, I saw some of those kids take their first steps, Harriet. That shouldn't have been me, that should have been their mothers. You want some more carrots, honey?" She turned her attention back to Libby, who was opening and closing her hands rapidly like she always did when she got excited. The first time Harriet had seen her do that, she laughed. "Wow, how does she move her hands so fast?" she'd wondered aloud. "What'd you put in the kid's bottle, speed?" Celia had laughed too and told Harriet she called it "Libby's hands of delight."

"Of course, we never told any of the parents that we saw their kid's first step," Celia went on. "We were instructed to say, 'She *almost* walked today, Mrs. Parker. You'd better keep a close eye on her. It could be any minute now.' I mean, I would just *die* if I missed Libby's first step."

"But, Celia..." Harriet couldn't bring herself to say what was on her mind. Some mothers *had* to work. As Celia would have to if she didn't have Harriet's help. Harriet supposed Celia could live on welfare and food stamps, but she would never let that happen. And didn't Harriet have what she wanted? For the most part, yes. But the part that was missing—the part about Harriet being in love with Celia but still afraid to say so—was getting to be more and more of a problem. Harriet knew she needed to tell Celia, but she just couldn't push out the words. And besides, Celia was changing. First it was not believing in day care, and then it was deciding to go to church. Harriet had been shocked to see Celia and Libby in matching flowered dresses early one Sunday morning.

"Where are you going?" Harriet had asked, stumbling into the kitchen in an oversize tie-dyed T-shirt, her hair held back with a rubber band she'd pulled off the rolled-up newspaper on the front porch. "I was going to make whole-wheat waffles."

"We're going to church," Celia said, straightening one of Libby's sleeves.

"You're going where?" Harriet wasn't sure if she was wide awake or dreaming.

"We're going to church," Celia repeated. "I want Libby to grow up with some kind of spiritual background."

"Not *Catholic* church?" Harriet groaned, but she was afraid she knew the answer.

"See you later," Celia called, and she and Libby were out the door.

It just got worse and worse. Soon Libby's wardrobe consisted solely of pink outfits, and the toy trucks and airplanes Celia had gotten at the baby shower vanished into thin air. And then, to top it all off, Celia started dating an older man she had met at Mass one Sunday, a man whom Harriet disliked on sight.

"I'm here to pick up my girls," he said the first time he came over and Harriet answered the bell.

"First of all, they're not yours," Harriet said, her arms folded like a sentry guarding her castle. "And second of all, one of them is a girl and the other one is a woman."

"Is that Phil?" Celia called from the kitchen. "I'll be right there." And when Celia caught sight of Phil, a light shone in her eyes that Harriet had never seen before. Even Libby's hands of delight started going a mile a minute when Phil smiled at her, much to Harriet's dismay.

"Phil, this is my roommate, Harriet."

"Charmed," Phil said, never taking his eyes from Celia and Libby.

"Can you hold her while I get my coat?" Celia asked.

"Of course," Harriet and Phil said at the same time. They both reached out, their hands colliding in midair. It would have been almost funny, Harriet thought bitterly, except of course it wasn't.

Celia started spending a lot of time with Phil, and Harriet saw less and less of her. She knew it was only a question of time before she lost Celia for good, but still she wasn't about to go down without a fight. And as far as Harriet could tell, they hadn't slept together yet. At least Phil had never stayed over at their apartment, and Celia hadn't stayed out all night. So there was still hope, as far as Harriet was concerned.

One night when Harriet was playing peekaboo with Libby in the living room, Celia came out of her bedroom in a new pink dress. Her shoes were the exact same color, and she clutched a matching pink purse as well. *You look like an overgrown Easter egg,* Harriet wanted to say. "Going somewhere special?" she asked.

"Phil's taking me to a fancy restaurant, and I think," Celia paused to study herself in the mirror over the fake fireplace and smooth a strand of hair, "I think he's going to propose."

"What?" Harriet had been staring at Celia, thinking, *Redheads really shouldn't wear pink*—she'd read that in a women's magazine years ago, and though she hated that this fashion tip was stuck in her long-term memory, she had to admit it was true. Celia, with her freckles and ironed-out hair that was sure to frizz by the end of the evening, looked awful. But Harriet wasn't going to be the one to tell her that. "Celia, you can't possibly be thinking of marrying Phil."

"Why not?" Celia, evidently satisfied with her appearance, turned from the mirror. "He treats me so well, Harriet. Not like all those other guys who only wanted to sleep with me. Phil doesn't believe in sleeping together before marriage."

"Since when did you become so old-fashioned?" Harriet covered her eyes then pulled her hands away and smiled at Libby. "Peekaboo! I see you." She wanted to cover her ears as well.

"And besides, Libby needs a father." At the sound of her name, Libby turned toward her mother and smiled.

"Why?" Harriet asked. "I can take care of you. Haven't I been doing a good job?"

"Oh, Harriet," Celia shook her head. "You've been great, but did you think this could last forever?"

Yes, Harriet thought.

"I mean, sooner or later we're both going to get married and you're going to have kids of your own..."

"Celia," Harriet's heart was beating in her throat like a small, trapped bird, "Celia, I love you."

"I love you too, Harriet," Celia said automatically. "Now, make sure you wind up Libby's mobile when you put her down. You know, the one that plays 'Jack and Jill.' She can't fall asleep without—"

"No, I mean I *love* you, Celia. I mean the way Phil does." There. She said it. Harriet looked down at her hands, and then, being a glutton for punishment, raised her head and stared with morbid fascination at Celia's face as her words registered. Shock, fear, disbelief, and finally what appeared to be disgust rearranged her features.

"That isn't funny, Harriet," she finally said.

"It wasn't meant to be," Harriet said quietly.

"You mean, you're like that woman, Orca?" Celia's voice rose in horror. Orca—whose name had been Cynthia until she came out and reinvented herself by shaving her head, letting her enormous breasts swing free, and tattooing a double women's symbol on her upper arm—had been in their consciousness-raising group.

"Well, not exactly," Harriet said, and then instantly felt awful for betraying a sister. "I mean, yes. Yes, I am like Orca. I'm a woman-loving woman too."

"Oh, my God." Before Celia could say anything else the doorbell rang. "I have to go." She glanced from Harriet to Libby and back again, and for a minute Harriet was afraid Celia wasn't going to leave her daughter with a baby-sitter who also happened to be a pervert. But Celia just said, "Be good," blew Libby a kiss, and was gone.

Harriet tried to stay up until Celia got home, but sleepiness got the better of her. When she stumbled into the kitchen the next morning, the diamond ring on Celia's finger woke her up with a start, like bright sunlight cutting into her eyes.

"Isn't it stunning?" Celia said, extending her hand. "We're moving in with Phil at the end of the month, Harriet. I can't wait to tell my mother."

Harriet blinked a few times, trying to absorb this information. Being not quite awake, it took her a minute to realize that "we" didn't mean her and Celia, it meant Libby and Celia. "Your mother?" Harriet asked.

"She's going to be so thrilled that I'm finally getting married and Libby is going to have a father." Celia spilled some Cheerios onto the tray attached to Libby's high chair. "Of course, she would have been a lot happier if I'd done things in the correct order, but that can't be helped now."

"I thought Phil didn't believe in sex before marriage," Harriet said, moving toward the coffeemaker in slow motion. Maybe if she didn't allow herself to fully wake up, she could convince herself this was a dream.

"Who said anything about sex?" Celia asked. "Phil just thinks—and I agree—that, that, umm…under these circumstances, it would be best if I moved in with him as soon as possible."

Under these circumstances… Harriet knew what that meant. But what was the point of saying anything?

There were only two weeks left in the month, and Harriet dragged herself through them. She hated being away from home, as she knew her time with Celia and Libby was drawing to a close, but she hated being in the apartment too. More often than not Phil was there making Harriet feel like a third wheel. A fourth wheel, really. Phil, Celia, and Libby made the perfect little family. And where did that leave Harriet? Nowhere.

On moving day, Celia let Harriet hold Libby as she and Phil

loaded the last of Celia's boxes into the van Phil had rented. "Aren't you going to give me your new address?" Harriet asked when it was time to say goodbye.

"Look, here's some cash to cover her share of the bills." Phil slapped a pile of money into Harriet's hand. She wanted to throw it at him, but the truth was she needed it too badly to make such a dramatic gesture.

"But how will I get in touch with you?" Harriet asked Celia, staring into Libby's clear green eyes.

"I'll call you," Celia said.

But of course she never did. She didn't even invite Harriet to the wedding. Not that Harriet would have gone. Once Celia and Libby were no longer part of her life, Harriet became a militant feminist lesbian and swore off anything to do with heterosexuality and the patriarchy. She made herself as unfeminine as possible by growing out the hair on her legs and under her arms, and cutting the hair on her head as short as possible. She started volunteering at a newly formed rape crisis center, joined a food collective, and moved into an all-lesbian household. Later Harriet grew less extreme; she grew out her buzz cut, put on a bra, and went back to school for the advanced degree she needed to open her own therapy practice (solely for women and girls, of course). She spent most Friday and Saturday nights in gay bars and over the years took many women home with her. Some stayed for a night and some stayed for a year or even longer, but ultimately Harriet found herself alone. She tried monogamy, non-monogamy, and serial monogamy, all of which worked for a while…until they didn't.

When she turned forty, Harriet decided to try two things she'd never tried before: sobriety and celibacy. It was time to do a little internal work, take some breathing space, fall in love with her new, middle-aged self. Harriet needed to find out who she was, where she was going, what she wanted. Somehow the time had flown and one day Harriet realized with a start that she'd been celibate for five years. Whoa. She looked into the mirror, stared long and hard into her deep-brown eyes, and uttered something she remembered her mother was always fond of saying: "Enough is enough." Harriet was ready to settle down, to be half of a couple, to have that part of her life settled once and for all. "Some smart, funny, sexy, fabulous woman is out there just waiting for you," she told her reflection. "And boy, is she lucky."

But where to find such a creature? It was the mid 1990s; no one went to the bars anymore. Harriet thought of all the advice her happily and not-so-happily married friends had given her over the years: take a class, read the personals, let us fix you up. And she thought of the advice she often gave her single clients: Just live your life fully. You'll meet someone when you least expect it. Above all, don't look desperate.

Harriet decided to take her own advice. She didn't really have time to take a class and couldn't very well answer a personal ad—what if it turned out to be one of her clients? And forget blind dates. The few she had gone on had all been disasters. Harriet had learned that someone could look awfully good on paper—be just the right height (ridiculous as it sounded, Harriet didn't want a girlfriend taller than she was), have the right interests, believe in the right causes—and still be an utter bore. Or worse, have no sense of humor. Or even worse, be lousy in bed.

One afternoon Harriet had a few hours to kill between clients and decided to while away the time in a café that had just opened up a few blocks from her office. The place was rather pretentious: dark and crowded with little round tables, each one occupied by someone nursing a cappuccino and trying to look as cool as possible, either by wearing sunglasses or by reading a book of poems by the likes of Allen Ginsberg, Sylvia Plath, or Ranier Maria Rilke.

The upstairs was standing-room only, so Harriet went down to the lower level and parked herself at a corner table. She switched on a little lamp, opened up a very uncool psychology journal, and promptly shut it in favor of looking around. *My shoes are probably older than half the kids in this joint,* she thought just as a server came to take her order.

"Coffee, tea, or me?" the young woman asked. Harriet chuckled as she looked up.

You, Harriet thought as she stared into the most incredible green eyes she had ever seen. Even in the semi-darkness, the woman took her breath away. She had wonderfully thick red hair and a million freckles that Harriet wanted to count with her tongue. But it wasn't just her features. There was a daring and an openness about her face that Harriet found enormously appealing.

"What's your name?" Harriet asked, startling herself.

The woman was unfazed by the question. "My friends call me L.B."

"And what do your lovers call you?" Harriet couldn't believe the words that were flying out of her mouth.

L.B. grinned. "Wouldn't you like to know?" she asked.

"Yes, I would. Very much." Harriet didn't know what had come over her.

L.B. wrote something down on her order pad and ripped off the top page. "Call me sometime," she said, handing Harriet her phone number.

Harriet resisted the urge to bring the scrap of paper up to her lips and kiss it. She felt dazed, drugged, in a time warp. "L.B.," she said, "I think I'm old enough to be your mother."

"Cool. I don't have a mother." L.B. looked over her shoulder. Customers were waiting. "So what'll you have?"

"An iced coffee, please."

"Coming right up." L.B. flounced off, and Harriet sat back

and enjoyed watching her in action for a good forty-five minutes. L.B. flitted from table to table, leaving, it seemed to Harriet, a string of admirers, both male and female, in her wake. Did L.B. give her phone number to anyone who asked? Was Harriet just one of many hopefuls?

At quarter to four, Harriet rose from her table. L.B. was immediately at her side. "On the house," she said as Harriet opened her wallet.

"Thanks."

"I have a thing for older women," L.B. said, moistening her lips with the tip of her tongue.

"I'll call you." Harriet could barely get the words out. She felt herself flush and prayed she wasn't having a hot flash.

"I'll be waiting." L.B. cleared Harriet's empty glass and used napkin with one sweep of her hand.

Harriet climbed the stairs and made her way to the front of the café, shaking her head in disbelief. She had never acted so outrageously in her life. She squeezed past a folksinger who sat near the door, wailing, his guitar case propped open with a sign that said IF YOU'RE AFRAID OF CHANGE, DROP IT IN HERE. Again Harriet chuckled, then tossed in a few coins. Wasn't she always telling her clients the only constant thing is change? And hadn't she sworn to herself she would take her own advice?

Before she could lose her nerve or talk some sense into herself, Harriet pulled her cell phone out of her shoulder bag and dialed L.B.'s number.

"Hey, you've reached the redhead. Lucky you. Leave your number and I'll call you back. *If* I feel like it."

"It's Harriet. From the café. The woman you treated to an iced coffee." Harriet felt all of twelve years old. "Listen, you are clearly someone I need to get to know. What are you doing tomorrow night?" Harriet left her number and shut off her phone. *I did it,* she thought, feeling more proud of herself than the deed warranted. Would L.B. call back? It was more important to Harriet than she cared to admit. She tried to tell herself it was just five years of horniness suddenly catching up to her, but she knew it was more than that. L.B. had gotten under her skin. Harriet hoped she was older than she looked, which was about twenty-five. It turned out she wasn't.

Over dinner at an Italian restaurant the following night, they exchanged life stories. L.B. had grown up in Pennsylvania but no longer had anything to do with what she called her "family of origin." She was taking some time off from school before going back for a master's degree in writing. "I'm majoring in life right now," she said as she tore a hunk of bread in half and used a piece to mop up a puddle of olive oil.

Harriet gave L.B. the nutshell version of her own life: her traditional, conservative, stifling childhood; how she had burst out of the closet in the seventies after college and became an ardent feminist; the political movements she'd been a part of; her recent success with becoming sober. L.B. listened intently and at some point in the evening started holding Harriet's hand. *I'm a goner,* Harriet thought, feeling her legs turn as mushy as the tiramisu she and L.B. were now sharing. It wasn't exactly robbing the cradle—L.B., it turned out, had been on the planet for a quarter of a century, but still she was a good twenty years Harriet's junior.

When it was clear which way the night was going, Harriet felt she had to ask. "Doesn't our age difference bother you?" She looked into her coffee cup rather than meet L.B.'s eyes. And then, being a therapist, she couldn't help wonder if L.B. was just looking for a maternal figure. "What did you mean yesterday when you said you didn't have a mother?"

Now it was L.B.'s turn to look down into her cup. "My parents disowned me when I came out. Both my mother and my father—well, he's not my real father, but he's the only father I know—anyway, both of them are very strict Catholics. I knew I probably shouldn't tell them I was a dyke, but I couldn't help it. I felt so hypocritical, taking their money to pay for college when I knew I was doing something they'd totally disapprove of. I guess I do have some Catholic guilt in me after all." L.B. smiled sheepishly. "Anyway, I haven't talked to them since I was a junior. I got financial aid and put myself through school. Been on my own for a long time. So I may be only twenty-five, but I'm kind of an old soul. And I've learned that superficial differences like age, race, whatever, really don't matter. Since I know what it's like not to be loved," she raised her eyes to Harriet's, "I know how to love very well. Very, very well." L.B. enunciated each word carefully. "I know it involves taking risks. Not being politically correct. Letting your head go and following your heart."

"Let's get out of here," Harriet said, waving for the check.

The next twelve hours were everything Harriet could have hoped for and more. L.B. was an absolute goddess with her eager young body that curved in and filled out in all the right places. She was open and willing, creative and energetic, and extremely attentive. Harriet felt good in places she hadn't been aware of in years, if ever. The hard knobs of her elbows, which until now had never been kissed. The backs of her knees. The ladder of her spine. L.B. told Harriet she was perfect and interrupted any self-deprecating and what she called "ageist" remarks Harriet made by putting her hand over Harriet's mouth. Harriet swallowed her words and kissed L.B.'s palm as her hands wandered up and down her magnificent, responsive body.

In the morning, after they made love again, Harriet grabbed the bathrobe hanging from the bedpost and rose to put on the coffee. She hunted around for the breakfast tray she hadn't used in forever, and popped two English muffins into the toaster oven.

Breakfast in bed, why not? Harriet thought, getting out her best cloth napkins. When she came back into the bedroom, a naked L.B. sat up and smiled.

"Umm, coffee," she said, reaching out with both arms, her hands opening and closing rapidly like high-speed lobster claws. Harriet raised an eyebrow and L.B. laughed.

"This?" she asked, looking down at her hands, which were still going strong. "I always do this when I see something I want. I've done it ever since I was a baby. My mother used to call it my hands of delight."

Harriet felt all the blood in her body rush to her feet as she gripped the handles of the breakfast tray tight. "What does L.B. stand for?" she asked, her voice a shaky whisper.

"Libby Bernadette. Why?"

"Oh. My. God."

❀

Harriet closes the newspaper and puts it on the kitchen counter. She'll finish the crossword later while L.B. does the dishes. It's Harriet's night to cook, and she outdoes herself with a vegetable lasagna that "rocks my world," as L.B. puts it. L.B. asks Harriet to rub her feet after dinner; the new inserts the doctor gave her to lift her arches are killing her. Later, after watching the ten o'clock news, they have dessert: Harriet nibbles a small dish of plain vanilla frozen yogurt, and L.B. devours two scoops of fudge ripple ice cream drenched with marshmallow topping and whipped cream. L.B. seems to take the news that Harriet attended her birth in stride, as she does most things.

"It's not like I didn't know you and my mother were roommates," L.B. says, as Harriet had told her that long ago, the first morning after the first night they had spent together. Their first night together had almost been their only night together, since Harriet was extremely upset about the whole thing. But L.B., whom Harriet referred to as "younger and wiser," convinced her to give their relationship a try. "What if I'm the one true love of your life?" L.B. had asked, looking directly into Harriet's dark eyes. "How could you risk not giving me a chance? Besides," she'd said, "this feels so good. Even though it's only been a night and a morning, I feel like I've known you forever."

Harriet winced. "I have known you forever," she said, wondering how something so unbelievable could feel so right.

And five and a half years later, it seems that L.B. is "Ms. Right," since Harriet has never been happier. Still, she worries how this new bit of information will affect L.B.

"I think it's cool," L.B. says later when they are lying in bed, side by side. "Besides my mother, you're the first person I ever saw. Maybe I should write a short story about it. Nah..." L.B. shakes her head. "No one would ever believe it."

"Truth *is* stranger than fiction," Harriet says, gathering L.B. into her arms. They lie there holding each other for a few minutes, and L.B. is so quiet, Harriet thinks she may have fallen asleep.

"L.B.?" Harriet strokes the side of her cheek.

"Hmm?"

"I know the circumstances of your birth, love, but you never told me if you've ever had a near-death experience."

"Oh, yeah." L.B. nestles into Harriet's shoulder. "I have one every night."

"Every night?" Harriet pushes back a little so she can look into L.B.'s eyes. "What are you talking about? Do you have sleep apnea or something?"

"No, baby." L.B. is smiling. "Don't you know I almost die of happiness every night lying here next to you?"

"You're too much." Harriet shuts her eyes and leans down to give L.B. a kiss. L.B. kisses her back, her front, and both her sides, tracing every inch of Harriet's body with her two greedy hands of delight.

Private Lessons

Woman
the round sound
in my mouth of you
resounds like clouds
around the moon…

She was my teacher. I knew being at the hot tubs with her would be considered inappropriate at best, but I didn't care, and obviously neither did she. She taught at a nontraditional East Coast college like Goddard or Bennington, though it was neither of those, and I was a nontraditional student, older though hardly wiser than the others in my class. Yet despite this, we were doing something that couldn't be more traditional: We were embarking on a student-teacher affair.

I had never been with a woman before, and she knew this. I suppose it was something she decided to teach me about, much the same as she was teaching me how to write poetry. She already had a lover, a blond buxom woman twice our age (she was only four years older than me), also a teacher at the college, over in the art department. She was away that semester, in Italy on sabbatical. And while the cat's away…

Her name was Cat. Catherine to the public, as that was the name she published under, but Cat to everyone else, including me. And she *was* cat-like, with those gold-green eyes, that skullcap of black hair, those long limbs, that muscular, sinewy back. Her body was the most amazing thing I'd ever seen as it wavered in the tub under the water, shimmering like the lilies in a Monet painting. She had taught me the power of comparison, of using like or as to describe something by way of simile, the irony that anything could be seen more clearly when presented as something other than itself.

I thought this over as I sat fully clothed on a wooden bench off to one side, my eyes riveted to Cat. She was naked, relaxed, her body submerged, her head leaning back, her arms outstretched along the tub's rim, her dangling hands making wet, splashy sounds as she lifted them in and out of the water and let cool, jeweled drops drip from her fingertips. We'd been lucky enough to get the one tub that was up on the roof; there was nothing above us but a mile-high sky full of a thousand glittering stars and a glowing, full-to-bursting moon. Cat loved the moon, had insisted we wait until it was full so that everything would be perfect. Now she raised her face to it as if she were tanning. Cat's most famous work, her signature piece that had garnered all those awards, was a series of twenty-eight poems, each describing a different phase of the moon.

Praised be the moon
as she rises tonight
a round white pearl
in the velvet earlobe
of the world...

The moment was pure magic; Cat, the moon, an owl hooting nearby, the cool night air brushing my cheek. If she would have said something, anything—"Come on in, the water's fine," for example—the spell would have been broken. She knew this, of course. Hadn't she told us in class over and over that what *wasn't* said in a poem was just as important as what was? Hadn't she told us the week that she taught haiku to pay attention to the white space on the page—there was even a Japanese word for it, *yohaku*—and to the emptiness surrounding the poem, the distance between each line? Everything became crystal-clear that night as I watched her, as she allowed me to watch her, taking as much time and space as I needed to absorb her chiseled beauty with my eyes.

I knew she wanted me to join her in the water, but I was hesitant and this surprised me. Wasn't this the moment I'd been waiting for, the moment we'd been building toward all semester? The poets whose work Cat had suggested I read—Adrienne Rich, Audre Lorde, Marilyn Hacker, Chrystos—were all women I had never heard of, women who obviously took other women as lovers. I had wondered if she'd suggested the same poems to other students, and I burned at the thought. I wanted to be special to her. Her favorite. Her pet. And tonight, at long last, I knew I was.

The moon, half full
And I half-drunk
At the sight of you
Shimmering beneath it...

Finally, I started to undress. But first I moved to where she could see me, as I knew she wanted me to. I'd often caught her staring at me in class, her eyes lingering just a second too long at my nipples, which she could clearly make out underneath my sweaters—soft, low-cut cashmere pullovers I began to wear for her torment and her pleasure. I knew I was driving her crazy; she could barely keep her mind on the day's lesson, and this pleased me enormously as I sat in the front row and watched her watching me, my breasts beckoning to her as I sat straight and still in my chair. Her clothes were loose, billowy; it was impossible to know what her body looked like beneath those windy skirts and dresses, which, after a while, became as torturous to me as I hoped my tight, bright sweaters were to her.

She smiled now, leaning her head back against the tub's edge, as if she were about to enjoy a show. I began by loosening my auburn hair from its woven braid and removing my tortoiseshell glasses. Everything became softer, fuzzier; everything lost its edge. Somehow that made it all easier. Cat grew blurry, watery, less definite, less sure. I hadn't expected to be so shy, yet it made sense. Wasn't I about to cross the line, enter new terrain, embark upon an exciting yet terrifying adventure from which I could never return? I didn't remember feeling like this the first time I'd made love to a boy. I was seventeen and eager to get on with it, get it over with, as I was the only one of my friends who had yet to complete the task. I thought I'd feel different afterward and be a brand-new person, a woman instead of a teenager or girl. But I felt nothing. Unlike now, when I was shivering even though I was fully clothed, my heart racing, my face flushed, my palms sweaty, and Cat still halfway across the room.

I stepped out of my flats, removed my socks, stared at my feet, thought about Cat's. Her feet were the one part of her body I knew well, for she wore sandals every day, and her feet were lovely. Pale, delicate toes. High, elegant arches. I found myself staring at them in class, much to her amusement. She could say so much without uttering a thing. She'd see me staring at her feet and lift her eyes to catch mine briefly and silently ask, *Do you like what you see?* She knew the power of silence, of watching and waiting, of delaying and postponing, until the yearning was so exquisite you almost didn't want it to come to an end. But everything does come to an end, which is another thing Cat had taught us. She explained a principle of Japanese poetry known as *wabi:* the moment something begins it is already ending. Nothing is permanent, which is what makes everything so sorrowful and beautiful, so precious and rare.

Black cat in the night
Invisible save her two eyes
Glowing like two moons
In the dark...

Each moment came and went that night, moments I couldn't hold on to, moments I couldn't bear to let go. I locked eyes with Cat as I unbuttoned my sweater and slipped the sleeves down my arms. She tried not to gasp, but her breath quickened at the sight of my torso, exposed to her at last. I took my time, folded my sweater neatly and placed it on the bench before stepping out of my jeans and allowing her to behold me in my plain cotton underwear. I had never thought of myself as particularly attractive; I was too soft and round everywhere and envied the tight, lean bodies of women like Cat, but now, for the first time, standing under the spotlight of the moon and feeling Cat's unbridled admiration, I felt truly and utterly exquisite. The feeling was intoxicating, like the peach juice and champagne we had drunk at dinner earlier. At that moment I would gladly have done anything for her, anything at all.

Cat let me stand there—For how long? Minutes? Hours?—before she gave me the signal I was waiting for. She lifted one arm and held out her hand, white and pale against the darkness. I climbed out of my underwear and slipped into the water. It was hotter than I'd expected, or perhaps it was the juxtaposition of the steamy water against the chilly night air, a delicious combination that made me shudder. I kept my back to Cat and felt rather than saw her glide across the water to me like a swan.

Bits of moonlight on the water
Like diamonds around your neck
Ice-cold and delicious...

Without a word, Cat lifted my long, thick hair off the nape of my neck and licked the delicate, soft skin she found there. I swooned, melted, fell back against her, surrendered to her strong embrace at last. The feeling of Cat's body against mine was exciting and comforting; it was home and a place I'd never been to before. She floated me across the tub until she was sitting back on her bench and I was sitting on her lap. I listened to her breath in my ear, felt her fingertips against my skin, heard myself mewling like a kitten as she taught me the wonders of my own bones and flesh. We sank, we floated, we melded into each other, we let the water part around us, enter us, keep us afloat, wrap us in its warmth. And all the while the moon watched over us, pulled at us, called us, bathed us in its white, wondrous light.

Moonglow in the sky
Afterglow on your face...

Lifetimes later there was a knock at the door. "We're closing," a male voice informed us. It felt strange to hear words, as neither Cat nor I had spoken all evening. We continued our silence as we emerged from the tub, our bodies soft and glowing, our fingers as wrinkled as slept-in clothes. Cat dried me off tenderly, from head to toe, and then saw to herself as I got dressed. Back in our clothes, I felt distant from her, but then she embraced me again, and as her lips found mine everything between us fell swiftly away.

The moon slips
Behind a cloud
Like your pale arm
Inside a velvet sleeve…

Without asking, Cat knew I would come home with her. We drove through darkened streets in silence, her hand on my thigh, our wet hair streaming. Once inside Cat's house, it was only a matter of minutes before we were undressed again. Her bed was covered in white, and through a skylight above I saw a smattering of stars and the lovely translucent moon.

This time Cat let me touch her. I was surprised at the sound she made, something between a sigh and a grunt, as I explored her with my fingers and tongue. I couldn't believe how soft she was; I was unspeakably moved by the gift she was giving me, how completely vulnerable she allowed herself to be. I licked the beauty mark on her belly with my tongue, I placed my hand inside her warm, wet sweetness, I kissed the hinge where her hip met her thigh. Finally, we were filled with each other, the moon disappeared, and we slept, curled together like the two s's at the end of a long, tender kiss.

The morning light was bright and harsh as I opened my gritty eyes. Cat stood beside the bed holding open a kimono, and I rose to step toward her and slip my arms through the long silky sleeves.

You stood behind me
lifting a kimono to my shoulders
And I was the sky
A full moon rising
From my feet...

She made a pot of green tea, toast with blueberry jam, and small talk: the weather, the class she had to teach later, a film that had just opened in town. I listened to her chatter, mute with the wonder of it all. Cat was now my lover, and she acted like it was perfectly natural for me to be sitting at her table, drinking tea from her mug, eating toast off her plate, watching her move about her kitchen with ease, as she got me a cloth napkin, put another slice of bread into the toaster, opened a window to let in the morning air. It was all very strange and new to me, but I didn't let my confusion show, or if I did, Cat didn't seem to notice.

As Cat poured me a second cup of tea, there was a knock at the door. She excused herself, and I remained at the table, not knowing what else to do. It wasn't her lover, home from Europe for a surprise visit. That would have been too contrived, too melodramatic. It was a friend, another teacher from the English department, returning some books she had borrowed and asking Cat if she would loan her a particular volume of poetry. "Wait here," I heard Cat say, but as she moved into her study the woman stepped into the living room, peeked through the doorway, and saw me sitting at Cat's kitchen table, wrapped in the kimono, my hair unkempt, my face wearing a mixture of embarrassment, defiance, and pride.

"Uh, Cat, I'll see you later," the woman called, backing out the door.

Cat returned to the kitchen, poetry book in hand, but something had been interrupted, lost, the spell had been broken. I was already on my feet, heading for the bedroom, for the safety of my clothes, eager to put up a wall between us.

"I'd better get going," I mumbled, trying to ignore the hurt and bewildered look on Cat's face as I struggled into my jeans.

"Wait," she said as I reached for the door. "Don't go," she implored as I turned the handle. "I love you," she whispered as I opened the door and stepped through it, her hand on my arm unable to stop me.

"I have to run," I stammered, not bothering to shut the door behind me. And I did begin to run and then kept running, without once looking back. I never went back to her class, I never returned her phone calls, the letters she wrote me, the notes she tacked to my door.

Moonless night
Like my bed
Without you in it...

I dropped out of school and moved clear across the state without saying goodbye. What was I running so hard from? I couldn't explain it to her because I didn't understand it myself. All I knew was that I couldn't bear to face her. Sure, I identified as bisexual, but that didn't mean anything. Everybody did—after all, it was a nontraditional school. But embracing a label was very different than embracing an experience. And that's what Cat was to me, just an experience, an experiment, a litmus test, wasn't she? Or was she?

Cat had her own theories about my disappearing act. Perhaps it was because she was my teacher. ("Don't be ridiculous," she said in a letter. "We're practically the same age, and it won't matter once the semester is over.") Or perhaps it was because she already had a lover. (Cat informed me in another letter that they had an "understanding," and besides, they were on the verge of splitting up.) Was I afraid that we had gotten carried away by the moon, the champagne, the water, and that her feelings for me weren't real? (She assured me they were.) How could I tell Cat when I couldn't even tell myself I wasn't afraid it was those things, I was afraid it *wasn't* those things. I was afraid that whatever was between us was real, too real, as real as the ache in my heart every time I thought of her. I kept running from the questions that plagued me, running from the answers I didn't want to hear. But there was one thing I couldn't run away from, and that was the moon.

Moonlight spilling through my window
Filling my empty teacup
Stroking my sleeping cheeks
As I reach through my dreams
For someone who is not there...

Every night the damn moon rose high in the sky, making it impossible for me to forget what had happened with Cat. There it was, just a sliver, like a disembodied smile. Then it was half-full or half-empty, depending on your point of view. Next it grew fat and bulging, almost as if it were pregnant with itself. Finally it was full, a silver coin, an incandescent opal, Cat's smooth white cheek glowing in the sky. Then all at once the moon disappeared completely, giving me a night of peace, only to return again just as suddenly, forcing me out of my denial. It took months for me to realize I wasn't running from Cat, I was running from what Cat had taken a great risk to teach me: that I was just like her; that I needed the warmth, the comfort, the thrill of another woman beside me. It hit me sudden and hard, without warning, like turning the corner and coming upon a golden harvest moon bigger than a house in the sky. How powerful and peaceful, how tremendous and true. And so a year later I gathered my courage and went back to find Cat, to thank her, to apologize, to beg for forgiveness, to explain.

Twelve full moons
Have risen and set
Since you have been away.
An old woman greets you
At your young lover's door.

Flight of Fancy

Anyone who says they love to travel doesn't travel for work. Take it from me. I fly at least five times a month, and the more I do it the less I like it. It's not that I'm afraid to fly—I feel safer in the air than I do on the freeway—it's just that it's so damn unpleasant. The seats, for example. They're so close together that if the person in front of you decides to recline, you're a good candidate for knee surgery before your flight has landed. And take the food. Or, if you're smart, you won't take the soggy sandwich, rotten apple, and crumbled potato chips that are waiting for you in a little container in the cooler you pass on the way to boarding your aircraft. See what I mean? The flight attendants (who in my opinion were much nicer when they were called stewardesses) don't even serve you anymore. Unless you're sitting in first class. Then all you have to do is snap your fingers and they'll fall all over themselves to bring you your complimentary martini, complete with a smile and a wink. But if you're sitting behind that obnoxious blue curtain the flight attendant always makes sure she closes right after takeoff, forget about it. You can try ringing for assistance, and she might answer your call if she has nothing better to do. But she won't have what you want anyway. No blanket, no pillow, no bottled water. Never mind that you've seen all these items and more as you passed through the holier-than-thou section, whose members are all nicely settled in with their drinks and newspapers and pretzels by the time you finally get to board. If this were the Titanic you know you would go right down with the ship along with all the other coach passengers, no questions asked. But you try not to think about that as you buckle up and make a feeble attempt to strike a bargain with God (whether you believe in Him or not). You'll be good, you'll be very, very good if only He'll give you a break and allow the seat next to yours to remain empty so you can spread out, relax, and enjoy the flight for once in your life. But the minute you promise God the moon and the stars and your favorite vintage beaded cocktail dress, the flight attendant's voice comes over the sound system loud and clear, welcoming you aboard and telling you that the flight is completely full, so you'd better get over yourself and put all your carry-on items under the seat in front of you or in the overhead compartment.

I sigh, fold my coat in two, and rest it on my lap carefully so as not to wrinkle it. Then I run my hands through my hair and try to fluff up my flattened tresses, but it's hopeless. Airplane air, the little there is of it, really does a number on your locks. Not to mention your skin. Lotion, lotion, lotion is the name of the game, 30,000 feet in the air. And speaking of feet, if you want my advice, don't remove your shoes while you're zooming through the clouds if you know what's good for you. Once, a while back on a cross-country flight, I decided to give myself a pedicure, and boy, what a mistake that was. First of all, I was chastised up and down and sideways by a flight attendant who didn't even know I was alive until I unscrewed my bottle of "Rubyfruit Red" and began polishing my little right toe. Before I had a chance to dip my brush and move on to toe number two, she was right in my face, ranting and raving about how flammable nail polish was (who knew?) and saying that the plane would surely blow sky-high (and she didn't even laugh at her own joke) unless I put my polish away that very second. And then hours later, after I had finished my pedicure in the bathroom—I couldn't very well go on with one polished toenail and nine naked ones—when I tried to put my pumps back on, my tootsies had swelled so much, I felt like one of Cinderella's evil stepsisters, trying to squeeze my big, fat foot into that delicate glass slipper. *Serves you right,* I can just hear that self-satisfied flight attendant from hell smugly say.

I sigh again and look out that window—I make sure I always get a window seat—and pray that the person who will undoubtedly sit next to me won't be too annoying. If they fall asleep, I hope they won't snore. If they stay awake, I hope they won't be interested in conversation. Just the fact that they'll be sitting so close to me *breathing* will be annoying enough.

When I was a teenager, my father flew off on a rare business trip, and when he got back, I asked him who had sat next to him on the plane.

"I don't know, sweetie," he mumbled as he riffled through the mail.

"What do you mean you don't know?" I asked. "Didn't you talk to him?"

"No," my father said as he tore open the phone bill with a wooden letter opener.

"No?" I was furious. "But he could have been someone famous, Dad. He could have become a good friend. He could have been the messiah. He could have been anyone!"

"Honey," my father sighed an apology, "I was tired."

All I could do was groan, roll my eyes, and shake my head. Now that I think about it, I'm sure my frustration stemmed from adolescent angst over being stuck in the small, unexciting suburb I grew up in. Here my dad had had a chance to meet someone interesting (i.e., anyone who didn't live in our town) and he'd gone and blown it. I made him promise that next time he flew somewhere he'd talk to the person sitting next to him and bring me a full report. Which he actually did, though I'm ashamed to say I can't recall one word of that conversation.

And now, of course, I've grown up and turned into one of those people who has to admit that her parents were right. I never talk to whatever poor, unfortunate traveler, through luck of the draw, winds up sitting next to me on a plane. I make sure my nose is buried in a book or magazine long before my seatmate can even think about saying, "Are you flying for business or pleasure?" There are those who can't take a hint, however, which is when I bring out the big guns. It does you no good to say, "Can't you see I'm reading?" to these people; obviously they can see that you're reading and they don't give a damn. So I hold up a book I carry just for this purpose, something like Eve Ensler's *The Vagina Monologues* or Holly Hughes's *Clit Notes,* and say, "Have you read this? It's really good." That usually shuts them up for the rest of the flight, and if it doesn't—if the person happens to say, for example, "I loved that book"—well, then, I've lucked out for a change and actually wound up sitting next to someone worth talking to. Which has never happened yet, in case you're wondering. But one can always hope.

I feel the weight of something settle next to me—my seatmate's carry-on bag, no doubt—and keep my head turned toward the window. Making eye contact on a plane is as unwise as making eye contact on the streets of New York; you're simply asking for trouble. But then I hear a voice—a sexy, husky, two-packs-a-day older woman's voice—say, "Honey, do you think you could help me with this?" and before I turn around, I know I'm a goner.

She's gorgeous. Breathtaking. A real knockout. I try to keep my tongue in my mouth as I scramble out of my seat and undo $200 worth of chiropractic work by hoisting her forty-pound carry-on up into the compartment above our heads. I break a nail in the bargain too, but I hardly notice (and I've sued people for less). If this woman—no, that's too common a word—if this *goddess* asked me to bite all ten fingernails down to the quick, I'd do it in a heartbeat. Hell, I'd give her my whole arm—both arms—if she asked. I mean, this heavenly creature, who is now smiling and standing in the aisle so I can settle back into my window seat before she sinks herself down beside me—*me*, the luckiest woman on the planet—is really something else. Mere words can't describe her, but for your benefit I'll try.

Let's start with her hands, which I am now staring at because I can't bring myself to look at that face, which I'm sure could launch a thousand ships, airplanes, and then some. She's got long, slim, tapered fingers, ending with polished nails the color of coral one could only find off the coast of a tropical island called Paradise. A few age spots dot her silky skin here and there, perfectly placed, not flawing her hands but giving them character. Her left hand sports a wedding ring, of course—a woman this drop-dead gorgeous would never be unattached. The ring is one of those "forever" affairs, probably from Tiffany's. You know the kind; it has about twenty tiny diamonds or so set in a white gold band that goes all around her strong yet delicate finger, which is supposed to mean that whoever gave her this ring loves her forever and ever with no beginning and no end, et cetera, et cetera, ad nauseam. (I tend to become very cynical when I'm insanely jealous.)

I watch her hands buckle her seat belt and remember to do the same. And then before I can stop myself, I ask the dumbest question in the world: "Are you flying for business or pleasure?"

She looks at me then, and I swear I feel every molecule in my body rearrange itself to take in this experience, which I'd never even dreamed of before. Her eyes—and I don't usually go for blue eyes, but what the hell, I don't usually go for femmes either—are astonishing. They're all the blues of my childhood box of 64 Crayola crayons rolled into one. They're the periwinkle blue of the tiny flowers painted on my grandmother's good china plates and the pastel blue of the eye shadow my mother wouldn't let me wear when I was ten. They're the same light, light blue as the eyes of the husky dog I had as a teenager and loved more than anything or anyone in the world. They make Paul Newman's aqua orbs look dull as dishwater. They're the ocean and the sky and all the other corny images you've ever heard of that I see at this moment are absolutely, undeniably true.

"I'm flying home from visiting my grandchildren," she says, answering the question I've already forgotten I've asked.

"Grandchildren? You don't look old enough to have grandchildren," I say, racking up at least fifty demerits with the politically correct police in my head but scoring big points with her.

"Oh, honey, you're sweet," she says, brushing my forearm with the tips of her fingers for the briefest of seconds before I swoon and she takes her hand away.

We settle back then as the flight attendant instructs us what to do in case of an emergency. (*Don't worry,* I want to say to my traveling companion. *If anything happens, I'll save you.*) I can feel my heart banging against my chest and my palms beginning to sweat, even though it's freezing in here. (Airplanes are not known for their heating systems.) I can't believe I'm falling for a femme. As a rule, I don't even like femmes. It's a well-kept secret—well, maybe not that well-kept—that most femmes don't really like each other. I know we're supposed to be feminists and everything, but to tell you the truth we've been brainwashed about our looks just like every other red-blooded American female (you think Gloria Steinem and Naomi Wolf wake up looking like that?), and I don't know a femme—though none will admit it—who doesn't walk into a room and check to see if she's the best-dressed, most attractive, not to mention sexiest chick at the hen party. (There go the PC officers groaning in my head again.) Even though I'm out of the running, since I've been with my butch for a good seven years, and no femme worth her weight in eyeliner would make a move for my beloved (it's not for nothing I keep these talons nice and sharp), you bet I still like to keep my eye on the competition.

Seven years—can this be a seven-year itch I'm experiencing? I don't understand it. I've never been with or even wanted to be with another femme. If anything, this is the kind of woman my butch would fall for. And believe it or not, I'm feeling very butchly at the moment. I want to take care of this little lady, who I'm sure is anything but helpless. Still, I've got a mad urge to sprint up the aisle and get her a soda. Search every overhead compartment for a blanket and pillow. Hit the guy in front of us over the head with my purse and steal his magazine. Dash back into the airport and buy her favorite candy bar. Hell, I'd even trade places with her, and I never give up my window seat for anyone.

So what's so butchly about wanting to do all that? Ah, clearly you, like so many others, are misguided. Everyone thinks femmes are so maternal, so giving, so nurturing. I don't know where you people got that idea. (Do you want to know how nurturing I am? When my butch is sick and I tend to her, she calls me Nurse Ratshit and begs me to leave her alone.) Femmes, or at least this femme, like to be the center of attention. This femme likes to be fussed over and waited upon. This femme knows that allowing her butch to take care of her is what makes her butch feel good. But I never knew how good. Right now I want to puff out my chest with pride and be milady's Prince Charming, her Don Quixote, her knight in shining armor. I want to be debonair, dashing, gallant. In fact, I'm so close to leaning over and unfurling my coat down the aisle so that she can step on it if she needs to leave her seat and go to the bathroom, I'm actually starting to scare myself.

"How about you?" the object of my idol worship asks. *How*

about me what? I wonder. I've completely lost the thread of our conversation, which must be obvious because she quickly bails me out (she must be used to having this effect on people). "Are you traveling for business or pleasure?"

"Business," I say, and then luckily we start taxiing down the runway before she can ask me what kind of business I'm in. The words "educational consulting work" are not even worthy of uttering in her presence. I should be saving the rain forest, feeding homeless children, building shelters for battered women, doing something—anything!—to make this world a better place for her to walk around in. *Boy, do I have it bad,* I think as she closes her eyes and grips the armrests as we pick up speed. I take advantage of her position and study her profile—have I ever even seen a nose before? What a marvelous invention. And her lips—to die for, as my ancient Aunt Tillie would say. Perfect, like the wingspan of a rare bird that would leave the world bereft if it ever went extinct. She's wearing that same pale shade of coral on her lips (of course, my girl knows the first rule of makeup is your nails and mouth must match) as well as the faintest hint of blush and a touch of mascara. Her shoulder-length hair is a luxurious shade of brown with just a hint of red highlights glinting in the sun, courtesy of a bottle perhaps—not that I care—and held back from her face with a small gold clip. As I stare at her I suddenly remember what I look like, and I'm horrified. If I were traveling *to* my business appointments, I'd be all dolled-up too, in heels, full makeup, and a sharp business suit. But I'm on my way home now, and I'm wearing black stretch pants so old they've faded into gray and an even older, greenish-gray baggy sweater even the Salvation Army would probably reject. My face is devoid of any makeup, and my hair is one step below rat's nest. What was I thinking?

The first time my butch picked me up after a business trip, she was surprised that I was so unkempt. I explained to her that I'd had to be dressed up all weekend and I just wanted to let my hair down on the way home.

"But I thought femmes liked wearing makeup and all that," she said as we walked through the airport toward the baggage claim, her arm looped across my shoulder.

"We do," I reassured her, as I realized what she was getting at: She was disappointed and maybe even slightly hurt that I hadn't bothered looking my finest for her. "You know what I like about you?" I purred as we waited for the baggage to roll. "I know you think I'm irresistible, whether I'm in a low-cut sexy gown and five-inch heels, or baggy sweatpants and sneakers without a smidgen of makeup on my face." What, after all, could she say to that?

So now I've trained my girlfriend not to expect too much, but the glamour-puss sitting beside me doesn't know that this isn't what I normally look like. Do I have time to sneak on a bit of lipstick and blush before she opens her eyes? Before I can reach for my purse, we're in the air and the angel whose aura is brushing mine is looking past me out the window and smiling.

"I'm glad that's over," she says, and her teeth—even her teeth!—are beyond compare. "I hate taking off and landing. Once we're in the air, I'm fine."

Let's never land, I think—me, who usually can't wait to get out of the air, onto the ground, and into the arms of my butch, whose name I can't seem to recall at the moment. But with *her* beside me, I could stay in the air forever. I make a mental note to have my forearm laid out upon the armrest for the last part of the trip so she can grip my flesh instead of the cold plastic that I'm sure offered her little comfort as we took to the friendly skies. I imagine her apologizing after it's all over for squeezing my arm so tight, my skin sporting little black-and-blue marks (may they never fade!). I'll just shrug and say, "Don't worry about it" and be rewarded with another of her dazzling smiles.

We break through the cloud cover (I'm in heaven!) a moment later, and the flight attendants start making their way down the aisle with the drink cart. It'll take them a while to reach us (I'm in seat 34A, my bra size, which I knew was lucky), so I recline my seat back and rack my brain for something to say. *Will you marry me?* comes to mind, but I restrain myself. The diamond band strangling the fourth finger of her left hand announces loud and clear that she's taken. As am I, I hasten to remind myself. *Think, think, think.* Normally I am not a shy, tongue-tied kind of lass. But this babe-and-a-half has me completely beside myself.

As I sit there trying to think, she bends down and reaches into her oversize straw bag. This does not bode well: I know if she pulls out a magazine or book, it'll all be over. "Do you have any pictures of your grandchildren in there?" I ask, knowing the way to a grandmother's heart is through the offspring of her offspring.

"Do you really want to see them?" she answers, surprised. "Most people are so bored with pictures of other people's grandchildren. I know I am." She leans closer, as if she's going to confide something, and I lean in too, eager to hear her most intimate secret. "I don't even like children that much," she says, and I fall even more in love with her than I already am, if that's possible. "I mean, I love my daughter, of course, and my daughter's daughters too. But as a rule, I'm not much for other people's kids."

"Me neither," I blurt out. "I hate kids." I'm giddy as a nine-year-old who's made a new best friend in thirty seconds because she and the other girl have so many things in common: *You like chocolate ice cream the best? Me too! Your favorite color is purple? Mine too! You like kittens better than puppies? I do too!*

"Well, then, let's not bother with pictures," she says, and I'm afraid I've come on too strong.

"No, no, I do want to see them. Really. I don't exactly *hate* children." I hasten to correct myself and not come off as the heartless cretin that I am, though to tell you the truth I'm about ready to strangle the kid two seats over who's been whining "I want a cheeseburger, I want a cheeseburger" since the minute we left the ground. "I just prefer the company of mature people," I say, and then to my absolute horror my eyeballs, as though they have minds of their own, look her up and down.

"I know what you mean," she says, as she starts digging through her purse and I continue to stare at her breasts. How did I not notice them before? That's further testament to the beauty of her face. But now that her magnificent bosom has come to my attention, I'm really beginning to feel faint. She's wearing one of those blue-and-white-striped boat-neck pullovers that always make me think of France, with white slacks and shoes. As she leans down again to put her bag back under the seat in front of us, my eyes catch a glimpse of her cleavage, and I actually start to hyperventilate.

"Are you OK?" she asks as she sorts through an envelope of photos.

"Yeah," I gasp, trying to get a hold of myself. "I think we just hit an air pocket."

"Look, this is Tracy. She's four." She points to the photo with a feminine finger. "And this is Sarah. She's eight."

"They're cute," I mumble, trying to muster up some interest. She's got a lot of photos there, and I hope one of them contains what I'm dying to see: her husband. Is he worthy of her? As if any man could be. Still, I've got to know.

"This is my daughter."

"She's pretty," I say, and she is, but she can't hold a candle to Mama.

"Let's see…" She flips through the photos, and I bravely put a hand on her wrist to stop her.

"No, let me see. Who's this?"

"Oh, that's me and Lloyd. That's our wedding picture. That was almost thirty years ago."

If I were alone, I'd hold the photo against my lips or perhaps press it to my own bosom. But then again, if I were alone, I wouldn't be looking at a picture of the most stunning woman I've ever seen. Not that time has faded her beauty—in fact, I think it's added to it—but as a young, blushing bride, she was truly a sight to behold.

"You look so happy," I say, when I find my voice.

"Oh, those were the days," she says, staring at herself. "Poor Lloyd. I left for Europe the very next day on a photo shoot—"

"You were a model?" See, just in case you were doubting my taste, or thinking I was exaggerating about how amazing she is, herein lies the proof.

"Oh, yes, Paris, Rome, New York—I did it all. It's a horrible life. Glamorous, my ass. But it paid well. Set me up for my dotage." She laughs and puts the pictures away.

"Something to drink?" At last the cart has made its way to us.

"What have you got there, handsome?" Even though our flight attendant, with his bleached-blond hair, diamond stud earring, and gold pinkie ring, is probably known to his friends as Queen Mary, he falls fast under her spell.

"Well, for you…" He pretends to search through his cart. "We've got whatever you want. Cranberry juice, apple juice, Coke, Pepsi, Diet Pepsi, Sprite…"

"How about something a little more exciting, honey?" She sits forward and gives him her full attention. "It's going to be a bumpy night."

He grins all over himself, and I've got to give her credit: Throw a fag a line from *All About Eve* and you've got a friend for life.

"How about a little wine for the lady?"

"Now you're talking."

"You got it. White or red?"

"White, please. And one for my friend too."

Now I know I'm a goner, because I don't say a thing. If a guy tried to buy me a drink on a flight I'd slug him, then immediately ring a flight attendant and demand to change my seat. But I'm so delighted that she called me her friend that I just sit by her side, mutely grinning like an idiot. Normally I hardly drink at all, let alone on an airplane. I figure there's a chance this might be my last night on earth (or above it), and if that's the case I want to be in complete control of my faculties. Which clearly I'm not, wine or no wine, so what the hell. I accept the drink graciously.

"To us," she says, clinking her glass against mine. Since they're both plastic, they make a very unsatisfying sound. She winks at me before taking a sip, and even though I'm desperate to believe she's flirting with me, I know better than to fool myself into thinking that's what's going on. No, let me correct myself. She *is* flirting with me, but it doesn't mean anything. I could be male or female, gay or straight, plain or attractive, old enough to be her mother or young enough to be her child, and still she'd act the same way, touching my arm lightly with her hand when she's making a point, or leaning in close, breasts first, to listen to what I have to say. I know these tricks of the trade all right—after all, I'm a femme too—but I've never seen anyone work it quite like this. She just exudes sexuality; it's oozing out of her every pore.

She continues to talk about her granddaughters and all the cute things they said during her visit. ("Tracy counted to ten for me, and I asked if she could count higher. 'Of course,' she said. Then she stood on her toes and counted to ten again.") As she prattles on, I study her and myself at the same time. What is so goddamn attractive about her? And why am I so mad all of a sudden? Because I want what she has, I realize with a start. I want it so bad I can taste it. And just as soon as I understand that, I know what *it* is, and furthermore I know *it* is something that I can never have, no matter how deeply I long and crave and want.

She's straight. That's why she can be so free and easy with her sex-words and her body. She walks through the world knowing her sexuality is welcome and wanted and appreciated. If I started to flirt with her—and now there's no denying that's what she's doing, in a harmless straight girl to straight girl (or so she thinks) kind of way—I'd be worried that she'd be thinking I was coming on to her, and that I was offending her. She, on the other hand, can throw all that flesh around without a care in the world.

And now I understand butches in a way I never have before. Especially those butches (including mine) who've gotten themselves in trouble with straight girls. Who swear up and down and sideways they've sworn off the hetero ladies forever, but then somehow find themselves tangled up with another broad who's either got a man waiting in the wings for her or knows she can bail out anytime and find herself a lover with a dick (that isn't kept in a drawer). Who wouldn't want to be with someone who can walk through the world so free and easy? Who wouldn't want to share in all that la-di-da, hip-swinging glory? I know I long to take this doll's arm and walk through the streets, laughing in the breeze, just a couple of chicks out having a good time, making everyone we pass smile because our joy is so infectious. But even if the world thinks I'm straight because I enjoy being a girly-girl, I know I'm not. And there's always a part of me that stays alert to the fact that I'm in danger of being found out, so I can never truly let my guard down one hundred percent.

"I'll be right back, honey." She breaks through my thoughts, touching my arm yet again before standing up. "If I don't return in ten minutes, come get me in the ladies room." Now there's a great dyke pick-up line if I ever heard one, but again I know better than to twist her words into something that isn't true. I lean across her seat (I can't help it) to watch her stupendous ass make its way down the aisle, and I'll be damned if not every single passenger does the very same thing. This woman could, and probably does, stop traffic. Fucking Lloyd is one hell of a lucky guy, I think as I settle back into my seat and wait for her to return.

And when she does, she's all curiosity. "What are you reading, sweetheart?" she asks, and I show her: this year's *Best Lesbian Erotica.* Her eyes widen—with interest? Disgust? It's hard to tell.

"Have you read it?" I ask nonchalantly. "It's really good."

"No, I haven't." She finishes her wine with one gulp and puts the glass down. "I think I'll shut my eyes for a few minutes," she mumbles. "Wake me when it's over."

She closes her baby blues, and I shut my book, wondering what I've done. *Are you happy now?* my mother's shrill voice screams in my ear. Why did I purposefully put some distance between us? Crazy as this sounds, I miss her. I miss that sweet, gravelly voice hitting my ear; I miss those warm, slender fingers pressing my arm. I miss her laugh, her smile, her eyes. I feel they're gone forever, and when we land she'll get up without a word, maybe toss her lovely locks in a huff, and just march right off the plane without a word.

Or, drama queen that I am, maybe that's what *I* want to do. Maybe I want to show her somehow that she can't have everything. Fuck this flirt with no dessert. She can't have her cake and eat it too. She can't have everyone. I, for one, am not going to be taken in by her (considerable) charms.

But my outrage lasts only as long as the rest of the flight. As soon as she opens her eyes, I'm Silly Putty in her hands.

"Are we almost there?" she asks in a little-girl voice, like she's a kid on her way to the circus.

Before I can answer, the flight attendant's voice fills the cabin, telling us to buckle up and bring our seats and tray tables forward.

"Ooh, I hate this part," she says—the cue I've been waiting for.

"Here, hold my hand," I offer. "It's not so bad." I don't know if I'm talking about the landing or my hand, but in any event she takes it, and I take the cheap thrill of pressing my palm against her own.

We start to descend and she inhales sharply, like I've just discovered her G-spot. I squeeze her hand tightly, she squeezes mine back. Then (and I'm not imagining this, I swear to God) she starts caressing the pads of my fingers with the tips of those sleek nails of hers. She does this so softly and imperceptibly that it takes me a minute to catch on to what's happening here. But then her middle finger travels down to the center of my palm and starts moving in a slow, circular way that's impossible to mistake—she's definitely turning me on. Is she getting a thrill out of this? I know I am. But is it wrong? Do I care? I think even my butch would understand this is an opportunity of a lifetime and I'd be a fool to turn away.

She continues to lightly and not so lightly touch my hand and arm, sending little shock waves to my hinterlands, and suddenly my inner butch wakes up and takes over. Without thinking, I grasp her hand and lift it to my face, turning toward the window so the passengers across the aisle can't see what's going on. Then before she can say or do anything, I tongue the center of her palm with all the love and lust I can muster and then some. I flick my tongue lightly and quickly, I press it against her flesh hard and powerfully, I suck the sweetness from her skin and graze her flesh with my teeth. She tastes like nectar, honey, manna from heaven, and I can't get enough of her. When she doesn't pull her hand away, I really go to town, sucking the tip of each long, strong finger, licking my way down to the fleshy crevices between each digit, spending a long time pleasuring the delta of her thumb, nibbling her bone china knuckles, nuzzling her slim, tender wrist, showing her exactly what lesbians *do* do in bed. (After all, isn't that what every straight woman really wants to know?)

When we come down with a sudden bump, both of us are breathing hard. Luckily the plane is noisy enough to mask the sounds we're making, not that I really care. I plant a loud smack of a kiss in the center of her palm as a final farewell, then lay her hand gently in her lap. I can't look at her, in case I just made an absolute idiot of myself, but her words are very reassuring.

"You don't happen to have a cigarette, do you?" she asks in that raspy, gaspy voice.

"No," I say, turning toward her. And even though I know I should, I just can't stifle my grin.

"I really should quit," she sighs, and looks me directly in the eye. "But sometimes there's nothing like a cigarette."

"How about a peanut?" I offer her the tiny untouched bag the flight attendant left with my drink.

"That'll do," she says, and holds out her hand, palm up, which almost makes me start in all over again.

A bell rings twice—bing-bong—the signal that we can all unbuckle and deplane, but my seatmate doesn't move. "What's the rush?" she asks, smiling at me. *Hey, I've got all night,* I think as disheveled passengers make their way past us and hurry up the aisle.

"I really enjoyed the flight," she says, still sitting pretty in her seat.

"Ditto," I respond, which is something my butch often says when she's in the mood to annoy me. Since we only have a few minutes at most left together, I definitely want the upper hand.

"Maybe I'll see you on another flight sometime," she says.

"Maybe." I remain noncommittal.

"Well, if I don't see you again, have a nice life," she says, and then she kisses me softly, then not so softly, right on the mouth. *Whoa,* I think as my head starts to spin. *Is this what straight girls do in bed?* Luckily, or not so luckily, she pulls away before I collapse in a boneless, blob-like heap.

"Shall we?" she says, rising. I get up too and help her get her two-ton carry-on down from the overhead compartment. Of course I insist on lugging it down the aisle for her, even though I've got more than my hands full with everything I brought on the plane. We make our way to the front of the aircraft, where both flight attendants as well as the pilot light up at the mere sight of her.

"Bye-bye. Bye-bye. Bye-bye," they chorus, their voices full of wistfulness. Me they ignore completely. Under normal circumstances, this would really get on my last gay nerve. After a long, uncomfortable flight, complete with lousy food and an even lousier movie, I'm deprived of my very own bye-bye too? "What am I, chopped liver?" I actually once said that to a flight attendant when she snubbed me in favor of a richly dressed businessman who was leading me up the aisle. But today they can stick their bye-byes where the sun don't shine for all I care. *I know something you don't know, I know something you don't know,* I chant silently as I quickly pass by.

My chest puffs up with pride as I follow her out into the airport, still clutching her suitcase like a prize. But then I see my butch, and the minute her handsome face breaks into that old familiar grin at the sight of me, I come to my senses and drop my beauty queen's bag like a hot potato. Before she even glances at it, another admirer picks it up.

"I'm tired," I whine to my butch, giving her my backpack, briefcase, shoulder bag, and assorted other paraphernalia.

"You poor baby," she murmurs, engulfing me with her strong, princely arms.

"Carry me," I beg, and she bends down to offer her back.

"Hop on," she says, and I smile, knowing she would gladly cart me away if I really wanted her to. "How was your flight?" she asks as we make our way down to baggage.

"OK. Ordinary. Uneventful." *Yeah, right.*

We stand at the baggage claim area and wait for my suitcase.

As I chat about my business trip, I notice my butch's attention wandering. I follow her eyes, and sure enough she's spotted *her,* the femme fatale I long to be.

"Wow, she's a knockout," my butch says as I give her a dirty look. "Though she isn't as pretty as you," she hastens to add, lying through her teeth.

"She sat next to me on the plane," I brag, as the luggage begins to circulate.

"No kidding." I know my butch has just added a fantasy to the wet dream file in her brain's overworked hard drive. "Did you talk to her?" she asks, knowing how much I hate conversing with strangers on airplanes.

"A little," I say. "But we both preferred silence."

A minute later my suitcase makes its way toward us, and my butch hoists it off the conveyor belt. I watch Lloyd grab his babe's bag as well. Then, just as I turn to go, the crème de la femme lifts her left hand, the one still glistening with my saliva, and waves farewell to me.

Bye-bye, I mouth, my lips still stinging with the taste of her. Then, happy as can be, I let my strong, mighty butch take my hand and firmly lead me home.

Keeping a Breast

You are lying on your back, in bed, your hands behind your head, your lover moving over you softly like a summer breeze. She plants tiny kisses along your jaw, under your chin, in the carved-out hollow where your shoulder meets your neck. You sigh, shift, watch her out of half-closed eyes, think, not for the first time, how lucky you are. Your lover moves to your breasts with her hands and her mouth. Your nipples stand at attention, eager for her to begin. You have been together long enough for her to know just how to please you, but not so long that the thrill has disappeared. Your lover knows every inch of your body, every hair, every wrinkle, practically every pore. You sigh again, your whole being reduced to a puddle of pleasure. You could do this forever and you know she could too. So when your lover stops what she is doing, you think she is teasing and play along. "Don't. Stop. Don't. Stop. Don't stop." But your lover has stopped. She studies you, her forehead furrowed in three crooked horizontal lines. You want to write *I love you* on those three little lines, and lift a finger to start tracing the letters, but then your lover speaks, and you stop before you begin. "What's this?" she asks, her voice not curious but concerned. You are not worried. What can it be, a beauty mark, a pimple, a mole? Your lover takes your hand and moves it to the outside of your right breast, which has fallen back into your armpit as it always does when you lie on your back. "Feel that?" she asks. You shake your head, and she presses your hand harder until you can no longer deny what she has found: a lump. A lump that presses against the flesh of your fingers like a small irritating pebble in the bottom of your shoe.

Talk about killing the moment.

❀

You have always had breasts. Of course you know that isn't true, but you can't remember life without them. There must have been a time, though, when all you had were two tiny nipples small as snaps sewn onto your chest. Then breast buds, though you don't think they called them that when you were growing up. You remember a lot of talk about "developing" when you were a teenager—as if you are film in an instant camera. You hate your plump, less-than-perfect body and despise having your picture taken, but your father tells you to stop being silly and snaps you out in the backyard in your bathing suit working on your tan, or coming down the living room steps on the first day of school in a brand-new skirt and sweater. His camera spits out the photo, and you watch in dread and fascination as the image on the shiny paper slowly takes shape. You develop right in front of your own and your father's eyes. And there isn't a damn thing you can do about it.

❀

"It's nothing," you tell your lover. "It's just my lumpy mashed-potato breasts." That's what the doctor calls them every year during your physical exam as her fingers ply your flesh. "Do you do a self breast exam?" she always asks. Some years you lie and say yes.

Other years you 'fess up and tell her the truth. You can't tell the lumps from the bumps, you say. It feels like one big mass of stuff. "If you do it regularly," your doctor tells you, "you'll get to know your breasts. Then you'll be able to tell if anything changes." She uses the flats of her fingers to press your breasts around and around. You do not think of your lover. You think of your cat, who kneads you with his paws every morning using this same amount of pressure. "Your breasts feel perfectly normal," the doctor finishes up. "Like lumpy mashed potatoes. What you're looking for is a hard lump. Like a pea, bean, or marble." You nod, vowing to turn over a new leaf. You'll do a breast exam every month, eat more vegetables, drink more water, take up jogging. Of course you do none of these things.

"It's nothing," you tell your lover again, hoping she'll go back to what she was doing. But your lover has a built-in bullshit detector. She hears the fear in your voice. She sees through you so easily, you might as well be Saran Wrap. It is one of the things you love and hate about her.

❀

Your breasts arrive the summer between fifth and sixth grade. You spend all of July and August at sleep-away camp. You laugh at the girls who are so homesick they live for the mail and cry themselves to sleep. You love being away from your parents. You feel incredibly free. You even have a boyfriend. His name is Jed, and he is the first person (besides your father) to call you beautiful. He loves it when you gather up all your long, thick black hair, hold it aloft for a split second, and then let it tumble over your shoulders and neck. Jed is a good five inches shorter than you, but you don't care. It only matters when you slow-dance, and instead of putting your head on his shoulder, he puts his head on yours. He also puts his hand on your breast one night down by the lake when you sneak out to meet him. You are lying on the ground; he is lying on top of you, and before you know it, he has snaked his hand between your bodies. Your breath slows and quickens at the same time. So does your heartbeat. You wonder now which breast it was, the right one with the I'm-sure-it's-nothing lump, or the left one, which will be the one that's left if the right one has to be taken away.

When your parents pick you up from camp, you stop at a Howard Johnson's on the way home to get something to eat. You wait for a table with your mother, while your father goes "to use the john." As soon as he is gone, your mother grabs you by the arm, digs her fingers into your skin, and whispers loud enough to make your cheeks burn with shame, "I don't care what you did in the woods down there, but now you're back in civilization and the first thing we're going to do when we get home, young lady, is buy you a brassiere." You don't know how she knows, but she does, and you blame her for the fact that even though Jed promised he'd write, call, and visit, you never hear from him again.

❀

"Do you think it's cancer?" you ask your lover when it's clear she isn't going to pick up where she left off. She shakes her head. You know what she is thinking, but you can't help it: You're a pessimist, you always assume the worst. When you lost your job last year, you immediately feared becoming a bag lady; when the cat didn't eat or use his litter box for three days last month, you thought the end was near (it wasn't).

"It's probably just a cyst," your lover says, but you know her as well as she knows you, and her voice is less confident than you'd like it to be. "Call the doctor tomorrow and have her take a look at it."

"OK." You give in and lie quietly in your lover's arms for a few minutes, letting her stroke your back and smooth your hair. You feel safe in her arms; nothing bad can happen as long as you are wrapped up like this. You wish you were your cat so you could purr. Your lover kisses your forehead, your nose, your cheek, your chin, and soon she resumes what she was doing before, much to your relief. You come fast and hard, your orgasm over almost as soon as it begins. Afterward, you cry.

❀

Your best friend reads about the pencil test in *Seventeen* magazine and wants you both to try it. You climb the steps to her bedroom, and she closes the door behind you. Without a word, you turn back to back and take off your shirts. You wait for her to go first. She puts a pencil under her breast and you hear it clatter to the hardwood floor. You wait as she tries again. Once more the sound of wood against wood. Now it's your turn. You lift your flesh and slide the pencil under your breast. It stays put. You try your other breast. The pencil is cold against your skin, where it seems to have found a home for all time. You even jump up and down a little, as a joke, sort of, but it isn't funny and the pencil doesn't move. You both get dressed and accept your fate: your best friend is too small to wear a bra; you are too big to go without. The pencil test is over and both of you have failed.

❀

The next morning you call your doctor's office. Of course, you're put on hold. You listen to the Muzak, one hand holding the receiver, the other wandering over your breast. Maybe it's gone, you think. Maybe you imagined it. After all, no one in your family has ever had cancer. Not even your mother, who smokes two packs a day. What are the other high-risk factors? You can't remember. But it doesn't matter. The lump is still there, hard, stubborn, undeniable. You quickly take away your hand, afraid that you'll irritate the lump, afraid that worrying it will make it grow. But like a child who can't help wiggling a loose tooth with her tongue, your hand finds its way back to the upper, outer quarter of your right breast, where trouble has been brewing—for how long?—without your knowledge. Don't they say that by the time you can feel a lump it's been growing inside you for two years? Or is it ten? Again you can't remember.

Finally the nurse comes on the line and sets up an appointment for next week. Next week? But what about the lump? She assures you one week won't make any difference one way or the other. You don't know whether to feel panic or relief.

❀

The lady in the lingerie department at Macy's has glasses perched on the tip of her nose and a measuring tape looped around her neck like a snake. She measures your bust size by pulling the tape tight around your back and bringing the two ends around in front. You almost die as the back of her hand accidentally brushes one of your nipples. "Thirty-four," she reads aloud to your mother, "and I think she's a B cup already."

"Thirty-four B?" Your mother's voice is full of shock and disdain, as though you've done something wrong, as though you grew your breasts on purpose, all by yourself. You tell her to wait outside the dressing room while you walk through the curtain and pull it closed tightly behind you. You take off your shirt and put your arms through the straps of one of the white, lacy bras the saleswoman handed you. Now what? You reach behind your back, your bent arms flapping up and down like useless wings as you try to match hook and eye, but it's impossible. Just when you think you're going to need your mother's help after all, you figure out how to put on the bra by fastening the hooks around the front of your waist and then swiveling them around to the back and pulling the bra straps up over your arms. There.

You suck in your stomach and study yourself in the mirror. You look like what your older sister would look like if you had one. You gather up all your hair, hoist it above your head, and let it rain down around your shoulders. You arch your back and put your hands on your hips like a girl modeling a bikini in *Seventeen* magazine. You purse your lips at your own reflection and just as you are about to blow yourself a kiss, your mother's arm appears through the slit in the curtain. The rest of her follows. "How are you making out?" she asks, the saleswoman standing behind her like a shadow.

"Mom!" you shriek, rushing to cover yourself. Your mother backs out, stepping on the saleswoman's foot. This would all be funny, you think, if it were happening in a movie instead of to you.

❀

The week before your doctor's appointment, your lover can't keep her hands off you. You tease her about a second honeymoon as she leaves the dishes after supper to carry you into the bedroom. You grab and claw and clutch at each other, yet you are soft and tender too. The last time you were like this was when your grandmother died. You drove down to New York, checked into your hotel room, and as you and your lover undressed to change into good clothes for the funeral, something came over the two of you. You don't know who started it, but in an instant you were thrashing around on one of the double beds in the room, rolling from side to side, first you on top of her, then she on top of you. You were the last ones to arrive at the funeral parlor, and though your mother couldn't possibly have known what you'd been up to, you could hardly look at her. You were sure everyone in the room could smell your lover on your hands.

Your lover's hands are on your breasts now. She asks if it's all right, and you nod. You want her to touch them and only them. You leave your jeans on so that you are topless and barefoot. Your breasts are very sensitive; you are one of those women who can come just from having your lover touch your breasts. You are proud of this, as if it's some kind of talent, like wiggling your ears or curling your tongue. As you begin to melt under your lover's mouth, you think, *Please God, don't take this away from me.*

❀

You sit on the exam table, your clothes folded on a chair, replaced by a white johnny dotted with small blue flowers that ties in the back. Paper crinkles under your legs and your butt; you have been waiting for a good twenty minutes, after sitting in the lobby for just as long. Not only that, you had arrived early for your appointment. Your lover wanted to come with you, but you nixed the idea and sent her off to work. There are only a certain number of days she's allowed to take off from her job and you want her to save them, just in case, though of course you didn't tell her that. She would have only teased you again for thinking the worst. You sigh, shut your eyes, let your left hand find its way to your right breast one last time. It's still there. The lump. Your mind whirls: One lump or two? Is that a lump in your breast or are you just happy to see me? Don't just sit there like a lump on a log. "Stop it," you say out loud, just as your doctor enters the room.

"How are you?" she asks, and you don't know why but tears

well up in your eyes. She studies your chart, giving you a minute to get hold of yourself. Then she sighs too, as if you are both resigned to something. "Let's have a look," she says, coming over to the table and motioning for you to lie down.

You let her slide the johnny to your waist as you lift your arms over your head. She feels your right breast, starting in the center near your nipple and working her way out in a clockwise spiral. You know when she has come to the lump, not because you can feel her feel it, but because her expression changes and she utters a little "hmm," something she has never done before. Usually she makes idle chatter when she examines your breasts: the weather, an upcoming holiday, whatever. You are both lesbians, and though you do not travel in the same social circles, it's still a bit awkward. You and your lover have joked about the good old doc and how many pies she's put her fingers in. Professionally, of course.

But this is nothing to joke about. You'd been counting on her to dismiss your concerns with a little chuckle and maybe even chastise you for being a hypochondriac, but she does no such thing. She feels your other breast, and you remember her telling you that if you feel something suspicious on your right breast, feel your left breast to see if there is something similar there. Clearly there isn't; now the doctor is feeling your right breast again, and again she mutters "hmm." Then she tells you to get dressed.

"I am concerned about this," your doctor says when she comes back into the room. "When was your last period?" She looks at the chart again. "Three weeks ago." She answers her own question. "So you're due next week. Why don't you come back in three weeks, after your period, and we'll see if anything changes. In the meantime, I want you to cut out coffee, take 400 units of vitamin E per day, and have a mammogram." You nod as she fills out a slip of paper. "Do you have any questions?"

Only one: When will this all be over?

❀

Breasts, bosoms, bazooms, bazookas, boobs, boobies, boobalas, teats, tits, titties, titskis, titskilehs, nipples, nippies, gazungas, headlights, hooters, hangers, jugs, knockers, maracas, milk duds, mams, mammies, mammos, mondo busto, eggplants, pamplemousse, melons, boulders, pimples, udders. Flat as a pancake, flat as a board. Hey, want a bust in the mouth? She's like a third-world country: undeveloped. Buxom, busty, built, stacked, ripe for the pickin', well-endowed. Do your boobs hang low, do they wobble to and fro? Victoria's Secret. Frederick's of Hollywood. Tit-slinger, harness, over-the-shoulder-boulder-holder. Ze-bra. Bra mitzvah. Two men were walking abreast. Keeping abreast of the situation. Breast friends. Bosom buddies. It was the breast of times, it was the worst of times. Breast Area: Enter here.

❀

You haven't had a mammogram for five years, since you were thirty-seven. Your doctor told you it was silly to have one then; you were too young, your breast tissue too thick, but you had insisted because your friend Viv had found a lump in her breast that turned out to be malignant and it freaked you out. Viv was a health food nut, she'd had a child before the age of thirty, there was no cancer in her family, she exercised regularly, ate no chocolate, drank no coffee or soda; in other words, she did everything she was supposed to do and still her body betrayed her. After her diagnosis, Viv became a breast cancer activist. She let everyone feel her lump before she had it and her breast removed; she didn't wear a hat, scarf, or wig to cover her bald, shiny head; she organized a group of survivors who held potluck dinners once a month and made special visits to women who needed to have mastectomies.

"Every time we visit a woman who's about to have surgery, the same thing happens," Viv tells you one day at lunch. Viv eats an enormous seaweed and sprouts salad and sips bancha tea; you gulp coffee with your gooey grilled-cheese sandwich. "The woman looks around," Viv says, "and slowly it dawns on her: She's the only person with two breasts in the entire room. Then—you can almost see it on her face—she realizes she will survive, that a breast is only a breast, it isn't your life. And then she cries with relief."

You don't tell Viv what you suspect: that the tears she witnesses over and over again might not be tears of joy, and that you hope and pray she belongs to a club that would never have you as a member.

❀

You arrive early for your mammogram and are shown into a dressing room with lockers, almost like a gym. But instead of a swimming pool or Nautilus equipment waiting to welcome your body, there is only a cold, hard mammogram machine. The technician is very nice; she apologizes for what she has to do. She places your left breast onto a smooth, ice-cold plate, then lowers another plate, and tells you to take a deep breath as she squeezes the plates together. You hold on tightly to a metal railing beside you and try to keep breathing. Was it this bad the last time? You can't remember. The technician leaves, then comes back to release you and change the plates. She positions your right breast, and as she leaves the room you begin to feel dizzy. The room is growing dark, your head is spinning; all of a sudden you're nauseous, you actually see spots before your eyes. Your hand begins to lose its grip, and the next thing you know you are sitting in a chair with your head between your knees, the technician's hand rubbing your back.

"Are you all right?" she asks.

You are so embarrassed you want to die, you think, then you hasten to correct yourself in case anyone, like God, is privy to your thoughts. You don't want to die; that's why you're here, isn't it? Slowly you sit up and face the technician. "Did you eat anything this morning?" she asks. You shake your head; you never eat breakfast. Then you remember the time you gave blood a few years ago—you'd fainted then too. They pumped you up with orange juice and doughnuts afterward, and that's what the technician offers you now. You eat, drink, sit in the waiting area for a while, watching other women go in, come out, get dressed, and leave with their prize: a pink carnation for a job well done. After half an hour, the technician asks if you think you're up for trying again. You nod and follow her in. This time you complete the procedure without incident. Later you will joke about the whole thing and tell your lover how you were hanging there by your tit, the technician all aflutter. Again your lover will see right through you. She will zing your favorite movie line right at you, the one spoken by a distraught Katherine Hepburn in *A Lion in Winter* that you yourself are fond of quoting: "Laughter is how I show my despair."

❀

What do they say, one in every ten women gets breast cancer? No, they say one in every ten women is a lesbian. Is it one in nine? One in eight? How do they come up with those numbers anyway? You find yourself studying women on the street. Every one you see has breasts. Round floppy breasts. Small perky breasts. Whatever the shape, they definitely come in twos. Maybe all the cancer survivors have had reconstructive surgery. Or maybe they're wearing falsies. You're sure they don't call them that anymore. Prosthesis. Breasts. Such hard words to say. They don't exactly roll off the tongue. Prosthessssisssss. Breast-st-st-st-stssss. You have to hiss the words out, like a snake.

You remember a poster from your early feminist days. It showed a photo of a woman who'd had one breast removed. She'd covered the scar across her flattened chest with a flowery tattoo, and under the photo was a poem she had written. You can't remember much of it, something about a tree. That poster hung on the walls of every women's bookstore you'd ever been to. Viv had one over her bed. You remember lesbians talking about Amazons who had chosen to remove one breast so they could be better archers. Now women are having their breasts taken off and calling themselves FTMs or tranny boys. You once saw a news story about a woman whose mother, grandmother, aunt, sister, and cousin all died of breast cancer. The woman had a double mastectomy even though she had no signs of cancer. If all these women could go through it, so can you. You still don't know what *it* is. It could be nothing. It could be everything.

❀

Your lover brings in the mail and hands you your stack. Phone bill, credit card statement, *People* magazine, letter from the health center. You wait until your lover goes into the other room to listen to her phone messages before you tear open the envelope. You unfold the single sheet of paper and see immediately that it is a form letter, telling you that your mammogram showed "no definite signs of cancer at this time." Does that mean it showed indefinite signs of cancer at this time? You study the letter intently, but it offers you no further information than the standard advice you already know: Do monthly self-breast exams and have a mammogram every year.

Your lover comes back into the room, talking about dinner. You show her the letter. "That's good, isn't it?" she asks, her voice cautious. You suppose so, yet you still feel glum. Your period has come and gone, but the lump has not gone with it, as you had hoped. You'd been counting on it dissolving like a lump of sugar in a cup of tea, and you'd spent more time than you'd care to admit fantasizing about canceling your next doctor's appointment. You imagined yourself telling her over the phone that the lump was gone, vanished into thin air, hocus-pocus, abracadabra, now you see it, now you don't. But as your lover, who is in one of those relentless twelve-step programs, is fond of saying, "Denial is not a river in Egypt."

❀

The morning of your doctor's appointment, you spend a long time in the bathroom. You wash, scrub, rinse, shave, moisturize, powder, and puff. You baby your breasts. You talk to them. You coo, cajole, tell them not to worry, whisper that everything will be OK. Still, your mind gets the better of you. You force yourself to imagine the worst: what it would be like to lose your breast. It's hard to go there. You are extremely squeamish about blood. You remember taking a friend with stomach cramps to the emergency room a few years ago. The friend insisted you stay with her, and for some reason the doctor let you. As soon as the nurse put the IV into your friend's arm, you hit the floor. When you came to, you saw the nurse was not amused. "That's why we ask friends to stay in the waiting room," she scolded, showing you the door.

How would you handle an operation? And how would you handle being lopsided? You know many women decide to have reconstructive surgery, and you imagine that you would too. A former lover of yours had breast reduction surgery a year ago. She told you more than you wanted to know: how the doctor had taken off her nipples, made her breasts smaller, and then reattached them.

You imagine your ex-lover's luscious brown nipples on a cold, metal tray, like two Hershey's kisses waiting to be returned to her body. She wanted to show you her new and improved breasts, but you declined the offer.

You get dressed and convince yourself to eat something before you leave for the doctor's office. There's not much in the refrigerator, just a few Tupperware containers with leftovers in various edible and inedible states. You put a glop of mashed potatoes in the microwave before the irony of the situation hits you and you hear your doctor's voice in your head, talking about your "lumpy mashed-potato breasts." Some comfort food, you think, as you shovel in bite after bite after bite.

❀

You know the routine by now—fill in the form: name, address, date of birth, date of last period, method of birth control, why you are here today? Under birth control you put your usual flip answer: *lesbianism—100% foolproof!* You ponder the next question, biting the tip of your pen. I'm here because I'm queer because I'm here because I'm queer. The little chant spins round and round your brain. You shake your head to clear away the noise. I'm here because my lover made me come. I'm here because I always do what's on my calendar. I'm here because I ate too much fatty food when I was growing up. I'm here because I did something in a past life that screwed up my karma. I'm here because what goes around comes around. I'm here because I don't know what else to do.

Finally, you fill in the line next to "Why are you here today?" with four little words, "Because of my breast," but you accidentally omit the "r" and the word "breast" reads "beast." Because of my beast. Is that a sign? Of what? You really should start meditating again, you tell yourself. You need to quiet your mind.

As soon as you hand the receptionist your form, your name is called and you are ushered into an exam room. This time your doctor does not keep you waiting long. She glances at your chart then tells you to lie down. She is all business today as she explores your body. She asks if you would mind if she brought an intern in to feel your breast, and you are so detached from your body you say you wouldn't mind at all.

She goes out and returns a minute later with the intern, who looks about seventeen and is a man, besides. You can't believe the possibility the intern would be male never even occurred to you. Your doctor is a lesbian just like you: Doesn't she know most lesbians don't like men touching their bodies? But you aren't really angry at her—you're angry at yourself. How could you be so stupid? But it's too late. Your doctor is already showing him where to feel and suddenly you are no longer in the room. You are at college twenty years ago. You see a sign posted in the student center: FEMALE STUDENTS: MAKE $50 IN TWO HOURS. CALL NOW: 555-0978. You call and are told to come to the science building the next day. You lay splayed across a table, topless, while half a dozen young men in lab coats—the future doctors of America—file by, each of them examining your breasts. One boy—you can still see his bespectacled, pimply face—gets very excited. "I think I found something!" he exclaims, and everyone rushes over. The professor, a tall, middle-aged man with wavy salt-and-pepper hair who reminds you of your father, pushes him gently aside and uses his expert hands. "That's nothing," he tells his students. "These breasts are perfectly normal." You get dressed, receive your fifty dollars in cash, go home, and crawl into bed even though it's the middle of the day. You still don't know why you did it. Sure, fifty dollars went a long way back then, but still, your parents had set you up with a bank account. You didn't need the cash.

You felt proud of your breasts twenty years ago. Had you

hoped the students would all be bowled over by your beauty? Were you looking for love, admiration, acceptance? A week later you see one of the students on the street and your eyes meet. "Do I know you?" he asks, and you think it's a pickup line, except he does look familiar.

"Are you a student?" you ask.

He nods. "Pre-med," he says proudly, and then it hits you both at the same time. Even though you can't see your own face, you're sure it's as red as his is, as he mumbles something and rushes away. As red as you're sure your face is now as the intern thanks you and backs out of the room.

After you get dressed, your doctor comes back to give you the news. "It doesn't feel really suspicious to me, but it doesn't feel unsuspicious either. Since we can't be sure, let's just go ahead and remove it."

"My breast?" you shriek, your hands automatically flying up to protect it.

"No, no, no. The lump."

"Oh." You are so relieved you don't ask about other options. It's like that old coming-out strategy—call your parents and say you have something very important to tell them: You only have six months to live. After they get completely hysterical, say you were only kidding. The news is: You're gay. No big deal. Right? Right? Right?

❀

Your lover takes the day off and drives you to the hospital. You're glad she'll be there in the waiting room, though you feel guilty for making her miss a day of work. She tells you to stop being ridiculous, but you still feel this is all your fault. There must have been something you could have done to prevent it. Been nicer to your mother? Given more to charity? My karma ran over my dogma, you think as you hug your lover goodbye and let them take you away.

You don't look as they put the IV into your arm. As you begin to feel nauseous, they tell you to count backward from 100 and you get to 97. The next thing you know you are in the recovery room, and the first thing you see is your lover's face. "Your sister's here," the nurse says, all smiles.

"I don't have a sister," you say before you recede into a drugged-out fog again.

When you take the bandage off the next day, your breast is black-and-blue. You are not really in pain, but still you take the Tylenol they sent you home with, just in case. You have to wear a bra day and night, and you are squeamish about having anyone hug you. Friends come and go, send cards, flowers. You are the hostess-with-the-mostest, making sure everyone has what they want to drink, entertaining everyone with your war stories. Some women from Viv's group show up, even though Viv has moved out of state. Somehow they always know where to find you. They tell you about their latest achievements and defeats: They've convinced several local lingerie stores to have plastic breasts imbedded with cancer-like lumps in their dressing rooms so women can feel them and know what they're looking for; they've haven't yet been able to convince Mattel to put out a Breast Cancer Barbie. They tell you when their next meeting is and invite you to join them. But you are not ready for your membership card, a voice inside your head gloats. Until another voice pushes that one aside and reminds you: not yet.

❀

Your doctor gives you the good news: Your tumor is benign. The news startles you; it's the first time she's used the word "tumor." You thought you had a lump, but no, you had a tumor. A benign tumor. It's called a fibroadenoma—such a big word for such a little lump. But it's gone and you're out of the woods. For now. Yes, your doctor tells you, it can come back. No, there's no way of telling whether it will or won't. You should do breast exams every month and have a complete physical once a year, including a mammogram. Cut down on caffeine. Eat five servings of fruits and vegetables a day. Exercise regularly. Be grateful.

❀

That night you feel euphoric, giddy, goofy. When your lover gets home, you seat her at the kitchen table. "What's this?" she asks, motioning to the cardboard square and plastic chips you've put at her place.

"We're playing bingo," you tell her, and though she looks puzzled—what in the world?—she goes along, to humor you.

"A, one," you call out. Your lover puts a chip in the corresponding space on her card.

"B, nine," you say, watching her face. She puts down a chip with no response.

"B, nine," you call again.

"You already said that," says your lover.

"B, nine," you repeat, ignoring her. "B, nine," you say even louder. "B, nine. B, *nine. BEEE*, NINE." You say it again and again, until your lover finally gets it.

"Benign?" she asks.

"Bingo!" you yell as your lover leaps up, knocking over her chair in her haste to embrace you.

"Benign! Benign!" You both scream the word over and over, as you jump up and down all across the kitchen floor with your arms linked around each other's waists, laughing like maniacs.

❀

You didn't know you would have a bright-red scar that would, over time, fade to pink but never completely heal. You didn't know the area around the scar would remain angry-looking and hard. You didn't know it would be a long, long time before you could look down at your right breast and not think about dying. You didn't know your lover would become less spontaneous and somewhat hesitant, more likely to ask rather than grab like she used to. You didn't know that she, the strong, silent one, had been scared out of her wits too.

You didn't know you would never be the same but that some parts of you would actually be better. You're more aware now. You don't take things for granted. You have been given a second chance, and you embrace it eagerly, your face lifted toward the sun, your arms flung to the skies, your mouth open wide to greedily gulp great fistfuls of air, like life.

Prelude

"The first fifty years were a prelude to my life."
—Yoko Ono

It had been a good day, a wonderful day, an extraordinary day in fact, though I hardly thought of it that way back then. Back then, which seems like a lifetime ago, I wouldn't have given a second thought to that Friday. Or if I did, I would have called it a typical day, an average day, a day not unlike any of the thousands of days Toni and I had spent together since we became a couple nine and a half years ago.

The day began like any other workday: The alarm rang at seven o'clock; I slapped the snooze button and snuggled down into the blankets for a few more minutes of blissful unconsciousness before Sophie butted her hard, furry head against my back. Somehow Toni had conveyed to Sophie that I was the one to be nudged, and it worked because it never took more than three head-smacks to get me sitting up and reaching for my robe. Sophie and I got out of bed together, leaving Toni to her daily struggle of rising from the sheets versus returning to dreamland, and made our way into the kitchen, where cat food and coffee beans awaited can opener and grinder.

It was going to be a sunny day, which made me happy and

Toni cranky. "Why waste a sunny day at work?" Toni always asked. If it was raining, Toni didn't mind being indoors, but to me there was nothing more depressing than standing inside the store where I worked and looking out the plate-glass window at the rain coming down in sheets, people hurrying by huddled under umbrellas with no time to stop in a bookshop and browse. On clear, sunny days, as it looked like this one would be, people strolled down the street like they had all the time in the world, paused to peek in the window, came in to check out the new best-sellers, thumb through some used paperbacks, or simply purchase a magazine or newspaper to read with their lunches in the park.

I poured myself a cup of coffee, sat down at the kitchen table with a bowl of cereal, and tuned my ear for the rustle of blankets being pushed aside and Toni's feet hitting the cool, wooden floor. If she wasn't up by twenty after seven, I had permission to wake her; otherwise I left her a wide berth, as my girlfriend was hardly what one would call a morning person. I, on the other hand, love the early morning and would wake up singing if Toni hadn't threatened divorce the first time I leapt out of bed belting out an off-key version of "Oh, What a Beautiful Morning" the day after we'd seen a friend star in a local community theater's production of *Oklahoma*.

At exactly 7:20 according to the neon-blue numbers on the microwave, I heard movement from the bedroom. A moment later Toni shuffled into the kitchen, sat down, folded her arms onto the table, and lowered her head on top of them. I got her favorite hand-painted, midnight-blue mug down from the shelf, poured her coffee, and set it in front of her.

"Did you feed Sophie?" Toni mumbled into her cup.

"Yes, dear," I said in my best Donna Reed voice, before I remembered. "Oh, shit."

"What?" Toni looked up, bleary-eyed.

"I forgot to say 'rabbit rabbit.' It's the first of the month."

"You forget every month," Toni reminded me.

"I do not."

"Yes, you do." Toni cupped her hands around her mug and stared at it as though she couldn't remember how to get the warm liquid up to her mouth. "Anyway, it doesn't matter."

"It does so." I moved toward Toni, who circled my waist with her arms and leaned her head against my belly. "If I don't say it, we won't have good luck this month. You shouldn't have asked me if I fed Sophie. Why do you ask me that every morning?" Toni didn't bother answering me, so I stopped talking and just stroked the top of her head with my palm. Toni relaxed against me, and if I didn't know better I'd swear she had fallen back asleep. "Drink your coffee," I told her, moving away gently. "Can you believe it's the first day of May? I never thought spring would come. Maybe this weekend if it warms up we can dig up the garden and—"

"Shh." Toni held up one hand to stop my chatter. "Roberta, please."

"OK, OK."

Every morning Toni asked me to be quiet, and every morning I had to remind myself not to take it personally. "I just can't hold a conversation in the morning," Toni told me over and over. "Just because a person is sitting up doesn't mean she isn't asleep." Of course, femme that I am, I used Toni's allergic reaction to mornings to my advantage by asking her to agree to things I knew she ordinarily wouldn't, such as spending New Year's Eve at a party at my ex-lover's house. Toni would agree to practically anything before ten o'clock in the morning in exchange for a little peace and quiet.

I left her at the kitchen table and went to take my shower. By the time I was done, Toni had downed her coffee and was looking a little more lively. Sophie was sitting on her lap, and Toni was rubbing her spotted little head between the ears and down under her chin, and even clear across the room I could hear the old girl purring with delight.

"Bathroom's all yours," I said, flouncing across the kitchen in my birthday suit. "Hands off the dry goods," I said, slapping away Toni's fingers as I passed her on the way back to the bedroom. I was all set to put on black slacks and a white sweater, until I saw that Toni had laid a similar outfit across the ironing board for herself: a white button-down shirt and freshly pressed black jeans. We seemed to do that at least once a week and had recently become more conscious of it because a street musician playing a kettledrum had made up a song about us as we walked by him about a month ago: "Two girls in leather jackets and jeans / Both of them looking fine as queens." We'd looked down at our matching outfits horrified, and Toni had insisted on taking off her jacket, even though it was barely forty degrees out and windy besides. I told her she was being ridiculous; we were hardly the kind of couple that confused people. I can't recall anyone ever calling me Toni or anyone ever calling her Roberta. About the only thing we had in common was that we were both female. Toni was a tall, handsome butch with short black hair that stuck straight up in a crew cut like my brother wore when he was twelve, dark brown eyes, and a cleft in her chin that made this femme glad she was alive. I'm short and round and fair, with silver hair cut in a Liza Minnelli bowl, a sprinkling of freckles across my nose, and hazel eyes that change from brown to green depending on my mood. (Toni always said that when I wanted her my eyes became goldish-green.)

I stepped into a green jumpsuit, slid a jade bangle bracelet onto my wrist, and pushed a pair of matching jade posts through the holes in my ears. As soon as I slid into my shoes, I heard Toni come out of the bathroom, a signal that it was my turn to go back in and apply my makeup. Our morning routine was like a dance, perfectly timed and coordinated. As I stepped past Toni, she reached for me and buried her face in my hair.

"You look like a luscious green goddess." She stepped back and bent at the waist in a formal bow.

I laughed and shook my head. A couple of years ago, Toni had read in a magazine at her dentist's office that children need to be complimented every day. "Why only children?" she asked me, opening her mouth so I could admire her newly polished teeth. "Why not adults too?" And from that day forth she said something nice about me every morning, something about the way I looked, the way I smelled, the way I walked… And it wasn't only a habit. Toni meant it. I basked in her appreciation, like a houseplant in the window soaking up the sun.

"Hey, want to be late for work?" Toni asked, unbuttoning the top button of my jumpsuit. "What's in here?" She reached inside my black lace bra. "Oh, it's the ladies. Hello, ladies. Nice to see you both." She buried her face into my cleavage, causing my knees to buckle.

"Toni, you're going to be late." I slapped her shoulder and tried half-heartedly to push her head away.

"Mgwff," she mumbled into my skin.

"What?"

"I said, 'Let them fire me.'" She raised her head long enough to utter those six words before getting busy again. I gave in (who wouldn't?) and afterward shook my head and grinned at her.

"What's gotten into you?" I studied her in the mirror as I rebuttoned my jumpsuit and tried to unflatten my hair. Toni and I hadn't done something this spontaneous in a long time. Not that I was complaining. Toni and I were pretty steady once-a-weekers, which was pretty damn good after nine and a half years.

"I don't know," Toni shrugged, looking quite pleased with

herself as she opened her bureau drawer and dug through her undershirts. "Maybe I wanted you to get lucky even without saying 'rabbit rabbit.' "

"I'm never saying it again." I threw my arms around her waist as she bent over to pull on her socks, both of us innocent of the truth of those words, because the fact is I've never said "rabbit rabbit" again. No, after what happened I've stopped believing in luck or lucky charms or pretty much anything at all.

But I don't want to get ahead of my story. In fact, if I had a magic wand I'd wave it over my head and go right back to that ordinary day and stay there forever. I wouldn't change a thing, except of course the day would never end. Because if the day had never ended...but I'm getting ahead of myself again.

Toni and I got it together and left the house after calling our respective bosses to say we'd be about half an hour late. The bookstore is never busy in the morning, so it wasn't a problem for me. And since Toni is usually not more than ten minutes late and hardly ever calls in sick, her boss wasn't too concerned either. She knew if Toni needed a little extra time in the morning, she probably had a good excuse. And if necessary, I certainly could vouch for that.

Toni dropped me off, then headed on to The Tip Top Copy Shop where she's worked ever since I've known her. Between my managing the bookstore and Toni being the head typesetter at Tip Top, we knew just about everyone in town. Burnsville is one of those small, arts-oriented, liberal New England pockets, so it's no big deal to be a lesbian couple here. Everyone knew Toni and I were an item, and no one made a big deal about it. But wasn't a "don't ask, don't tell" situation either. We were treated pretty much like any other couple. When a dozen roses arrived at the store on our anniversary last year, my boss found a vase in the back for me and said, "Toni sure knows how to treat a lady, doesn't she?" even though I hadn't yet told her who had sent the flowers.

And when I would stop in to see Toni at work, whoever was at the front counter would yell back, "Toni, Roberta's here," before I even had a chance to open my mouth.

I poured myself a second cup of coffee and got busy unpacking the cartons of books that were waiting for me in the back. I love everything about books: the feel of them, the smell of them, the weight and heft of them in my hands. Even before I worked in a bookstore, I was a voracious reader, the kind who devours every single word between a book's front and back covers. The copyright page. The acknowledgments. The list of the author's other titles. Even the ISBN number and the Library of Congress cataloguing information. And I can't abandon a book, even if it's boring or predictable or horribly written. I hang on until the very last word, hoping somehow that the author will rally at the end. You never know. Books, like life, are full of surprises. And of course I'm a closet writer. Everyone who works in a bookstore dreams of being an author, the one the customers stand in line waiting to talk to, copies of her book clutched tightly in their hands. Yes, I've practiced signing autographs; yes, I've rehearsed my National Book Award acceptance speech; yes, I know exactly what I would wear on TV if Oprah picked my work for her latest book club selection; no, I haven't written a single thing since college.

The morning flew by, between unpacking the new shipment from our distributor and going through the bags of used paperbacks customers had dropped off over the weekend. This was another task I thoroughly enjoyed. Old paperbacks were like old friends, and it surprised me that people so easily discarded them. Who, for example, would give up their well-worn, dog-eared copy of *Catch-22* so soon after Joseph Heller had died? Who had left off a bag of Russian classics, including Dostoevsky's *Crime and Punishment, The Selected Poems of Mayakovsky,* and Tolstoy's *Anna*

Karenina? My favorite discoveries were books that had personal inscriptions and this morning I found several, including a copy of Pablo Neruda's *The Captain's Verses,* which in my opinion is the most romantic book of love poems ever written. The half-title page bore the inscription: "Darling Laura, my love for you is as deep as the sea. Love and kisses, your Captain, Sidney." Unfortunately, Laura must have thought Captain Sidney's love was pretty shallow, since she was willing to exchange his token of affection for less than a dollar. I felt bad for Sidney, whoever he was, but hoped he would find a more appreciative lover, just as I hoped his book would find its way to a more appreciative audience.

After going through the paperbacks, I sorted through the ever-growing pile on my desk—distributor invoices, catalogs of upcoming books, back issues of *Publishers Weekly*—and then Toni called to see if I wanted to have lunch together.

"It's so nice out," she said. "Let's have sandwiches in the park."

"I'll pick some up and walk over." I glanced at the cat-shaped clock on my desk. "Give me half an hour."

I called in our sandwiches, and as soon as Jocelyn, the owner of the Good Belly Deli, heard my voice she asked, "The usual?" That's what kind of town this is. My usual is smoked Gouda on rye with lettuce, sprouts, and a dab of mustard; Toni's was egg salad on pumpernickel with tomato and mayo and a sour dill pickle on the side. By the time I got to the deli, our lunches were bagged and ready; by the time I got to the copy shop, Toni was standing out front, leaning against the building, her face tilted toward the sun.

"Hi, love." Her words warmed me more than the rays beating down through my jacket. "Sure wish I didn't have to be inside today."

"Let's take the rest of the day off," I suggested as we started walking.

"OK." Toni was always game. "Where do you want to go?"

"The beach." The ocean was my favorite destination. "Want to drive to the coast this weekend?"

"Don't you have to work on Sunday?" Toni asked as we sat down on a bench in the park facing the sun.

"Oh, yeah," I said, sinking my teeth into my sandwich. "Reality bites."

After we ate, we sat on the bench a while, not saying much, just enjoying being outside on the first really warm day of spring. We watched some kids goofing around on skateboards, a businessman yakking into his cell phone, a young mother pushing a stroller, stopping every three feet or so to fuss over her child. A black-and-white puppy wagging its tail-less butt sixty miles an hour bounded across the park to us and practically jumped into Toni's lap, trying to lick her face. The dog's owner appeared a moment later, leash in hand, apologizing. Toni waved her away as the dog dashed off in another direction, and I laughed, remarking to Toni how irresistible she was.

"What can I tell you?" Toni shrugged. "Dogs love me, children love me…"

"Femmes love you…"

"Femmes love me," Toni repeated with a self-satisfied smile.

"Hey!" I poked her in the arm.

"I mean one femme loves me," Toni hastened to correct herself. "Which is all that matters to me."

Lunch ended too quickly, as it always did, and Toni walked me back to the bookstore. "Pick you up at six, dollface," she said, ruffling my hair. Toni never kissed me in public, and though I understood her caution, I wasn't pleased by it. Then again, I wasn't the one who had the word *lesbian* practically tattooed on my forehead simply because of the way I cut my hair and wore my clothes. Tolerant as this town was, I didn't blame Toni for wanting to be careful.

I have floor duty in the afternoon, and the store was pretty busy. Several die-hard Stephen King fans stopped in wanting his latest and were none too pleased when I told them they had to come back next Tuesday, the official release date. A woman came in asking about a Toni Morrison title, studied the book for a good fifteen minutes, then left the store empty-handed. I watched her go, knowing she was either on her way to the mall where she could get a steeper discount at one of the chains, or on her way home to order the book over the Internet. There's really nothing I can do about readers like that. I try to focus instead on our loyal, faithful customers, people like Mrs. Wolinksy who buys a book from us either for herself or as a gift at least once a week. (Today she was in for Sue Grafton's latest.)

When things got slow, I worked on a display of gardening books, always big sellers this time of year. And then it was six o'clock, and my Toni was walking through the door with that smile on her face, the one she swore was reserved only for me.

"Chicken or fish?" she asked by way of greeting. It's a joke that started way back at the beginning of our relationship when I said I never wanted to become old farts like my parents.

"They're so boring," I'd explained to Toni. "Every day my mother calls my father at the office around four o'clock to ask what he wants for supper. 'Fish or chicken? Chicken or fish?' I swear, when I was a kid it drove me insane." And then before you knew it, I was asking Toni the same question, only since we're vegetarians it was "Pasta or stir-fry? Stir-fry or pasta?'" The first time I called to ask her, she replied, "Humble pie," reminding me that we weren't so different from my parents after all.

"Let's go out," I suggested as I gathered my things. Since I was always reminding Toni that we had to watch our budget, she raised one eyebrow in surprise. "Hey," I said, "what the heck, it's Friday night. And," I cocked my head to the side, "who says you're the only one full of surprises?"

We left the car where it was and walked two blocks over to our favorite Chinese restaurant. We ordered mu shoo vegetables and vegetarian lo mein and talked about my upcoming birthday.

"So, birthday girl..." Toni began.

"Don't rush me," I admonished her, waving my chopsticks in the air. "I'm still in my late forties, and I want to stay here as long as I can."

Toni laughed to herself as she poured us some tea. "Let's see. According to my precise calculations, you have one month and seven days until you officially become the prettiest fifty-year-old woman in the world."

"Well, when you put it that way it doesn't sound so bad." I smiled and watched her load some mu shoo vegetables onto a pancake, add the sauce, and roll the whole thing up. "I still can't decide if I want to throw a big party or have you take me on a trip."

"Why not both?" Toni asked, never one to deprive herself of pleasure, as opposed to me, Miss Practicality.

"Toni, we can't afford to do both," I reminded her.

"Says you." Toni pointed a chopstick at me. "Don't you worry your pretty little head about it. This is a special occasion, and I want my girl to have everything her heart desires."

We finished dinner, drank our tea, and read our fortune cookies. Toni went first. "*A great adventure awaits you,*" she read, holding the little slip of paper at arm's length as she had yet to give in and buy herself a pair of reading glasses.

"See, maybe we should go on a trip for my birthday," I said, cracking open my cookie. "Mine says," I unrolled the little slip of paper, "*A great adventure awaits you.* Hey." I looked up at Toni. "I don't think we've ever gotten the same fortune before. Do you think this means we're meant to be together?"

"Till death do us part." Toni raised her water glass and clinked it against mine. "*L'chaim,*" she said, taking a long sip.

"Now you have to break it." I motioned for her to put the glass underfoot like she did at our commitment ceremony. "Remember?"

"Of course I remember. How could I forget the happiest day of my life?" Toni wrapped her fortune cookie up in her napkin and smashed her fist down on top of it. "*Mazel tov!*"

Now that I think back to that dinner, I'm amazed by our conversation. *Till death do us part...* Did Toni know, on some level, what was going to happen to us? I once had a friend named Pamela who died of insulin shock when she was only thirty. She lived in New York City, and I hadn't talked to her in more than a year when out of the blue she called and left a message on my answering machine: "I just wanted you to know I was thinking of you and that our friendship has always meant a lot to me, even though we don't see each other very often anymore." And the next day she was dead. A mutual friend called to tell me. Pamela had been diabetic since birth and knew exactly how to handle her diet and medication, so it was a mystery to everyone how she could have run out of insulin. I've always regretted not calling her back right away, and I've always wondered about the timing of her call. Did she have some kind of unconscious premonition? Or was it merely a spooky coincidence?

Not that I gave much thought to what Toni said at the time. Right then I just felt warm all over, completely safe in Toni's love for me and in our secure, ordinary, mundane, and sometimes downright boring little life. A life that fit me like a glove ninety-nine percent of the time, though once in a while I grew restless, particularly in the spring when the change in the weather made me think about making some other change in my life—apply for a new job maybe or move to a bigger, more exciting town. Whenever I brought up the idea, Toni would joke about it: "Maybe we should take up bungee-jumping." When I told her to be serious, and that I thought our life was growing a bit stagnant and stale, Toni, the most content person I had ever met, just shook her head, unable to understand what in the world I had to be dissatisfied about. "You don't know how good you have it," she'd say, and then remind me of the words of a Holocaust survivor we'd once seen interviewed on television. When asked what she missed the most during her days in the camps, the woman said, "All I longed for was the luxury of a long, boring evening at home." And now of course I've learned my lesson: I'd give anything to have just one more day of the boring little life I shared with Toni and didn't fully appreciate until it was fully and irrevocably gone.

Toni and I walked back to the car and headed home. Once inside, we drifted through the house in different directions: Toni went to get the mail; I wandered into the kitchen to give Sophie her supper. Then Toni settled in the living room to read the paper, and I went into the bedroom to make a few phone calls. At nine o'clock we watched an *I Love Lucy* rerun on Nick at Nite, and as we sat on the couch side by side with Sophie asleep between us, I again pondered the ordinariness of our lives. This was a pretty typical Friday night for us. We weren't out there smashing the patriarchy or recruiting innocent children into our deviant lifestyle or doing whatever else Pat Robertson and company liked to think we evil lesbians were up to. If only the Pope could see us now, I thought, staring at Toni's and my feet, all four of which were encased in dorky, fuzzy, zebra-striped slippers we'd bought on sale at Filene's Basement. Not that I wanted His Holiness in my living room at the moment, thank you very much. It's just that I was awfully tired of being seen as horrible, sick, and disgusting by him and everyone else who didn't think we were worthy of our civil rights. Toni and I often joked about how "radical" we were. We both had worked the same job for more than a decade and were die-hard monogamists. *What's to hate?* I wondered, not for the first time. Civil rights, hate crimes, and all the rest of it were on my mind lately (they were on everyone's minds) because yet another lesbian had been brutally beaten up recently, this time out in California. It made national news because she was the daughter of some bigwig CEO-type at a Fortune 500 company. As though that made her more important than some dirt-poor lesbian who got the crap beaten out of her in Nowheresville, USA. In any event, Toni and I had gone to a local vigil for the woman on the steps of City Hall (*that's* what kind of town this is), and then we hadn't talked that much about it. It was too painful, especially for Toni, since the woman was butch and by all accounts was brutalized for no other reason than that. And for being in the wrong place at the wrong time.

"Ready to go to bed?" I asked Toni, leaning against her shoulder and stifling a yawn.

"Yeah, I guess." My darling stretched her arms over her head then brought them down around me. "First I think I'll have a little *nosh.*" Toni smiled at me, pleased with herself like she always was when she used a Yiddish word correctly. "Sophie," she imitated my grandmother's Yiddish accent as she addressed the cat, "let's go into the kitchen and have a *bissl* pound cake, a bagel or two or seven, what's bad?" Toni got up and Sophie leapt off the couch.

"You certainly didn't have to ask her twice." I got up too and followed my family into the kitchen, where Toni was already foraging.

"Care to join me in a sandwich?" she asked, slicing the end off a loaf of sourdough rye.

"I'd rather join you in the bedroom," I said, stifling another yawn.

"Why don't you go get ready for bed? Sophie and I will be along in a minute." Toni tossed a bite-size bit of Swiss cheese to the cat and laid a few thin slices onto a piece of bread.

"Toni, don't feed her that." I bent down to snatch the cheese away from Sophie, but I didn't stand a chance.

"Oh, Roberta, let the poor girl enjoy life. How would you like to survive on that?" She pointed to Sophie's bowl, the brownish-gray contents of which, I had to admit, didn't look very appetizing.

"But people-food isn't good for her," I reminded Toni as I did almost every night.

"One little bite of cheese isn't going to kill her."

"But you give her one little bite of something every day."

"I do not."

"You do too."

"Hey, don't we have any milk?" Toni changed the subject, like she always did when she knew I was right.

"I must have used it up this morning," I called over my shoulder as I headed into the bathroom. "I thought we'd be going to the store after work, but we went out. Sorry."

"But I was going to make my famous French toast tomorrow morning," Toni whined. Even though I couldn't see her, I knew the corners of her mouth were pushed down into a frown.

"I'll run out and get some when I get up," I offered, spitting out a gob of toothpaste.

"No, no, no." Toni crossed the kitchen and stood in the bathroom doorway. "That's the best part of Saturday morning, not having to take a shower and get dressed until we feel like it. We can read the paper, eat breakfast, get back into bed..."

"I don't mind." I pulled back my hair with a black headband and smeared my face with Noxzema.

"I mind," Toni said. "I'll go get some now."

"I'll come with you."

"Like that?" Toni pointed to my gooped-up face and laughed. "You just get into your little pj's and I'll be back before you know it. You need anything else at the store?"

"I don't think so. Hurry back."

"OK. See you soon." Toni kissed the top of my head, grabbed her sandwich, and was gone.

I finished my beauty routine and got into bed, with Sophie curled at my feet. I hoped I'd sleep well that night, but I was in the throes of menopause, so anything was possible. Usually I had no trouble falling asleep, but I had a lot of trouble staying asleep because more often than not I'd wake up drenched with sweat, and once that happened it was impossible for me to get any more shut-eye. The previous night I had woken up at precisely 4:43 according to the clock at my bedside, and I had tossed and turned from that moment until 7:02 A.M. when the alarm went off.

"Good night, little Sophie-cat." My eyes were closing despite the big, fat, juicy new collection of poems by Grace Paley I was holding on my lap. I put the book aside, shut the light off, and must have fallen asleep immediately because all I remember after that was dreaming of standing next to Toni at the beach, the pounding surf getting closer and closer and closer, roaring so loudly it woke me up. And then I realized someone was knocking at the door.

"Toni, did you forget your key?" I asked as I stumbled out of bed. But Toni wasn't at the door. A police officer stood on the front porch, his uniform dark as the night surrounding him.

"Are you…is everything…where's Toni?" My words tumbled out on top of each other.

"There's been an accident. You'd best get dressed and come with me," the officer said.

In a daze, I threw on some clothes and rode in the police car to the hospital, already feeling guilty that I'd been fast asleep while Toni was…Toni was what? I had no idea, and I wanted—and didn't want—to find out.

The rest of that night is a blur, though at the same time I remember every horrible little detail of it. The waiting room with its ugly plastic orange chairs and out-of-date magazines with glamorous celebrities mocking me from their glossy covers. The *whoosh* of the automatic doors as they opened and shut, with nurses in crisp white slacks and soft-soled shoes strolling endlessly in and out. No one would tell me anything, even though I kept waving papers around: the health care proxy and power of attorney forms Toni and I had filled out a year after we first got together, which I'd somehow managed to remember to bring along, though they weren't doing me a bit of good now.

Finally a doctor came out and sat next to me. She asked if there was someone I could call.

"Why?" I asked. "I'm her family." I showed her the papers, which she said she'd already seen, as Toni kept a copy of them in her glove compartment.

"I can't really tell you anything unless there's someone here with you."

"Oh, my God!" She didn't have to say another word. I knew in that instant Toni was gone.

I'm sure you want the details, though they don't really matter. She was standing in line with the carton of milk in her hands when out of nowhere a car crashed right through the front window of the store, and Toni—my always-putting-other-people-before-herself Toni—had rushed to push a young woman with a baby in her arms out of the way. The driver of the car was old and confused and had mixed up the gas pedal with the brake pedal and driven right into the store. His wife had a little indigestion, and he was there to pick up some Pepto-Bismol. And because of that, Toni, my wonderful, loving, perfect, all-I-could-ever-dream-of-and-more Toni, is gone. Gone because she went out for a half-gallon of milk. Gone because she wanted to make me a special Saturday morning breakfast. Gone because I'd eaten a bowl of shredded wheat that morning. Gone because some poor old woman's dinner had disagreed with her, and so she'd asked her husband to go to the store to get something that would help settle her stomach.

I feel so incredibly guilty that I fell asleep so easily that night, clueless that Toni was lying on the floor of the 7-Eleven with her life—our life—already gone. I'd always thought Toni and I were psychically connected, that of course I'd know if anything awful happened to her. I'd know it in my bones. But I didn't know it. And it was so ironic. So many times when Toni was late (and she was chronically late) I'd think the worst: She was mugged, she was kidnapped, her car had broken down on a stretch of deserted highway. And it always turned out it was nothing. She had bumped into a friend, and they decided to go out for coffee. Or she'd gone out to put some gas in the car and had been distracted by a group of girls playing softball in the park. Toni never went directly from point A to point B. It used to drive me crazy. Once we were on our way someplace—to the movies, I think—and we were running late. I got into the passenger side of the car, and Toni, instead of getting behind the wheel, walked across the driveway out into the yard. I was just rolling down my window to yell at her when she made her way over to me, a peach-colored rose in her hand. "For you, love. The last rose of summer." And the smile on her face was so dazzling—more dazzling than the rose—my anger simply melted away.

Is it really true that I'll never, ever *ever* see that smile again? I just can't fathom it. But it must be so. The doctor said she died instantly. Didn't feel a thing. I hope that's true. I hope she had no idea she was leaving me forever because that would have been more than she could bear. We'd talked about it, of course. Talked about growing old together, joked about having wheelchair races down the hall of the Old Dykes' Nursing Home, where some young butch would be spoon-feeding me mashed tofu while a shapely young femme would massage Toni's callused, aching feet. The one time we spoke of it seriously, Toni said she wanted me to go first. "You'd be too sad without me," she'd said.

"And you wouldn't be sad?" I asked her. We were lying in bed on a lazy Sunday morning, tickling Sophie, who was sprawled belly-up between us.

"I'm stronger than you are," Toni said. "I'd just get myself a little cabin in the woods and live out the rest of my days like a hermit."

"You would not," I said, shaking my head. "You'd be fighting off the femmes with a stick."

"That's better than having an army of butches beating down your door," Toni said, rapping her knuckles on my stomach. And then we didn't talk anymore.

I'm so glad we made love the last day of her life. I think about that now—it was so odd, we hadn't made love on a weekday morning in years. Did Toni know? How could she? I wish I'd said "I love you" before she walked out the door that night. I wish I hadn't used up the milk that morning. I wish I had gone with her. I wish I had insisted she forget it and let me go for the milk in the morning. I wish I hadn't fought with her about feeding Sophie people-food before she headed out the door. I know I shouldn't blame myself, but still I keep coming back to it: If I hadn't gotten on Toni's case about giving Sophie that piece of cheese, maybe she would have left the house half a minute earlier and those thirty seconds would have made all the difference.

I keep thinking this is the kind of thing that happens to other people, the kind of thing you read about in the paper before you turn the page and see what Dear Abby has to say. I can't have lost my Toni over a carton of milk. Milk, for God's sake. Of all the things I dreaded might happen to her, something like this never crossed my mind. If Toni were here, we'd joke about it. "Don't cry over spilled milk," I'd say. Ha ha ha. And how about those matching fortune cookies from the Chinese restaurant? I just assumed we'd embark on the great adventure that awaited each of us together, not alone.

And I know this sounds bizarre, but I can't help thinking if Toni had been gay-bashed, like I'd always feared would happen, at least that would make sense somehow. At least then there'd be a reason why she died, at least she'd be a martyr like Brandon Teena or Matthew Shepard. At least then the whole world would know her name, and I'd have something to rail against. Sometimes I feel angry at the man who was driving the car (and who walked away with barely a scratch), but whenever I do I hear Toni's voice saying, "The poor guy. He has to live with this the rest of his life. He didn't mean to do it, Roberta. It was an accident. It could have happened to anyone." *But it didn't happen to anyone,* I want to scream at her. *It happened to you. It happened to us.* I don't know why it's easier for me to get angry at Toni than it is for me to get angry at her killer. ("Don't call him that," I hear Toni saying.) Why did she insist on going out that night? What the hell was so important about making me some lousy French toast? Why didn't she drive a little slower or a little faster so she didn't wind up in the wrong place at the wrong time? Why didn't she just mind her own business and get herself out of the way of the car? ("And let an innocent woman and child die?" I hear Toni's voice asking me in disbelief.) Toni would say it was her destiny and there was nothing we could have done to stop it—she was a great believer in fate; she always said she and I were simply meant to be. I can't believe I was meant to be so happy for such a short time—nine lousy years—and now Toni and I are meant to be apart.

Her last words to me were "See you soon," and my last words to her were "Hurry back." How I wish she could. I can't believe Toni isn't here today of all days, my fiftieth birthday. It was supposed to be such a huge celebration, but instead it's just one more day to get through. A day that starts like any other workday: The alarm rings at seven; I slap down the snooze button and snuggle into the blankets for a few more minutes of blissful unconsciousness before Sophie butts her hard furry head against my back, letting me know it's time for the day to begin. But I don't get out of bed right away, much to her chagrin. I keep my eyes shut for a few precious seconds as the nightmare that has become my life starts all over again.

Just Like a Woman

The screen door slammed behind Cassie, who winced before she realized with a jolt of relief that no one was home to yell at her. Her mother had taken the train into the city to go to a museum—she had signed up for some lecture series or something—and her father, the original Mr. Type A Personality, had gone into the office even though it was Saturday. Cassie rummaged through what her mother had dubbed the "flotsam and jetsam" that lay on the kitchen counter—piles of mail, old newspapers and magazines, potholders, coupons, and other assorted junk—looking for the wallet she'd forgotten, while her best friend Tammy and her mother waited in the car. Mrs. Ryan was driving them to the mall, and they'd gotten almost halfway there before Cassie realized she'd left her wallet at home. Mrs. Ryan had been pretty nice about it, saying everyone makes mistakes, no big deal, she didn't do it on purpose and blah, blah, blah, but Tammy had turned around to roll her eyes at Cassie in the backseat and proclaim, "Parker, you are so pathetic."

"Oh, shut up, Ryan."

"Girls, this isn't the army." Mrs. Ryan glanced sideways at her daughter and then met Cassie's eyes for a split second in the rearview mirror. "Must you call each other by your last names?"

"Sorry, Mom," Tammy mumbled. Then she swiveled around again. "*Cassie*, you are so pathetic."

"Oh, shut up, *Tammy*."

Mrs. Ryan laughed. "That's much better."

Cassie ran upstairs, taking the steps two at a time, almost tripping on the laces of her high-tops, which were forever untying themselves. Maybe her wallet was in the "shipwreck" of her room, as her mother called it. Cassie's mom had seen *Titanic* at least a dozen times. "Don't you just love that Leonardo DiCaprio?" she asked Cassie whenever they were in Stop and Shop and saw his face on the cover of *People* or some other magazine.

"Mom." Cassie would groan and shake her head like her mother was the teenager and she was the…the what? Parent? Yeah, right. That was the last thing Cassie ever wanted to be, someone who spent all her time yelling at someone to do her homework, clean up her room, get off the phone…

If your room wasn't such a disaster area, you'd know where your wallet was. Even though Cassie's mother was a good thirty miles away, her voice was right here, yammering inside her head. She threw aside dirty jeans, inside-out sweaters, mismatched socks, candy wrappers, and comic books, all to no avail. Just when she was about to give up, she spotted her purple backpack sprawled sideways in the corner with all its contents spilling out like it had just been in a terrible accident. Cassie plucked her wallet from the debris along with an old orange baseball cap her mother forbid her to wear out of the house. She stuffed the wallet into the back pocket of her baggy jeans and pulled the cap down low over her short, slicked-back hair. One quick glance in the mirror and she was ready. But just as she was about to run down the stairs, she heard something. Music. Coming from her parents' bedroom. *Did Mom forget to turn off the CD player again?* Cassie wondered. They were both getting so forgetful lately. Mrs. Parker blamed it all on hormones.

"Our bodies are changing, sweetheart," she said to Cassie one night when her father was working late and it was just the two of them. "Girls' night out," her mother called it, even though they didn't go anywhere—just ordered a pizza and ate it off paper plates at the kitchen table. "I used to bleed for five, six days at a time, sometimes even a whole week, but now it's drip, drip, drip for half a day and then I'm through. Oh, well." Mrs. Parker shrugged her shoulders at Cassie, who didn't know what to say to this information about her mother, which was way more than she wanted to know. "I'm like the last rose of summer," Mrs. Parker went on, then paused to sigh dramatically, "while you, my dear, are just beginning to bloom." Cassie's mother studied her wolfing down a slice of pizza. "After we eat, I'm going to give myself a facial. Would you like to join me?" Her voice was almost wistful. "I've got some ripe avocados we could mash up. They're supposed to be very good for the skin. Or we could give each other manicures. Or—"

"When's Dad getting home?" Cassie asked, eager to change the subject.

"Don't talk with your mouth full, honey." If Mrs. Parker couldn't get Cassie to stop being a tomboy, the least she could do was teach her to mind her manners. "Your father," she curled her lower lip inward, shook her head, and sighed again. "He's so afraid to leave that office if there's one thing left undone, if there's one last task he hasn't crossed off that never-ending list. He has to do, do, do like he's playing beat the clock with his own mortality." Mrs. Parker dropped her voice slightly, about to confide something else Cassie was sure she didn't want to hear. "There's definitely such a thing as male menopause, sweetie. It's not so obvious, since men don't have a period, of course. But they get cranky and moody too, believe me. Your father's been acting very strange lately... I don't know what to do with him. The other night I—"

"May I please be excused?" Cassie was still a little hungry, but her need to end this heart-to-heart conversation she never wanted to have in the first place was stronger than her desire for another piece of pizza.

Mrs. Ryan gave the horn two swift toots and Cassie hurried down the hallway. The door to her parents' bedroom was closed tightly, and Cassie hesitated. She didn't especially like going in there—that's where they did it, after all—but she knew she had to or she'd be the one to catch hell for leaving the CD player on, even though she hadn't been listening to it in the first place. "You were the last one to leave the house," her mother would be sure to say. Cassie turned the knob and opened the door gently, but before she could step into the room she saw something that froze her to the spot. Her father. At least she thought it was her father. Someone who looked an awful lot like him was sitting at her mother's dressing table, wearing one of her mother's long pink nightgowns with some sort of matching sheer pink jacket with lace at the collar and sleeves. Cassie blinked once, twice, as her mind reeled. *Mom's going to kill him for stretching out her clothes like that.* Then Cassie switched into logic mode. *Wait a minute. Those can't be her clothes. She's like a size two and he's almost six feet tall, not to mention a hundred and eighty pounds, besides.*

Then whose nightgown is that? Cassie wondered, though she guessed that didn't really matter. What mattered was that was definitely her dad, all pretty in pink with his face pressed up against the mirror like he couldn't get close enough to his own reflection. Cassie wanted to run, but instead she stayed put and watched her father outline his lips in a ridiculous shade of red, touch up his eyelashes with jet black mascara, and brush his cheeks with a rosy blush until he totally transformed himself into…into what? A monster, a weirdo, a fucking freak.

"Hey, Parker, you coming or what?" Tammy called through the screen door.

Cassie started, like she'd been shaken out of a dream—or a nightmare—and then ran downstairs and out the door before Tammy could run up. Had her father heard them? She doubted it. The music was pretty loud, and her father was singing along. "I Feel Pretty" from *West Side Story*—both her parents were completely into Broadway musicals—my God, how corny could you get?

"C'mon, girls." Mrs. Ryan's patience was finally beginning to wear thin. "I haven't got all day."

"Sorry," Cassie mumbled as she slid into the backseat.

"I don't know why you girls can't just ride your bikes to the Fairview Mall like everyone else. It's a lot closer than Riverdale, and then I wouldn't have to drive you."

"Mom, I've told you a million times, the stores are better at Riverdale."

"You'd get some exercise while you were at it and—Cassie, are you buckled up?" Tammy's mother paused her hand on the ignition key, waiting to hear a reassuring click from behind before she started the engine. Mrs. Ryan had been in an accident last year, nothing serious, just a little fender bender, but ever since she wouldn't even back out of the driveway until everyone's seat belt was on.

"Sorry," Cassie said again, fumbling for her strap.

"I don't know why you care so much about the shops anyway, Tammy." Mrs. Ryan turned back to her daughter. "It's not like you ever come home with a pretty sweater, or a skirt, God forbid. You too, Cassie. I know it would make your mother very happy if you bought yourself a nice outfit."

"Sorry," Cassie muttered for the third time. She knew Mrs. Ryan thought she was a bad influence on Tammy, who, until she started hanging out with Cassie, had kept her hair long and even worn a dress once in a while.

"What's with you?" Tammy flung herself sideways in the front seat so she could glare at Cassie, who usually bailed her out when her mother started in like this. They couldn't tell Mrs. Ryan the real reason they wanted her to take them to Riverdale—they could barely admit it to themselves—but Cassie was usually a lot more talkative and good at distracting Tammy's mother. Today she was no help whatsoever.

"You sick or something?" Tammy asked, narrowing her eyes at her friend.

"No," Cassie said, but her voice was caught somewhere down in her throat and came out in a little squeak.

"You OK, honey?" Mrs. Ryan stopped the car at a red light and turned to look at Cassie.

"Yeah," she said softly, then repeated it louder, "Yeah, I'm fine," in order to convince them. Or to convince herself, because the truth was, Cassie wasn't fine at all. She felt sick to her stomach and a little dizzy, like she had just stepped off the Drop of Fear, a ride Tammy had dared her to go on at Six Flags a couple of months ago. The man running the ride had motioned to Cassie to take her place on a bench-like contraption, and once she was seated he lowered a metal safety bar around her that clicked into place with a loud, final clank. Then the man started the ride, and Cassie, along with eleven other brave souls, was raised up, up, up into the air before she could change her mind. The bench rose so high that Cassie had a great view of the entire amusement park, including Tammy, who looked no bigger than the microscopic whitehead she had popped on her chin that morning. The bench finally came to a standstill at the top of the ride, and just as Cassie relaxed, thinking, *This won't be so bad,* the bench plunged to the ground like a crazy elevator let loose from its shaft. Cassie's arms and legs flew straight up in the air as her body raced toward the ground. After the ride landed, she managed to climb down from her seat, but her legs were wobbly and her stomach was queasy the rest of the afternoon. Of course she hadn't told Tammy that; then she'd know she was nothing but a big baby. "It was great," she said to her, thinking that the Drop of Fear was exactly like life: Just when you think everything's going to be okey-dokey—wham! The bottom gets dropped right out from under you.

Like today. What was up with her father? Was he sneaking out to a costume party? Was he some kind of pervert like those freaks who were always on *Jerry Springer*? But how could that be? Her father was normal. Her mother was normal. They were the most normal people around, so normal they were downright boring. Cassie was the weirdo, the freakazoid, the one who marched to the beat of a different drummer. But that was another story.

Mrs. Ryan pulled into the mall parking lot and stopped the car at the east entrance. "I'll pick you up right here at four o'clock. Does that give you enough time?"

"Yeah, Mom. Great. See you."

"You're welcome." Mrs. Ryan tilted her head and waited. Tammy leaned across the front seat and reluctantly kissed her cheek.

"Thanks, Mrs. Ryan." Cassie lumbered out of the car and walked with Tammy toward the polished glass doors of the mall.

"So what do you want to do?" Tammy asked once they were inside.

"I don't know."

"Want to get something to eat?"

"I don't care." A fresh wave of nausea swept through Cassie's stomach. The lights, the music, the stores, the people—it was all too much for her. "Can we just sit down for a minute?" She pointed to a bench next to a planter filled with artificial trees.

"What gives, Parker?" Tammy flopped down next to her and slung an arm around her shoulder.

"Hey, quit it!" Cassie jumped up as quickly as she'd sat down.

"What's with you?" Tammy frowned at Cassie, more puzzled than angry. "Nobody knows us here."

"I don't know. I'm just jumpy, I guess."

"Teenagers." Tammy shook her head in a perfect imitation of her mother, which made Cassie laugh and relax a little. These mall excursions, while they excited her, also made her somewhat nervous. But she could never tell Tammy that.

They headed toward the escalators and rode down to the Food Court. Cassie wished she could tell Tammy why she wasn't herself today—*And if I'm not myself who am I?* Cassie wondered—but this was a secret she wasn't ready to share yet, not even with Tammy.

They got two vanilla milkshakes and a large order of fries and sat down at a table to watch the shoppers stroll by. "Don't look over there." Tammy shifted her eyes to the left, and Cassie's head immediately snapped in that direction. "Hey!" Tammy grabbed Cassie's arm and Cassie yanked it away. "I said 'Don't look,' you dork. What's with you anyway?"

"I..." Could she say it? Tell Tammy what she'd seen? Or what she thought she'd seen? Maybe it had been a mirage, a vision, a figment of her warped imagination. But then again maybe it wasn't. "I have my period," Cassie finally said, taking the easy way out. "You know how weird I get."

"I'll say." Tammy picked up a French fry and traced a "W" for weird in the puddle of ketchup on the plate between them. "All right. They're gone anyway. Let's see." She swept the area with her eyes. "Ooh, over there. Three o'clock. The two with the pizza and the gigantic Sears box."

Cassie turned her head slowly to the left. "Where? I don't see them."

"You busy signal, that's because you're looking at nine o'clock. How many times do I have to tell you, twelve o'clock is straight ahead, six o'clock is behind you, three o'clock is to your right, nine o'clock is to your left..."

"OK, OK, I see them." Cassie studied the two women. "You think?"

"First of all, they both have short hair, and they're both wearing leather jackets, jeans, and workboots. Second of all, what do they have there? Some kind of appliance, right? An air filter, a toaster oven? I'd say they're members of the Pink Triangle Club. Definitely."

"I don't know. I guess so." Usually Cassie was more into this game, and she knew she wasn't being fair to Tammy. It wasn't Tammy's fault that Cassie's father was losing his mind, and it wasn't fair to let that spoil her day. "Hey, look over there. Ten-thirty."

"Ten-thirty?" Tammy laughed, raised her eyebrows, and glanced to her right. "Where?"

"The babes with the diet Cokes." Cassie didn't need X-ray vision to know what was in the giant plastic cups the two girls were sipping from. Girls like that always drank diet Cokes.

"Are you out of your freakin' mind?" Tammy scowled at the girls, who looked maybe a year or two older than her and Cassie. The blond one wore an orange fuzzy sweater, low-slung faded jeans, and three-inch platform shoes; her dark-haired friend was all in black: an off-the-shoulder leotard tucked into a pair of skin-tight pants. Both of them had perfectly manicured nails, perfectly made-up faces, and wore a ton of jewelry.

"You wish," Tammy said, popping a last French fry into her mouth.

"Yeah, maybe I do." Cassie stared at the girls—girls she knew wouldn't give her the time of day, with her short hair, oversize sweater, and ratty jacket and jeans.

"Hey, what's that supposed to mean?" Tammy asked in a voice full of hurt.

"Nothing. Hey, I have to go to the bathroom. Come with me?" Cassie softened her voice, giving Tammy the words she knew she'd been waiting to hear. Somehow it had been decided, even though they'd never discussed it, that Cassie would always be the one to give the signal. And so she did.

They stood up quietly, both of them in a hurry now, but nevertheless, each taking her time. Tammy put their milkshake cups one inside the other and wiped a smear of ketchup off the table with a paper napkin. Cassie made sure her wallet was secure in her back pocket and her orange cap was tilted at just the right angle while Tammy tossed the remains of their snack into a trash can marked "Please." Then without a word they rode the escalator up two floors and walked past a row of stores—The Gap, Victoria's Secret, Fashion Bug, The Disney Shop, Waldenbooks, The Body Shop—until they came to their destination.

Cassie pushed open the door of the women's room, strode inside, and then stopped short at the sight of a woman leaning toward the mirror over the sinks.

"Oof." Tammy collided with Cassie, who stumbled forward.

Just our luck, on today of all days, Cassie thought. There was never anyone in this bathroom; it was so out of the way. *Never say never,* Cassie's mother's voice chanted in her head. And for once in her life she was right, because this woman was big as life, frowning at her reflection as she pulled at a clump of mascara on her eyelashes with her forefinger and thumb.

"Hey, this is the ladies' room." The woman turned to face them, a wand of mascara paused in midair. "You can't bring your boyfriend in here." Though the woman was staring at Cassie, it was Tammy she addressed.

"My boyfriend?" Tammy spat out the word. "What are you, blind?"

"Don't get fresh with me, young lady. Do you want me to call security?"

"Oh, for chrissake," Cassie mumbled. She reached up with one hand to whip her cap off her head like she usually did in these situations. But then she got a better idea. With both hands, Cassie ripped open her jacket, the snaps popping like tiny firecrackers, and flung her sweater up over her head, leaving her bare chest exposed for a good ten seconds before covering herself up again. "There. Satisfied?" she asked the woman, whose face was as red as the small stain of ketchup on the sleeve of Tammy's white sweater.

"Oh, dear, I'm so sorry. It's just with your short hair and your baggy clothes and that cap and all—"

"Yeah, yeah, yeah. Tell it to the Marines." Cassie motioned with her head, indicating for Tammy to follow her into the handicapped stall. No need to wait—the woman surely wouldn't bother them now.

Tammy bolted the door behind them, then fell back against it, laughing. "What's *with* you today, Parker? I can't believe you did that."

"I can't believe it either." A burst of laughter flew out of Cassie's mouth. It wasn't the first time she'd been mistaken for a boy—far from it—but it was definitely the first time she'd ever done anything like that before.

"Did you see her face? Oh, man." Tammy cracked up again. "Why didn't you just take off your cap? Or let her hear your voice?"

"I don't know." Cassie felt so weird today, she might do anything. "C'mere now." She shrugged off her jacket and laid it on the floor as she heard the door to the bathroom close. Alone at last. Tammy plopped down on Cassie's jacket and Cassie did the same. Both girls curled their legs under them so they wouldn't be automatically seen by anyone waiting to use the stall.

Suddenly the bathroom got very, very quiet. Cassie looked at Tammy and felt the same ache in her chest she always did when they were finally together. It was this strange physical sensation, like her heart was getting bigger and smaller at the same time. Or like there was a hole in her heart that could only be plugged up by being as close to Tammy as possible. Cassie slowly took off her cap, then wrapped both arms around Tammy and hugged her as tightly as she dared.

"Hey." Tammy smiled and shut her eyes, waiting for Cassie to kiss her. Cassie let her wait a few seconds, then blew on her eyelids. Tammy's smile widened. Cassie always teased her like this.

"I missed you," Cassie said, tracing the softness of Tammy's cheek with the pads of her fingers.

"I missed you too," Tammy murmured, her eyes still closed. Cassie loved to look at Tammy, to study her, to drink her in. Tammy was so breathtaking, with her smooth skin, high cheekbones, and full, movie-star lips. She wasn't a misfit like Cassie, not by a long shot. Even with her short hair and sloppy clothes, she would never be mistaken for a guy in a million years. No, if anything Tammy could have any guy she wanted, but for some mysterious reason Cassie couldn't even begin to figure out, Tammy didn't want a guy. Tammy wanted *her.*

Cassie leaned toward Tammy and gave her tickling butterfly kisses with her eyelashes. Then she rubbed Tammy's nose with her own and then, finally, placed her lips on Tammy's. A sweet little groan began at the back of Tammy's throat.

"Shh," Cassie whispered. "We don't want company, do we?"

Tammy looked up at Cassie with wide eyes and shook her head. Then she squeezed her eyelids tightly together, and in one second Cassie was all over her, kissing her and touching her with an urgency that was new and exciting. Almost dangerous.

"Cassie," Tammy breathed out her name, letting her know she

was willing, more than willing, for Cassie to touch her everywhere. She let her unbutton her sweater and unhook her bra, and now Cassie did feel like the teenage boy she was always being mistaken for. With the soft lushness of Tammy's breasts under her hands, Cassie knew her life could end right now and she'd die perfectly happy. Tammy was running her fingers through Cassie's buzz cut and breathing quickly, and Cassie didn't care who heard them now. Anyone could walk in this very second and still Cassie wouldn't stop what she was doing. That bitch who was in here before, a security officer, the kids from school, Tammy's mother, Cassie's mother, Cassie's father—

At the thought of her father, Cassie felt something well up in her throat, and she pulled away from Tammy. She lay her head on Tammy's chest and felt her cool, smooth breast against her cheek.

"What's wrong, babe?" Tammy stroked Cassie's face with the flat of her hand.

Cassie let out a long, deep sigh. She didn't know what was wrong exactly. So her father liked to wear makeup and lacy nightgowns. Big deal. Who was she to judge? If anything, Cassie should sympathize. After all, she knew only too well what it was like to look different, to act different, to want different things. *But that's different,* Cassie thought. *He's my father.*

"I just wish we could hold hands and walk around like everyone else, you know?" Even though this wasn't what was on Cassie's mind, it was true. "I mean, we have to sneak around in a bathroom stall, for chrissake. It's pathetic."

"I know, babe, but I don't care. And anyway, it's only till we're in college next year." Cassie and Tammy had applied to the same schools, and even if they both didn't get into their first choice—Antioch—they'd promised each other they'd go to schools that were, at the most, only an hour apart. "And besides, you can hold my hand if you want. Everyone thinks you're a boy anyway."

"I know, but it's not like I can relax or anything. I mean, I'm always afraid someone's going to catch on and then beat me up."

"My poor baby." Tammy continued to caress Cassie's cheek.

"Let's get out of here." Cassie sat up and buttoned Tammy's sweater gently, like her body was a sleepy child that needed to be tucked in.

"I have to pee." Tammy shooed Cassie out of the stall, and Cassie used the next one over. When they went to the sinks to wash their hands, the automatic faucet Cassie stood in front of didn't work. She moved to the next sink, but nothing came out of that one either.

"What the...?" Cassie thrust her hands into every sink but couldn't get a drop out of any of the faucets.

"What's the matter now?" Tammy came up beside Cassie and rubbed her hands together under a faucet. Instantly water rushed out.

"Hey, I thought that one didn't work." Cassie put her hands into the sink and immediately the water stopped.

"What are you, an alien?" Tammy asked, laughing.

"I guess so." Cassie frowned, and her chin quivered like she was about to cry.

"Hey, it's no big deal." Tammy put her hands back in the sink so the water would run for Cassie, but she turned away. "Hey," Tammy said again. "You are acting really weird today. Are you sure you're all right?"

Cassie nodded, not trusting herself to speak, afraid she'd voice the thoughts running through her mind. *Was* she an alien? Was her whole family from Planet of the Wackos? Cassie wondered if her father was gay, if that's where she got it from. But what would that make her mother? A fag hag? A lesbian? And did all this mean she could now tell her parents that she liked girls? She doubted it. They still asked her insane questions like "Any boys call lately?" and "Who's taking you to the prom?" It was so ridiculous. *Look at me,* she wanted to shout at them. *Open your eyes! Your daughter's a dyke!*

"You ready?" Tammy asked.

Cassie nodded again, reached for Tammy's hand, and just for kicks held onto it as they left the bathroom. *This is what it feels like to be normal,* she thought as they started walking through the mall. But as soon as she saw some kids their age walking toward them, she squeezed Tammy's hand once and then dropped it.

"What do you want to do?" Tammy asked, looking at her watch. "We still have about an hour."

"I don't know." Cassie said. "Don't you have to buy anything?"

"Like what?"

"I don't know," Cassie said again. It seemed that was all she ever said these days. I don't know…I don't care…

"Let's get a cookie," Tammy said, steering Cassie in the direction of the Cookie Shack on the other side of the mall.

"OK." Cassie wasn't really hungry, but at least it was something to do.

They rode the escalator down one flight and fell in step with the rest of the shoppers: young mothers pushing babies in strollers, pairs of middle-aged women lugging enormous shopping bags, packs of teenagers teasing each other. As they passed Lord & Taylor, a woman in a white lab coat with a wicker basket slung over her arm accosted them. "Free makeovers today," she said in a singsong voice, handing Tammy a card.

"Get real," Tammy singsonged back, tossing the card over her shoulder.

"Tammy, I'm surprised at you," Cassie said, shaking her head. "Every woman can stand a little improvement." It was something Cassie's mother had said to her many times.

"Right this way." The woman extended her arm toward the

store as if she were inviting them to enter the land of their dreams.

"C'mon, Tammy," Cassie said, heading inside.

"What are you doing, Parker?" Tammy couldn't figure out if Cassie was kidding or not.

"I'm getting a makeover, Ryan." Cassie slid onto a stool in front of a counter piled high with lipsticks and eyeshadows.

"This I've got to see," Tammy said, taking a seat next to Cassie.

"Can I help you?" A woman with eyebrows that looked drawn with a black magic marker and bright fuchsia lips smiled at Tammy. She had a nametag that said "Crystal" pinned to her white lab coat.

"My *girlfriend,*" Tammy exaggerated the word as she gestured toward Cassie, "wants a makeover."

"Great." Crystal looked over at Cassie and paused. Cassie could just imagine what she was thinking: *Oh, shit, this'll be a challenge!* Or, *Christ, as if my day hasn't been hard enough.* But Crystal merely shook her head slightly as if to compose herself, smiled, and asked, "What's your name, honey?"

"Tiffany," Cassie said, removing her cap as Tammy burst out laughing. "Don't mind her," Cassie glared at Tammy. "She doesn't get out much."

"I see," Crystal said, two worry lines creasing her heavily powdered forehead. "So, Tiffany, do you want an everyday look, or is this for a special occasion?"

"She's getting married." Tammy folded her arms.

"Really? How exciting. Congratulations."

"Yep. Soon she'll be Mrs. Michael Williams," Tammy said, nodding. "Tiffany Williams. Tiffany Cassandra Williams." Tammy paused between each word and moved her hand through the air as if she were tracing the name on a marquee.

"That's lovely," Crystal said. "Can I see your ring?"

"Uh…"

"She left it at home. It's huge, and you just can't be too careful these days."

"Of course."

"Bite me," Cassie whispered to Tammy as Crystal turned her back and started rummaging through a drawer full of compacts and brushes. Michael Williams was the biggest dickbrain in their class. He was always busting Cassie's chops by making up little chants like "Parker eats pussy" and "Cassie is a lezzie" and singing them out whenever he passed her in the hall.

"I'd love to," Tammy said, clicking her teeth together and leaning toward Cassie.

"Now then..." Crystal turned back around and pushed up her sleeves like a woman who knew she had her work cut out for her. "You don't really need foundation, you have lovely skin. So, let's start with the eyes. They are the mirror to the soul, you know." She narrowed her own eyes at Cassie as though she were an artist appraising a blank canvas. "Let's try Spring Rain and Autumn Dew. That's usually a good combination for hazel eyes." She leaned toward Cassie and applied the eye shadow with a tiny foam applicator. "What do you think?" Crystal took Cassie by the shoulders and turned her toward Tammy.

"Just darling," Tammy said.

"Now, I think a dark eyeliner and mascara, don't you?" Crystal directed the question to Tammy as if she were some kind of expert. Somehow—and Cassie couldn't quite figure out how this had happened—Crystal and Tammy had become conspirators, and she, the one getting the damn makeover, was still the outsider. She remained silent as Crystal wiped, brushed, smoothed, and smeared gooey-feeling products all over her: cover-up, blush, pressed powder, and God only knows what else.

"And now for the finishing touch." Crystal uncapped a lipstick tube with a flourish. "This is the cherry on the sundae, the icing on the cake. It's called 'Just Like a Woman' and I haven't found anyone it doesn't look good on yet."

There's always a first time, Cassie thought and would have said out loud if Crystal hadn't been messing with her mouth.

"There." Crystal dabbed Cassie's nose one last time with a small foam sponge and stepped back. "Ta-da!" She whipped a big round mirror out from under the counter and held it up in front of Cassie. "What do you think?"

"Whoa." Cassie recoiled from her reflection, all the makeup in the world unable to hide the startled look in her eyes. *Christ,* she thought. *Even with all this stuff on my face, I still don't look like a girl.* No, in fact Cassie looked more like a boy than ever, only now she looked like a boy who'd been caught red-handed playing with his mother's makeup. *Jesus.* Cassie shut her eyes for a few seconds then opened them again, but her reflection remained the same. *Well, what did you expect?* she asked herself silently. *I'm damned if I do and damned if I don't.*

"It is kind of a shock, isn't it?" Crystal put the mirror back under the counter. "Makeup can do amazing things to a face."

"I'll say," Tammy chuckled.

Cassie remained mute as Crystal started putting her supplies away and launching into her sales pitch. "Now, Tiffany, if you don't want such a heavily made-up look for every day, you can just use lipstick, blush, and mascara. That's what I'd recommend for someone your age." Clearly Crystal hadn't bought the wedding ruse for one second. "The mascara is twelve, the blush is fifteen, and the lipstick is ten, so that would only come to thirty-seven dollars."

"She'll think about it," Tammy said, hopping off her stool. "C'mon, Parker, wipe that shit off your face and let's go."

"Tammy." Cassie's voice was full of reproach. "I told you," she turned to Crystal, "she has no social skills whatsoever. Especially when she doesn't take her medicine." Tammy hung her head loosely from her neck, stuck her tongue out of one side of her mouth, and blew a spit bubble. "I'd better get her out of here before she starts to drool. Thank you very much." Cassie slid off her stool, took Tammy by the arm, and led her out of the store.

"What the hell was that about?" Tammy looked at her girlfriend, her head cocked at a questioning angle. "Oh, my God, Cassie, you look just like a woman...*NOT!* C'mon, let's go wash your face. We have to meet my mother."

"Why would I want to wash my face? Don't I look pretty? I feel pretty." Cassie started singing. "I feel pretty, oh, so pretty. I feel pretty and witty and *gay.*" As Cassie sang out the word "gay," she flung her arms wide and raised her voice. People turned to look at her.

"Cassie, I think you're the one who needs medication." Tammy kept her head down as they walked to the east entrance of the mall. "Seriously, you're making me kind of nervous."

"Not as nervous as some people are going to be," Cassie muttered, opening the door for Tammy.

"What did you say?" Tammy raised one hand over her eyes and skimmed the parking lot for her mother's car. "She's late. Figures."

"There she is." Cassie nodded toward the green station wagon rounding the corner. She put on her cap, pulling the visor down over her face as low as it would go. "Don't want to give the poor woman a heart attack."

"Hi, girls." Mrs. Ryan barely glanced at Cassie as she slid into the backseat, focusing instead on her daughter. "Where are all your packages?"

"They didn't have anything good."

"In the entire mall?" Mrs. Ryan frowned as she pulled away from the curb. "Tammy, you need some new clothes. You can't go around in the same pair of filthy jeans all spring."

"OK, OK." Tammy turned away from her mother and stared

out the window without saying another word until they pulled up to Cassie's house. "See you, Parker. Call me later?"

"Yeah, sure." If it weren't for the makeup, Cassie would have tipped her hat to Tammy, but she wasn't in the mood to deal with Mrs. Ryan, who would definitely say something if she saw what Cassie looked like. "Thanks for picking us up, Mrs. Ryan."

"You're welcome. Say hi to your mom for me."

"I will." Cassie shut the car door and they were gone.

Time to face the music. Cassie yanked off her cap and put it in her back pocket—no use having her mother yell at her for wearing it—and put her key in the door. She knew by the white Dodge in the driveway that her mother was home; she wasn't sure about her father since he kept his car locked up tightly in the garage.

"Hello-o-o," Cassie sang out as she stepped into the house.

"Is that you?" yelled her father.

"We're in here," her mother called from the kitchen. "Come help me make a salad."

Cassie walked toward her parents' voices and stopped in the doorway. Her mother stood at the sink washing a handful of tomatoes and her father was sitting at the table, his head buried behind *The New York Times.* Cassie knew without even looking that he was reading the business section.

"How was the mall?" Cassie's mother asked, as she moved from sink to cutting board, wet tomatoes in hand.

"Fine."

"Here, slice these up for—oh, my God, what happened to you?" Mrs. Parker froze, the knife she had just taken out of a drawer clenched in her fist like she was just about to stab someone. "Cassie, what in the world did you do to yourself?"

"What happened?" Mr. Parker put down his paper and looked up. At the sight of his daughter leaning against the doorjamb, his mouth dropped open. Cassie watched a sea of emotions wash over his face: disgust, anger, guilt, shame…or were those the emotions she was feeling?

"Cassie," he barked, his hand flying up to his own face. "How could you?"

How could I what? Cassie wanted to ask, but before she could get the words out her mother sprang back to life.

"You look just like your father," Mrs. Parker whispered, before turning to address her husband. "Are you happy now, *Tootsie*?" she shrieked.

"As happy as you are, *Mrs. Robinson,*" Mr. Parker replied.

"What's that supposed to mean?"

"You know exactly what it means." Cassie's father slapped both his hands down flat against the newspaper. "Museum trip—yeah, right. You wouldn't know a piece of art if it bit you in the ass. Which is probably exactly what a certain young man is doing while I'm—"

"While you're what? Working?" Mrs. Parker laughed bitterly. "Maybe I wouldn't have to go into the city every weekend if I wasn't married to a—"

"To a what?"

"To a…" Whatever Cassie's mother was going to say was swallowed up by a great big sob that burst out of her throat. Without another word, she brushed past Cassie and ran up the stairs.

"Honey, wait." Cassie's father dashed out after her without even a backward glance at his daughter. Cassie heard her parents' bedroom door slam, and then the house was silent except for the loud humming of the refrigerator and the steady ticking of the kettle-shaped clock on the wall. *Shit,* she thought, letting her body sink into a kitchen chair. She put her arms on the table, rested her head on top of them, and shut her gunky eyes. What was going to happen now? Cassie had no idea. Was she going to get in trouble? She didn't know that either. She stood up slowly, and with a deep sigh stepped over to the cutting board to pick up the knife her mother had dropped. She sliced a tomato in half and then halved the halves and then halved them again. The rich redness of the fruit swam before her eyes as she realized with a start that she knew much less about her parents' lives than they knew about her own.

A Stone's Throw

You think you're queer—well, get over yourself, girlfriend. I'm beyond queer, queerer than queer: an authentic, genuine, pasteurized, homogenized 100% *perv.* Not the kind of girl your mother warns you about—the kind of girl your *friends* warn you about. Yep, I'm somewhat proud and somewhat ashamed to admit it, but it's the gospel truth (take *that,* Mr. Falwell). What exactly makes me so queerer-than-thou? The fact that I'm a butch who longs to make another butch melt in my mouth. And in my hands.

Hard for you to picture what two boys could do together in bed? Use your imagination, toots. Think it's just a phase I'm going through, and once I meet the right femme I'll come to my senses and get with the program? Like I said, get over yourself. I've had plenty of femmes, let me tell you. I am good-looking, if I do say so myself. In fact, the last little lady I diddly-bopped said I was a "hipless wonder with bedroom eyes and the handsomest hands on the entire East Coast." She went on to say that a good butch is hard to find (tell me about it) and that I was her Prince Charming, the boy-girl of her dreams, her fantasy come true. So why didn't I bed her and wed her and ride off into the sunset to live happily ever after? Because the problem with this femme was, like most femmes, she wouldn't lay down, spread her legs, and shut the fuck up.

Now, don't get me wrong—I'd never force someone into the

ungodly act; I'm not *that* kind of pervert. It's just that most femmes can't stop talking long enough for me to get my lips anywhere even close to theirs. One particularly frustrating femme told me talking was her favorite form of foreplay. Puh-leeze. Whatever happened to good old first and second base? Talking, for chrissake. And if that isn't bad enough, once you finally do get down to business, nine out of ten femmes are still yapping away: "To the left. To the right. Slow down. Speed up. There. There. No, there." Christ, I feel like I'm in the car with a backseat driver who's getting on my nerves so bad I want to dump her out as soon as we get around the next bend.

I know what you're thinking right about now: I'm nothing but a selfish bastard who couldn't care less about pleasing her lover. You couldn't be more off-course if you were trying to stick a tampon in your ear. There's nothing I like better than knowing I've satisfied a woman who gave me the honor of taking her to bed and exploring all her secret places. But I don't want to be directed like I'm some lousy actor and my chick is Barbra Streisand. I want to be in control. I want to *discover* what makes a woman weep with joy and then beg for more. I don't want to be told what to do; I want to be on top.

Another butch would understand this. That's why I'm sure another butch would be the perfect fuck buddy. If I ever convince a butch to come to bed with me, she'll know what I want because she's been there before. She'll know I want to be in total command, the captain of the ship. She'll understand that being the daddy is what gets me off. And what will get her off is knowing I'm getting off by getting her off. A vicious, delicious cycle.

You see, not many people know this, but the truth is, inside every butch there's an inner femme just dying to get out. A little lady who's sick and tired of always being the strong one, the one who takes care of everything, the one who's always in charge. Don't you think every once in a while even the strongest, toughest,

Arnold Schwarzenegger type of butch wants to lean her head on somebody's shoulder and say "You take care of it"? That's the butch I'm looking for. Sure, it's nice to have a femme on your arm, but to have a butch make herself that vulnerable…hey, I more than anyone know the courage that takes. It's an honor to be the recipient of that much trust. Believe me, it's not something to be taken lightly. And besides, why should femmes have all the fun?

So where do I find the butch who doesn't even know how much she wants me yet? At the bar, of course. I've got my eye on a young lad who hangs out at the pool table on Friday nights. Wears a backward baseball cap, white T-shirt, and faded blue jeans. Hangs her keys off her belt loop and chains her wallet to her back pocket. Oh, she's cool, all right. Knows how much the femmes admire her biceps as she sinks the old eight ball smack-dab in the side pocket. Swigs her beer straight from the bottle, lights her matches off her fly, parks her cigarette on the edge of the pool table while she's lining up her shot. You know the type. Short, sharp hair; kick-ass boots—a real ladies' man. Ha. That's what she thinks, anyway.

She calls herself Danni. Short for Dani*elle*. I bet she can *yell*, all right. Maybe tonight will be the night I get lucky and find out.

So at about 9:30 I start to get dressed. Black jeans pressed to kill. A black muscle T-shirt. Spit-shiny black shoes. Hell, if this was another era, I'd be wearing spats. I can see you shaking your head, hear you thinking, *That's no way to snag a butch. You should be wearing something short and tight with something soft and lacy underneath.* Well, I've gone that route, and let me tell you, there's nothing more sorrowful-looking than a butch in a dress. You thought Lea DeLaria looked pathetic in femme drag? Well, I make even her look good. Plus, the one time I tried it I damn near killed myself in those three-inch heels. I don't know how the hell you femmes do it, I really don't.

So I hop on my bike and roar off to the bar, which is actually called The Bar—guess the owner wasn't first in line when the originality genes were being handed out. The Bar is where all the girls go, and I'm sure tonight my girl will be there too. Hell, there's nothing else to do in this town on a Friday night (or a Saturday night, or a Sunday night…). Unless of course you've got a gal you want to get all warm and cozy with at home on the couch in front of the fire. Most of the girls who hang at The Bar are single. Once in a blue moon one of 'em will get lucky and disappear for a while, only to resurface a few weeks later looking all forlorn and tail-between-the-leggish. We'll buy her a few drinks, hear her war stories, clap her on the back, and before she knows it she'll be damn glad she's free and easy to hang with the butches again.

I park my bike in the lot, tuck my helmet under my arm, and ease my way into The Bar, looking cool. One must look cool at all times, at all costs. Mustn't ever let on that I'm on the prowl. Especially on the prowl for another steel-toed diesel dyke like *moi.* That's where the bike comes in handy. No one could ever fault a butch for wanting to check out another butch's bike. Nothing wrong with taking a little ride. I'll take her on a little ride, all right…a little ride straight to Paradise.

By now I'm betting you probably don't like me very much, all sure of myself and so goddamn cocky. Well, seeing that Danni has yet to make her grand entrance, why don't we sit down and I'll buy you a beer and tell you a story? Oh, come on, give it a shot. What the hell, you've got nothing to lose.

A long time ago, when I was a young pup, I met a short, sturdy, stiff-haired bull dyke who was everything I wanted to be. Strong. Tough. Cool. Hot. All she had to do was snap her fingers and the babes would come running. Single girls, married girls, straight girls, hell, even bitches (I mean real bitches—the four-legged kind) would go belly-up at the sight of her, wagging their tails and whimpering with no shame. Woman could've been a billionaire if she'd only figured out a way to bottle it and sell it.

So I started hanging out with her. Name was Lou, short for Lou Ann. Called me Squirt on account of how tiny I am. Or so I thought. Took me a long time to realize she had something else in mind.

Lou took me under her wing. Under her wing tips was more like it. Showed me how to dress. Taught me a butch has to look cool at all times, but she should never look like she gave more than two seconds' thought to her outfit. She's *naturally* cool. In fact, she should be able to walk down the street in a purple striped shirt and orange plaid pants and still look cool. Now, anyone else would look like a nerd in that getup. But all a butch would have to do is glare at anyone who thought she was dressing funny with a *What do you think you're staring at* look in her eye, and the next thing you know everyone in town would be wearing purple striped shirts and orange plaid pants. See, that's the power of the butch. That's what Lou had, and that's what I wanted too.

After a few months as Lou's protégée, after she taught me how to walk (think James Dean) and how to talk (think Marlon Brando), Lou decided it was time for us to double date. I was wondering where in the world we were going to find a mother-daughter act, since Lou was pushing 40 and I was barely 25, but boy was I in for a surprise. I never saw femmes fall all over themselves the way they did when Lou entered Where the Girls Are (now there's a decent name for a lesbian bar). It was "How you doing, Daddy?" "Got a match, handsome?" Even "Wanna lick my boots, mister?" I tell you, I must have been bug-eyed, 'cause at one point Lou took me aside, elbowed me in the ribs, and whispered, "Keep it in your pants, Squirt. Stay cool." I was a little embarrassed that one of the chicks might have heard, but believe me, I could have been sitting on that barstool stark-naked and not one of them would have noticed. They had eyes for Lou and Lou alone. I mean, those girls weren't throwing themselves at Lou—they were *hurling* themselves at Lou. I watched a group of them giggle and whisper in the corner until one femme got brave enough to cross the dance floor, undoing her blouse a button or two as she approached us at the bar. Lou just smiled, smoothed back her hair, and turned away to take another sip of beer, giving her a kind but firm dismissal. I was dying to see who Lou would pick to take home—hell, I was more curious about who she'd wind up with than who *I* would wind up with. It seemed like the whole bar was holding its breath waiting for Lou to make up her mind.

But Lou wasn't in any kind of hurry (that was something else she'd taught me—butches don't do anything in a hurry). She took her own sweet time finishing her beer, ordering another, joking with the bartender, motioning for me to wipe the corner of my mouth with the back of my sleeve. She didn't pay a whit of attention to the girls that were practically flailing at her feet. We could've been in a locker room surrounded by a bunch of sweaty, smelly butches for all she seemed to care.

And then a pair of lucky femmes walked in, only they didn't know they were the chosen ones yet. Which is why Lou picked 'em (of course, later they'd say they picked us, but that's an old butch trick: You let the femmes think they're in charge, but us butches know better). Lou knew how into us they were by how deliberately they ignored us. They sat at a little table clear across the room with their White Russians or Brandy Alexanders or whatever creamy concoctions they were drinking, bent their bleached-blond heads together, and started yammering away. Lou watched them a while, then slid off her barstool and motioned for me to do the same. I raised one eyebrow (a cool gesture it had taken me months to perfect), and Lou shook her head like I was the dumbest baby butch she'd ever pitied enough to teach a thing or two. "Squirt," she put her arm around me, "those femmes think they've won because we're making the first move, but they made the first move the minute they walked in the bar and gave us the cold shoulder. You gotta let go of your ego with femmes. Let them think they have the upper hand. No skin off your schnozz." She thumbed the left side of her nose for emphasis.

"Evening, ladies." You'd have sworn Lou tipped her hat, even though she wasn't wearing one. "May we join you?" Lou turned a chair backwards and swung her leg over it without waiting for an answer. I couldn't exactly mimic her style of sitting down without looking like an idiot, so I just dropped my weight onto a chair. "I'm Lou, and this here's Squirt," Lou went on. "And you're…"

"Cynthia," the blonder one said in a breathy voice. "And this is Laura." Poor Cynthia was trying to establish her position as leader of the pack, who therefore deserved the prize of Lou, while pitiful little Laura would have to settle for me. But Lou wasn't having any of that. She never was one to be told what to do. In fact, even if Cynthia was the one she'd originally had the hots for, she'd never let on to that now. Lou always went for the underdog.

"Pleased to meet you," Lou said, making it real clear that Laura was the one she was really pleased to meet. A pout immediately settled across Cynthia's lips and stayed there the rest of the evening. *Thanks a lot, Lou,* I wanted to say. Lou would've only answered, "You're welcome, Squirt. Hey, lighten up, man. If it wasn't for me, you'd still be in your lousy apartment watching a family of flies climb up the kitchen wall." And, of course, she was right.

Cynthia loosened up a bit after she got over having to settle for me, the consolation prize. I mean, I wasn't so bad, if you didn't waste your time comparing me to Lou. I knew how to dance, fast ones and slow ones, and I knew how to treat a lady. Ply her with drink (those femmes gulp those sickeningly sweet mixes like soda), hold her firmly but gently like she might break when you're out on the dance floor. Pull out her chair when you get back to the table, lean in toward her, and listen to her stories like she's the most fascinating woman in the world. And, you know, if you get into it, she really is. For that night, anyway, or for as long as you get next to her. Which is all a woman can really ask for. And all a woman deserves.

When it looked like the bar was about to close, Lou asked the ladies if they needed a ride home. By this time she had her hand under Laura's skirt clear up to the elbow, and I wasn't doing too badly myself (though, unlike Lou, I had yet to cop a feel of naked thigh). Lou helped Laura with her wrap, I did the same for Cynthia, and out the door we went, arm in arm in arm. Lou and Laura got into the front seat of Lou's car; Cynthia and I tumbled into the back. I thought Lou would start 'er up and pull out at once, but she did no such thing. Before I could even figure out where Cynthia's face was in the dark, Lou had her tongue halfway inside Laura's lovely mouth.

And here's where I got thrown for a loop, here's where my whole world turned upside down. There I was in the backseat with a good-looking femme—blond, blue-eyed, and stacked besides. She'd given me the green light by closing her eyes, tipping her head back, and puckering up tight. But I realized, even as I locked lips with the lady in my lap, that I was much more interested in what was going on in the front seat than what was going on in the back. And I don't mean going on with Laura. I mean going on with Lou. I'd spent days, weeks, months with the woman. We'd stood side by side in the kitchen less than an inch apart as she showed me how to flip pancakes. ("A butch that can cook, Squirt—it gets 'em every time.") We'd laid under a car together changing the oil of my 12-year-old Toyota. ("Don't ever want to be caught helpless, Squirt.") Hell, we'd even showered together at the gym. ("You call that a muscle, Squirt?" she laughed as she pointed to my upper arm.) But we'd never shared a sexual experience before. I found myself holding my breath, listening hard, squinting my ears, *praying* to catch a moan coming from deep inside Lou's throat. Of course, no such thing would ever happen. I should've known Lou would be the strong, silent type. And that Laura was just the opposite, yowling louder than a cat in heat on a hot summer night. *Shut the hell up,* I wanted to yell, but of course I did no such thing. Especially since Cynthia made no secret that she didn't appreciate the fact that my attention was so obviously someplace else.

"Over here, lover," she said with exaggerated patience, like I was 2 years old and couldn't find my favorite blankie that was right there in front of me. I tried hard to concentrate, but the only way I could even pretend to be halfway into what I was doing was to make believe that Cynthia was Lou. And it's not like I did so on purpose. My mind just automatically went there. And the rest of me was only too happy to follow.

It reminded me of my old days in high school when I double-dated with my best friend, Angela. Angie was one of those dark-eyed, raven-haired Italian beauties that every boy in town couldn't wait to get his hands on. She had a different guy take her out every Friday night. The hitch was, her guy had to come up with a boy for me, the pain-in-the-ass homely best friend that Angie insisted had to tag along. Not that I wanted to make it with a guy, you understand. I just couldn't stand having Angie out of my sight for two seconds.

So we'd go out with Joe and Shmo, take in a movie, a school football game, a party, whatever. It really didn't matter, because sooner or later we'd all wind up in somebody's parents' car, Angie and Joe in the front, me and Shmo in the back. It was worth the inevitable wrestling match I had to put up with from my date just to hear the sweet moans that started in the front seat and slowly filled the car when Angie and her boy du jour really got going. Just hearing Angie gasp and moan and sigh with pleasure was enough to make me gasp and moan and sigh as well. Of course, my guy thought this was all his handiwork, but I couldn't even remember his name the next morning. What got me off was being so close to the girl I knew I could never have. Angie was as straight as I was bent, not that that would necessarily stop me. As the weeks wore on, with Angie not knowing how badly she was torturing me, I hatched a plan.

One day I told her I was having trouble in the love department. "I don't think I'm a very good kisser," I told her, upstairs in her pinker-than-pink bedroom complete with candy-striped curtains and canopy bed.

"What do you mean, Mel?" In case I haven't told you yet, my name's Mel, short for Melody. My parents actually had that song "A Pretty Girl's Like a Melody" in mind when they came up with my handle. Boy, were they in for a surprise.

"I don't know, Angie. I just think I'm doing it wrong. You know, like I don't know when to open my mouth, what to do with my tongue..." I was looking down at my feet when I said this because I knew I couldn't face her with what I had to say next. "Do you, uh...think we could practice?"

"Practice?" Angie let out a nervous giggle. "I guess so."

I came over and sat next to her on the bed. My heart pounded so hard I thought for sure Angie could hear it as I took her in my arms. "Show me," I whispered, closing my eyes. And the next thing I knew, Angie's lips were on mine and we were kissing like there was no tomorrow. And when she opened her beautiful mouth and welcomed me inside, I remember every muscle in my body relaxing as the thought kept racing through my mind, *There's no place like home. There's no place like home.* My first girl-on-girl kiss, and I knew I had been transported to another world, a world more wondrous and magical than I could ever have imagined, just like the Emerald City in *The Wizard of Oz.* I knew that my first butch-on-butch kiss would be just as transformative too. And so I set out to make it happen.

"Lou," I said one Sunday morning after we had double-dated with (and you won't even believe this) twin sisters from out of state. "I'm having a little trouble in the love department—"

Lou shook her head before I even had a chance to get the rest out. "Squirt, Squirt, Squirt," she said, "what am I going to do with you?"

I looked down at the floor, trying to soothe my ego, which was smarting with the fact that Lou didn't even try to convince me that surely I was mistaken, surely I was just like her, a regular dyke Romeo. I let it go then and went on, thinking, *Hell, it worked once, maybe, just maybe, it'll work again.* "I don't think I'm a very good kisser, Lou. I just think I'm doing it wrong. You know, like I don't know when to open my mouth, what to do with my tongue…"

We were sitting in her kitchen, both nursing cups of black coffee. Lou was a coffee connoisseur and made the best joe I'd ever had. Mixed a million different brands together but wouldn't reveal her secret formula.

I took a sip, swallowed, put down my cup, and stared into my brew, the oily surface reflecting my sorry-ass face back to me. Lou dumped a teaspoon of sugar into her cup and stirred her spoon around and around and around. Time stood still as I waited to see what she'd say. Just as I stopped daring to hope, she took a deep breath, let out a sigh like she couldn't believe she had to do this, and said the words that practically made me come on the spot: "Well, I reckon then we'd better practice."

"Practice?" I asked, like the word was foreign to my ear. "You mean with each other?" As soon as I said that, I panicked, thinking maybe I'd gone too far. I didn't want Lou to think I'd had this in mind all along—she had to believe she'd come up with the idea herself—but I didn't want her to think the notion of kissing her disgusted me either.

"How else can I check your technique, Squirt?" Lou looked at me. "Unless you don't care that you're not pleasing the ladies."

She was giving me an out, and I knew it. I looked into her eyes and tried to read her, but Lou broke my gaze and stared down into her coffee cup, leaving it all up to me.

"I do care, Lou." I tried to sound sincere. "And who else would I want to teach me, Martha Stewart?"

That got a laugh. Which was followed by silence. A pregnant pause if I ever heard one. We sat together in the quiet, both drinking coffee that all of a sudden held as much interest for me as cold, squalid dishwater. Just when I thought I couldn't stand it any longer, Lou pushed back her chair and said, "C'mere, Squirt."

I always did what Lou told me, and now was no time to make an exception. I got up and came around the table until I was right in front of her. She looked up at me, and I met her gaze until my stomach dropped. "Sit down," she said, patting her knee. I did what I was told.

"Now," Lou shifted her weight a little bit until I was sitting sidesaddle, "you'll have to be the femme, of course."

"Of course," I echoed, my voice stuck somewhere deep in my throat.

"Pay attention to what I do," Lou instructed, as she put her arms around me. I guess I must've been pretty stiff, because Lou gentled her voice and told me to relax. "It won't hurt a bit, Squirt," she reassured me, and before I could reply her mouth came down hard on mine.

It was all I could do to keep from passing out as Lou kissed me long and deep, her tongue filling me in places I didn't even know were empty. I heard someone moaning and, after a minute, realized with embarrassment that those low, guttural sounds were coming from me. Lou ignored them and pressed on, caressing me with her mouth and tongue until I was panting like a racehorse. When I was so wet that I was afraid I'd slide off her lap, she pulled back and looked me in the eye.

"Now, Squirt," she said, her words coming out in short bursts, "you need some pointers in the below-the-neck department too?"

I couldn't get the word "yes" out, so I simply nodded.

"Now, all that hype about doing it on the kitchen floor is just crap. Trust me. A real lady wants a nice, comfortable bed. But you don't want to disturb the momentum you just created. So you stand up," and in one swift, smooth move, Lou was on her feet with me in her arms, "and carry her into the boudoir." And off we went, with Lou's mouth buried deep into the corner between my shoulder and neck.

"You paying attention?" Lou asked as she gently laid me down and rested her weight beside me.

"Yes, sir," I whispered, not knowing where the "sir" had come from. I had never called her that before.

"Ladies love it when you undress them," Lou informed me as she untied my high-tops. She took off my shoes and socks, then moved up to remove my T-shirt. "The ladies love to be teased," Lou whispered, as she ran her hands up and down my torso, tickling my belly, my neck, my throat, and the one-inch channel between my quivering breasts. "Take your time, Squirt," Lou said as she kissed me again. "You want them to be practically screaming for it."

I *was* practically screaming for it, and it took every ounce of restraint I had not to grab Lou's hands and plunk them right on top of my breasts. But I knew she needed to be the one in control, the one calling the shots. So I let her. And it didn't take me long to realize what a turn-on that was.

"You have to learn to feel when your lady is walking that fine line between pleasure and frustration," Lou said, her strong, callused hands barely grazing the outer edge of my breasts, then moving closer and closer to my nipples. "Then when you know she can't take it for one more second," Lou whispered in my ear, "you give her what she wants." And finally, *finally,* Lou put her hands where I wanted them.

"You can touch them gently," Lou murmured, her hands on my nipples soft as feathers, "or you can be rough." She pinched and pulled them hard. "Then, of course, there's lots of things you can do with your tongue." Lou lowered her head and lapped at me like a young deer at a salt lick, then sucked me like a lollipop. I was trying to hold back, but sounds I had never heard before were bursting out of my throat.

"You don't want to take her over the edge just yet," Lou said, clearly knowing I was about to come. "Slow her down." Lou came back up to kiss me on the mouth for a bit, her hands running through my brush cut. "Then you finish undressing her. If she's wearing a skirt, you got it made. If she's wearing jeans, like you," Lou paused as she unsnapped my fly and lowered the zipper, "you'll have to raise up her hips and slide 'em down. Don't ever let her help you." Lou slapped my hands away. "You need to keep reminding her that you're the boss and you're capable of anything." I relaxed as Lou proved her point by removing my jeans and underpants.

"Once she's naked and you're fully clothed, you have her just where you want her," Lou said, running her hands up and down the length of my body. "You keep her guessing for as long as you want, and then slowly, very slowly," Lou enunciated her words at a snail's pace, "you go in for the kill." Then there was no sound in the room except my ragged breathing as Lou's hands roamed the highways and byways of my body. Just as she brought me to the screaming point again, she zeroed in on the place I call home.

"If your lady's nice and wet, like you are, *Squirt,*" Lou went on, touching me high and inside, where it felt like I'd suddenly grown a faucet, "your job is almost through. Now, I like a clockwise motion on the clit and an in-and-out motion inside. That's usually a crowd-pleaser." Lou demonstrated her technique. "Of course, you can do a back-and-forth motion on the outside and a circular motion on the inside too." She switched what her hands were doing. "You've just got to read the dame, Squirt. Pay attention to what her body's doing to figure out what her heart wants. You get me?"

"Yes, yes, *yes,*" I screamed—and came and came and came. Lou kept her hand inside me while my body shook, shimmied, and shuddered against her palm. When I was finally still, she let me go and grinned.

"I'm pretty good, huh?" she asked, studying her hand, which was so wet she could have wrung it out.

"I'll say." I sat up on my elbows and looked at her in amazement. "You think I'll ever learn to please a broad like that?"

"Maybe," Lou shrugged. "But you know what they say: Practice makes perfect."

And so Lou and I continued to practice. She taught me different approaches, different techniques, different positions, always staying fully clothed and finding new and interesting ways to get me to howl with delight. We never called ourselves lovers, never really copped to what we were doing. I never even spent the night. After she made love to me Lou would leave the room so I could pull myself together and get dressed. And by the time I came back out to the kitchen she'd be brewing us some coffee, shuffling a deck of cards, or tinkering with a toaster or some other appliance that all of a sudden needed to be fixed.

This went on for a month or two, and then one night I announced to Lou over dinner that I was done practicing, I was ready for the real thing.

"What do you mean, the real thing?" Lou asked, screwing the top back on the ketchup bottle. We were having a basic butch meal of meat loaf and mashed potatoes, with a couple of beers on the side.

"I mean, we've been practicing for weeks, and I think I've got it down now. I'd like to give it a try."

"Fine by me." Lou opened the refrigerator to put some things away. "We'll pick up a pair of chicks and see how you do."

"Chicks?" I said the word like I'd never heard it before. "Lou, I thought I'd get to try my techniques out on you."

"On me?" Lou looked at me like I was nuts.

"Yeah," I said, like it was the most logical idea in the world. "How else will you know if I'm doing things right? How else will you be able to tell?"

"Nothing doing, Squirt." Lou picked up our plates and moved over to the sink, turning her back to me.

"But that's not fair." As soon as the words burst out of my mouth, I was horrified. Had my practice sessions with Lou actually turned me into a real, live femme? I sure as hell was sounding like one.

"I'm not even going to dignify that remark with a response," Lou said, turning on the water. As she washed the dishes I stared at her strong back, her long legs, those taut, muscular arms. And suddenly I knew what I wanted to do. Knew what I had to do. Hadn't Lou taught me that a butch is always in charge? And didn't she want me to show her that I had paid attention and learned my lessons well?

She couldn't hear me on account of the running water as I snuck up behind her. Flinched but didn't pull away as I kissed that tender, vulnerable spot of flesh at the back of her neck, right below her crew cut. Kept her hands in the sink as I reached around to unbutton her shirt and feel her chest muscles. Trembled but stayed put as I licked her velvet earlobe and stroked her breasts. Almost lost her balance but held on as I undid her fly. Didn't make a sound as my hands glided inside her pants. Growled low and deep in her throat as my fingers slid inside the waistband of her BVDs. And then, just as I felt her wiry pubic hair against my skin and was inching my way to the gates of Heaven, Lou whirled around with a roar that threw me clear across the room.

"What the hell you think you're doing, Melody?"

I just stood there blinking and rubbing my head, which smarted something awful from being smacked against Lou's kitchen cabinet. I didn't know if I was more stunned from Lou throwing me clear across the room without lifting a finger or because she had called me by my name. She'd never even called me Mel, let alone Melody, before.

"I'm being in charge," I sputtered, though I felt anything but. "Showing you my technique. Practicing."

"Just get the hell out of here," Lou yelled, her voice shaking. "And don't come back."

"But Lou—" I scrambled to my feet.

"But nothing. You heard me. Get out."

I backed away, staring at her, and she turned from me, but not before I saw her shoulders begin to shake. Damn if that big old bull dyke wasn't about to break down and cry. Not wanting to humiliate her further, I quietly let myself out her kitchen door and closed it softly behind me.

Yeah, I know, it's a bitch, ain't it? I don't know what else to tell you. I've thought this all out, replayed the scene over and over in my mind at least a hundred times. All I can come up with is that Lou wasn't paralyzed with passion or trembling with desire like I thought she was as I put the moves on her. She was paralyzed with fear and trembling with rage. The growl I'd heard was just that—a warning—not an expression of being turned on. I hadn't yet heard the words "stone butch" at the time, but now I feel like such an idiot. Of course Lou was stone. Lou was beyond stone. She was brick, she was steel, she was granite. So much so that she could never face me again because of what I'd done. She slammed down the phone when I called, wouldn't answer the doorbell when I rang, crossed the street when she saw me walking through town.

So there you have it. I never got to take Lou to that melted-down place she brought me to so many times. Never got to see the stone dissolve and the girl emerge. But ever since, I've been looking for a butch who's brave enough to show me what she's made of. Someone handsome, tall, strong…someone like you. Hey, you know what? It doesn't look like the dame I've been waiting for is going to show. Wanna step outside and check out my bike? C'mon, I'll take you for a ride. I've got an extra helmet. Sure, finish your beer, take your time, what the hell, have another. When you're ready, we'll go take her for a spin. Who knows where we'll wind up going.

Show Off

I love to watch them watch you. I stand in the back, leaning against the wall, one foot crossed in front of the other, arms folded, left over right. You are up on stage, of course, warming up the crowd in a fitted black jacket and tuxedo pants with a sexy silk stripe running down either side. You're wearing a white shirt and a burgundy tie, which you tied yourself this evening. Remember, it was me who taught you how to tie a tie. It was me who untwisted the knots your clumsy fingers made, who laughed as you cursed every time you didn't get it right. It was me who taught you to perfect your butch look, to swagger across the stage, to smile at the crowd and wink with one eye.

Your brush cut stands tall, short on the sides, long in front, stiffened with pomade. Only I know what it feels like to run my fingers through your crowning glory. Only I know how that stiff hair feels against the inside of my silken thigh.

Music fills the room, and you open your mouth and begin the first song. Women gasp, they swoon, they inch closer to the stage in one hungry wave. I can practically hear the disbelief churning through their minds: *A woman as handsome as that can sing too?* A femme in black Lycra wipes her chin with the heel of her hand as if she's drooling over you. She wouldn't be the first. Another femme sticks her tongue out as if she's panting like a dog.

You work the mike like it's an enormous clit, drawing it close to your lips, your tongue, caressing it with your hands, all the while singing words of love. I can feel all the butches in the room break into a collective sweat. They know they're in deep, deep trouble. How many of their femmes will wish they were going home with you tonight? How many of them will imagine it's you kissing them, you undressing them, you laying them down softly on the bed or you taking them roughly against the wall? How many of them will actually say, "Why aren't you more like *her*?" and gloat at the hurt the question brings to their butch's eyes? And how many of the butches will say to their femmes in a moment of self-doubt, "Am I as butch as *she* is?" knowing that the answer, "Yes, dear," is as transparent as Cinderella's glass slipper, an out-and-out lie.

I watch you flirt with a femme in the front, close to the stage. You pretend you're singing to her, only to her. You drop onto one knee and extend your right arm. You pretend she's everything you've ever wanted and more. You will never hurt her. You will never lie to her. You will never leave her. You will fuck her into ecstasy each and every night of her entire life. You will never fight with her over stupid things like money or the dishes. You are beyond all that. Your life is pure and simple lust. Nothing else matters. You will never say things like "I'm too tired" or "Honey, do you have to be so goddamn loud?"

The femme is dripping wet, watching you. Her eyes are big as nipples. She's wondering if you mean it, if she should go backstage afterward and rap on your dressing room door. Every girl in the room wishes she was that femme in front. You take her to the edge, reaching out with your fingertips as if to stroke her face, and then in a split second you turn and focus all your attention on someone else in the crowd. Every girl thinks she has a chance with you. Every girl is wondering, *Could I just ditch my butch for the night, let her fuck my brains out, and then go home in the morning with everything just like it was before?* Only everything won't be just like it was before. Believe me, I know.

You finish the set and promise to return. As you disappear backstage, I wander through the crowd, listening. I like to hear what they say about you. "I'd drink her bathwater," sighs a femme with a Southern accent. "Just looking at her curls my toes," says another. I notice the butches standing up a little taller, being more assertive, jostling each other as they wait at the bar for a beer. They don't fool me for a second, or their femmes, who are still mooning over you, the stage a magnet for their eager, impatient eyes.

The house lights go down, and the music goes up, promises that you are about to return. All the femmes jockey for position near the front of the stage. The butches roll their eyes at each other and hurry to claim their turf, to stand behind their femmes with their arms around their waists as if to say, *You belong to me, baby*, a fact that many a femme would just as soon momentarily forget.

This is the part of the show I like best. I'm almost drooling with anticipation. You make them wait for it. First they're standing quietly, politely; then they clap and cheer; and then, just before that split second when their eagerness turns to annoyance, you emerge. Like everything else about you, your timing is perfect.

As always, there's a pause, a heartbeat of silence, and then they gasp. Is it really you? It's really you, my darling. You, completely transformed in a tight, black glittery gown that shows off your to-die-for figure, complemented with elbow-length gloves and three-inch heels. Your hair is brushed out and fluffy, and there is a hint of mascara on your eyes. You are not a parody of yourself, not an exaggeration like Dolly Parton or RuPaul. No, you are truly, utterly beautiful.

Now it's the femmes who are getting nervous, as their butches relax. The butches puff out their chests, hold their chins high, surge forward as their femmes hold them back, hooking their hands into the crook of their butches' arms, as if to say, *You belong to me, baby,* a fact that many a butch would now like to momentarily forget. You begin to sing, and as you do you slink across the stage, perfectly at home in those three-inch heels. Only I know how many weeks it took you to master that walk; it was me who taught you, who nursed your twisted ankles, who laughed as you cursed every time you fell. It was me who taught you to wiggle those hips, it was me who taught you to bat those eyes.

You pick a butch from the audience and wag your finger at her. She tries to step forward but her legs are shaking. Her pals clap her on the back; even her femme, who's frowning, lets go of her arm. She's being a good sport, but they'll have words later, you can be sure. You hold out your arm, an invitation, and bring the butch up on stage. You place her behind you and wrap her arms around your waist. You sway as you sing and she sways with you. You move one of her hands up to your breast and let it linger for a minute before you slap it away, pretending indignation. But you got your point across by the look on the butch's face. It tells the audience what they want to know: You're just like Coca-Cola, baby. The real thing.

You indulge the butch for a minute more and then shove her offstage with a playful push and reach your arm out, beckoning to another, all the while singing words of love. The new butch bounds up on stage and takes her position behind you. You turn your head to gaze into her eyes through half-closed lids and pretend to sing to her, only to her. Your eyes and your body are saying you will never hurt her. You will never lie to her. You will never leave her. You will let her fuck you into ecstasy each and every night of her entire life. You will never fight with her over stupid things like money or the dishes. You are beyond all that. Your life is pure and simple lust. Nothing else matters. You will never say things like "I'm too tired" or "Honey, do you have to be so goddamn loud?"

And now it's the femmes in the house who are getting nervous.

The ones who wore pants tonight are cursing themselves for not wearing a skirt. They pat their hair, wipe their thumbs around their mouths to clear away any smudges of lipstick. They know they'd better keep their big mouths shut tonight. The question "Why aren't you as butch as *she* is?" can now easily be answered: "I don't know. Why aren't you as *femme* as she is?" For the butches are enthralled. Every one of them is dripping wet, watching you. Every girl in the room wishes she was that butch standing behind you, who is wondering at this very moment, *Could I just ditch my femme for the night, fuck her brains out instead, and then go home in the morning with everything just like it was before?* Again, the answer is no.

After several encores you bid the audience good night. That's my cue, and I hurry through the crowd, for I'm the lucky one who gets to go backstage and help you out of the dress. I'm the one who gets to watch you wipe all that makeup off your gorgeous face and slip your perfect body into a T-shirt and jeans. I'm the one who gets to go home with you, make love with you, sleep next to you all night long. I'm the one who gets to see you looking less than perfect, with sleep goop in the corners of your eyes, your hair all sticking up on one side, the side you slept on, like a baby bird. I'm the one who gets to argue with you about the grocery bill, the clothes left on the floor, the letter you forgot to send to your mother. I'm the one who gets to hear about your insecurities, your fears, your desires. I'm the one who gets to see through the illusion, who knows you are so much more than they think you are.

But not tonight. Tonight you are the star, and the real show is about to begin. That show in the bar is just foreplay, after all. The minute we're in the house we're all over each other, wet with the power of desire. All those women wanting what they can't have. You, my darling, neither butch nor femme tonight. Only mine. We kiss each other hungrily as we make our way down the hall to the bedroom, shedding clothes as we go. Your jacket lands on the kitchen table, my sweater on the living room floor. My breast finds your mouth, your fingers find my thigh. You lift me onto the bed and lay gently beside me. Finally we are together, naked, a little breeze ruffling our skin through the open window. We touch each other everywhere, fingers stroking, mouths caressing, skin on fire. When we enter each other, as if on cue, you sing out to me and I sing back. I'm the only one who gets to croon a duet with you. And even though I can't sing to save my life and your voice is a gift from on high, our fingers find their slippery rhythm and our songs melt together in one long chord of perfect harmony.

After we catch our breath I ask for an encore, and as you comply I clap my thighs around your handsome head while you sing a song my body loves. I want to give you the standing ovation you deserve, but my legs are too weak to hold me so I pull you up to look at your face, so close, so naked, so dear. I stare into your eyes and see my own tiny reflection mirrored there; I know you also see yourself in me. Our mutual admiration society is more important to you than a thousand fans will ever be. But that little secret is safe with me. Basking in each other's love, we draw the curtain of darkness around us tightly and sleep.

Bashert

“These are amazing.”

“Incredible.”

“I’ve never seen such fabulous paintings.”

“I’ve never seen such a fabulous model.”

Susan just smiled and tried not to spill the glass of white wine she was holding as an eager patron of the arts jostled her silk-clad arm in his haste to get a closer look at her work. And instead of sipping her wine, she drank in the moment many were calling her overnight success, though she knew it had begun with another moment more than twenty years ago…

❀

“You’re going to Israel for a year, to work on a *kibbutz*,” Susan’s parents said to her in 1977, the summer after she graduated from the State University of New York. “No need to thank us for this wonderful opportunity we’re giving you. Just go, see, enjoy, and maybe you’ll even learn something about yourself.”

What Susan’s parents didn’t tell her was this: *Over a million Jewish men in this country and you couldn’t find one to marry? What’s wrong with you? Twenty-one years old you are, with no boyfriend, no career…a B.S. in Art History—that and a token will get you a ride on the subway. What else can we do but ship you off to the land of milk and honey and see what God has in mind for you to make of yourself?*

And so Susan packed a few articles of clothing along with her charcoals, drawing pencils, and sketch pads, kissed her parents goodbye, and boarded an El Al jet filled with *sabras,* or native Israelis, who spoke the language of her people. Though Susan hardly understood a word, she knew from reading a travel brochure that a *sabra* was literally a fruit that was tough on the outside and sweet and tender on the inside, and she could understand why her fellow travelers were so dubbed—at least because of the outside part. They didn't talk as much as bark at one another, their words filled with the language's trademark guttural utterings, each one sounding like the beginning of a spit.

Susan leaned back in her seat and closed her eyes as the plane lifted into takeoff. She liked being surrounded by people she looked like—people with olive skin, dark hair and eyes, noses that hardly looked like ski slopes, and full lips—and she didn't mind being unable to communicate with them. On the contrary, she found it strangely comforting. Susan often thought of her life as a movie, a black-and-white foreign film with distorted sound and a grainy picture, shown at an art house with uncomfortable, creaky seats. Going to the Jewish homeland was simply the next scene in the film of her life that someone else was forever directing. Susan didn't try to protest, didn't try to rewrite the script, didn't ask for a different part. She didn't board the plane willingly or unwillingly; she took her seat and buckled up automatically, just as she had gone off to college, putting one foot in front of the other with a sigh, hoping for the best.

The flight, which lasted an entire day, was completely uneventful until the wheels of the plane touched ground. Then, as if on cue, the *sabras* burst into song: "*Hatikva,*" the Israeli national anthem, whose title Susan knew meant "The Hope." Even though she could have joined in—she knew the words and the melody from singing it in temple during the High Holy Days—she remained silent and let the fervor and passion with which the Israelis sang envelop her. By the time the plane got to the gate, Susan's eyes were brimming with tears. The song ended just as the FASTEN SEAT BELT sign was turned off. Then the moment was broken and chaos ensued, with everyone jumping up to grab their carry-on luggage and dash off the plane.

Susan made her way over to a man standing at the gate flashing a hand-lettered sign that read KIBBUTZ VOLUNTEERS. She showed him the letter she'd received assigning her to a medium-size agricultural *kibbutz* in the northern part of the tiny country, near a city called Haifa. Other people brandishing letters approached as well, and when a dozen of them had gathered the man herded them out to a van and whisked them off into the night. Susan slept through most of the bumpy ride, until she was handed off, like a baton in a relay race, to a volunteer waiting for her at the *kibbutz* entrance. She was driven by jeep to a dorm, and then led, stumbling, to the room she would call home for the next twelve months. She tried to be quiet, as three other girls were already sleeping in the small, crowded cubicle, but she couldn't help turning on the light for just a minute, and she was forever glad that she did, for there on her mattress lay a spider, a huge brown bristly-haired monster that she was in no hurry to share her sleeping quarters with.

"Oh, my God," Susan gasped in a stage whisper loud enough to wake the girl in the next bed.

"What is it?" the girl whispered back, her voice sleepy and annoyed.

"A spider. It's bigger than my fist. I've never seen—"

Susan's words were interrupted by a *thwack!* as the girl threw a shoe onto her bed, sending the spider scurrying away. "You'll get used to them," she murmured, rolling over and going back to sleep.

Susan didn't have much time to get used to anything, since she was woken up the next morning at five o'clock to get ready for work. She'd been assigned to the orange fields, which the *kibbutzniks* called *Pardis,* meaning Paradise. Susan introduced herself to her new roommates: Rona, who hogged the bathroom, blow-drying her hair for a good half hour even though it frizzed up the minute she stepped outside; Yael, neé Janet, who, though born and bred in Hoboken, N.J., now spoke English in short, broken sentences with a pseudo-Israeli accent; and Madeleine, who hailed from England and didn't understand why they had to wake up so early—it wasn't like the "bloody oranges" were going anywhere.

At six o'clock sharp a small truck arrived to pick up Susan and company. All the volunteers were dressed alike, in regulation *kibbutz* clothing: white T-shirts, khaki shorts, canvas workboots, and cotton hats. Susan, always sensitive to color or the lack of it, thought they looked like a studio full of blank canvases waiting to be painted. But as soon as they were dropped off in the orange grove, sleepy as she was, Susan saw the beauty of the contrast between the volunteers' drab clothing and their colorful surroundings. No wonder it was called Paradise: The trees were lush with emerald leaves that shone in the sun; the sky was a perfect cornflower-blue, the likes of which Susan had never seen; and to top it all off, the sweet, intoxicating smell of oranges wafted through the air like the perfume of an elegant woman who had just left the room. Susan felt a bit lightheaded from the aroma, the early hour, and undoubtedly a severe case of jet lag. She took a swig of water from the canteen hitched to her belt and tried to get hold of herself as she listened to the instructions a man named Shlomo was yelling in her direction. But it was useless to pay attention; she couldn't even figure out what language Shlomo was screaming in, let alone understand what he was talking about.

Each volunteer was given a rickety wooden ladder, a white canvas bag, and a row of trees. Somehow Susan figured out that her mission was to drag the ladder to the start of her row, lean it up against the first tree, climb to the top rung (despite her fear of heights), drop oranges into the canvas bag slung across her shoulder, climb down the ladder, walk to the end of her row, and dump the fruit into a crate the size of her new living quarters, all without injuring herself. This, she found out, was easier said than done—in Hebrew or any other language—since the more oranges she dropped into her bag, the heavier it grew and the shakier her balance became. As Susan tried to shift her weight, the ladder beneath her shifted its weight as well. Several times she held on for dear life as the ladder threatened to topple; twice she even found herself praying to a God she didn't believe in—but, she reasoned once her safety was secured, if God wasn't here in Paradise, where else would He be?

To her surprise, the skin of the oranges, even when they were ripe, were not orange in color, but rather a dark forest green. When she saw the other volunteers up in their treetops were snacking, she followed suit, digging her thumbnail into the thick rind of an orange and pulling it back to expose the pale orange pulp inside. Susan tore into a section with her teeth, and as juice dripped down her chin, she marveled at how sweet the fruit tasted—much, much sweeter than any orange she had ever eaten at home. There were two ways to tell if these green oranges were ripe: if they came off the tree easily (they had to be twisted by the stem, not yanked) and by their size. Shlomo—whom Susan learned from Madeleine was from Argentina and therefore spoke Hebrew with a thick Spanish accent—handed Susan a measuring tool made of wire, shaped into a circle like an oversize child's bubble wand. She was instructed to hold the tool up to orange after orange to see if the fruit was big enough to pluck. Of course it didn't take long for one of the male volunteers to hold up his wand to a girl's bosom, first one breast and then the other, to see if either one was ripe. The girl merely giggled, as did several other volunteers; some of them even called for the boy to bring his wand over to see if they measured up. Susan just ignored him.

By eight o'clock the sun was hot and bright-orange in the sky and a whistle was blown, signaling breakfast. All the volunteers clamored down from their ladders and made their way to a cluster of picnic tables set up outside a cabin-like structure where Shlomo had prepared a feast Susan couldn't believe: fluffy omelettes made with avocados grown on the *kibbutz*; huge bowls of creamy white yogurt topped with swirls of amber-colored honey; sandwiches made of *challah* and Nutella; and for dessert, *halvah*, a sticky sweet brick made of honey and ground sesame seeds. Susan, whose father was a dentist, wondered if she'd have any teeth left by the end of this "life experience" her parents had given her. Still, she chowed down with the best of them, passing the salt and pepper when motioned to, but mostly remaining silent as conversation and jokes in Hebrew, Spanish, Danish, Russian, and English swirled around her. Susan sat with the English and American girls whom she could at least understand, but she felt distant from them, and distant from herself. Of course she was awfully far from home—halfway around the world!—but that really didn't matter. Susan always felt removed from whatever situation she found herself in, like she was underwater or behind a window made of thick, smoky glass.

After breakfast it was back to work until noon, and then it was quitting time. The intense heat of the sun forced everyone down from their ladders and back into the truck to be driven from the fields to the main dining hall in the center of the *kibbutz*. Lunch was served at exactly one o'clock, and Susan, who barely ate breakfast at home—a cup of coffee and maybe half a buttered bagel—was surprised that despite her Paul Bunyan–size breakfast, she was ravenous. The *kibbutzniks* ate their main meal of the day in the afternoon—vegetable soup, broiled chicken, baked potatoes, cooked carrots, and of course dessert, a sheet cake with chocolate frosting that set Susan's teeth on edge. Still, she filled her belly then retired to her room for a much-needed nap.

Less than an hour after her curly head hit the pillow, there was a knock on the door. "*Ulpan!* Fifteen minutes," someone called. *Ulpan* meant Hebrew school. Susan dragged herself out of a deep sleep and rapped on the bathroom door.

"Just a minute," called a disembodied voice Susan recognized as Rona's.

"She lives in there, love." Madeleine gestured with an open compact then began powdering her nose. Madeleine was one of those women who tried her best to turn any getup—even a bland *kibbutz* outfit—into a fashion statement. A great deal of cleavage showed above the neckline of her white cotton T-shirt, and she'd tied the bottom of it up in a knot, so that her belly button peeked out over the khaki shorts that tightly hugged her abundant thighs.

"Rona. Hair." Yael pointed to her own scalp and shook her head in disapproval. The curls of her short "Jew-fro" bounced up and down with the motion.

Finally, Rona emerged and Susan entered the bathroom, which contained a sink with a mirror hanging over it, a toilet, and, instead of a shower stall, a spigot with two faucets underneath mounted right into the wall. When Susan showered, the toilet and sink got soaked, as did her clothing and towel. Not only that, a good two inches of water remained on the floor, until she figured out she had to push it all toward a drain in the corner with a rubber squeegee. The water moved slowly until Susan removed a glob of Rona's hair from the drain. "Dorm life, *kibbutz* style," she sighed as she hurried to get dressed and catch up with her roommates, who were also headed out to *ulpan*.

"Shalom, shalom," Ze'ev, the Hebrew teacher, greeted his students with great enthusiasm and motioned for them to sit down at the large circular table in the middle of the room. Ze'ev's classroom

was outfitted with a desk and a blackboard, above which hung green sheets of paper with the Hebrew alphabet printed in large white letters. Susan, who had dropped out of Hebrew school after only a year and never had a *bat mitzvah*, stared up at the letters, but try as she might she couldn't drag their sounds up from the dredges of her long-term memory bank.

"Ze'ev." Ze'ev pointed to himself, then pointed to Susan.

"Um…"

"He wants to know your name, love," Madeleine whispered.

"Susan."

"Shoshana." Ze'ev bestowed upon Susan the same Hebrew name she'd been given long ago by her childhood Hebrew schoolteacher. *"Ahnee Ze'ev. Aht Shoshana."* He pointed to Madeleine. *"He Malka."* Then Ze'ev turned to the class and asked, *"Me Malka?"* They answered in response, pointing to Madeleine, *"He Malka."* Susan was utterly confused until Madeleine explained in a whisper that *he* meant "she," *me* meant "who," and *who* meant "he." Other than Madeleine's explanatory whisperings, not a word of English was spoken during the entire lesson, and by the time the hour and a half was over Susan's head was spinning.

From 4:30 to 6:30, the volunteers had free time. Not knowing what else to do, Susan went back to her room and unpacked her things. There were no dressers or bureaus for the volunteers; instead each room had four metal, high school–like lockers along one wall. Susan opened the door of the only locker without a lock on it (she'd have to ask someone where to get one) and was touched to see a welcome packet inside. The packet consisted of a brochure explaining the history of the *kibbutz*, a chocolate bar, a package of cookies, and a pair of socks with the *kibbutz* logo on them.

After Susan unpacked, she grabbed her sketchpad and went outside to sit on the grass near the volunteer's residence hall. She'd promised herself she'd draw every day, even if only for ten or fifteen minutes. *A real artist has to be disciplined,* she reminded herself, though she knew she wasn't a real artist. Real artists were passionate. Real artists were creative. Real artists were driven. Susan knew she wasn't any of those things. Oh, she could render a passable likeness of a flower, a table, a rock, or anything else that was placed smack-dab in front of her. But her drawings were wooden; they lacked any kind of feeling or emotion. They didn't really *express* anything. That's what her college professors said, anyway. They kept telling her to loosen up. "Your still lifes have no life in them," one of them had said. "Just let your fingers go," said another, taking her wrist in his big, hairy hand and shaking it up and down until her arm flopped like a rag doll's. "That's it," he nodded in approval. "Now try and draw." She didn't think it made a bit of difference, and even though the teacher had said, "That's better," she could tell he didn't mean it.

Susan squinted her eyes against the bright sun and decided to draw some of the low, flat buildings around her. She needed to work on her perspective anyway. But as soon as she put charcoal to paper, she was interrupted.

"Drawing, eh? I'm Jeremy, from Canada. You're new here, eh?" Jeremy flopped down right next to her, crossed his long, skinny legs, and pushed his glasses up his nose.

"Yes," Susan said, reluctant to introduce herself.

"Susan, right? I sat across from you at *ulpan.* Which do you prefer, Susan or Shoshana? They call me Jacob, but I can't get used to it." Susan continued to draw without answering Jeremy, but that didn't stop him from keeping up a running conversation.

"I've been here about a month. It's all right, don't know how long I'll stay. They've already asked me about making *aliyah*, but I don't think I'll go that far, what about you, eh?"

"What's *aliyah*?" Susan asked as she shaded in the side of a building.

"Oh, you know, moving here. Permanently. Becoming an

Israeli citizen. You've heard of the Law of Return, haven't you?" Susan tucked a lock of dark hair behind her ear and shook her head, so Jeremy explained. "It means every Jew can become a citizen, no questions asked. They'll be bothering you about it before long, so you'd better start thinking it over. Hey, want to take a walk after dinner?" Jeremy abruptly changed the subject. "The nights here are very romantic."

Was he asking her out on a date? "Thanks, but I'm really tired. Still jet lagged. Sorry."

"All right. Maybe another time, eh?" Jeremy scrambled to his feet and stood over Susan for a moment with his arms folded, casting a long shadow over her work-in-progress. "I don't think you've got it quite right," he finally pronounced before turning on his heel and walking away.

"I think Jeremy fancies you," Madeleine said later as she and Susan walked to the dining hall for dinner. "He's cute. Do you fancy him as well?"

"Oh, I don't know. He was just being friendly," Susan said.

"Since when have you met a bloke who's just being friendly?" Madeleine shook her head and stuck her fists on her hips. "Watch out for the *kibbutzniks,* love, especially the married ones. They've heard you American girls are easy." She winked as she handed Susan a tray.

Dinner was a light meal, much to Susan's relief: plain yogurt with tomato and cucumber salad, matzo and *challah* with several types of mild cheeses, and fresh fruit for dessert. After dinner, Madeleine, who'd appointed herself Susan's personal welcome wagon, escorted her into the canteen, where the volunteers, as well as some of the young Israelis, gathered to drink coffee, eat sweets, and—Madeleine informed Susan in case she couldn't see for herself—pair off to take a walk in the woods and smooch.

"You see him over there?" Madeleine pointed with her cup as

she and Susan waited in the coffee line. "That's Mike. He's lovely, isn't he? But he knows it, thinks he's God's gift to women. He's from California, a real playboy type; he's been here about two months, and he's already been with several girls. Last week he was with her." Madeleine indicated one of the volunteers from Holland, who was tall and slim and had blond wavy hair down to her waist. "And now he's with her." She nodded toward a woman who could have been a carbon copy of the first one she'd pointed out, only her hair was flaming red. "Now, Jeremy, he was with Yael for a while, but she dumped him for that handsome *sabra*." Madeleine pointed across the room. "I fancy Stuart." Madeleine, who had been whispering all this time dropped her voice even further. "But he won't give me the time of day. Maybe you could talk to him for me, love, what do you say?"

"Oh, I don't know." Susan and Madeleine reached the front of the line, and Madeleine showed Susan how to make coffee the Israeli way: drop a spoonful of instant espresso into your cup, add five packets of sugar and about a tablespoon of hot water. Mix that up into a gooey paste, add another half a cup of boiling water, then top it all off with half a cup of milk. Susan's lips curled as she drank her concoction, but she forced herself to swallow, reminding herself, *When in Rome…*

"Here comes Jeremy," Madeleine raised her cup to him in greeting then started to sidle off but Susan grabbed her arm.

"Hello, ladies," Jeremy said, though it was clear he was speaking to Susan. *"Mah-nish ma?"*

"B'seder." Madeleine answered.

"How's everything? Fine." Jeremy translated for Susan. "Maybe I could be your tutor."

"Ooh, I bet he could teach you a thing or two," Madeleine nudged Susan's arm. "Go on, you two. *Lila tov.*"

"Lila tov." Jeremy replied. "Good night."

"I'm really tired. I'm going to bed. Excuse me." Susan rushed out of the canteen and headed to her dorm room. She wasn't interested in Jeremy, and she hoped he'd get the message soon. As she walked down the path lit only by moonlight, she caught sight of several couples strolling arm in arm and several others standing perfectly still, not strolling at all.

Susan hurried along, trying to make herself invisible and not disturb anyone. She wasn't particularly interested in romance, and she hoped the *kibbutz* wasn't going to be a repeat of college, which had basically been a repeat of high school. Girls getting all giggly and googly-eyed over boys who thought they were good for one thing and one thing only: Wham, bam, thank you ma'am.

Not that Susan was a prude or anything. She'd had her share of sexual experiences; after all, it was the seventies, the height of the sexual revolution, and everyone was screwing around. But for some reason the boys who "scored" with a different girl every night were revered as studs, and the girls who brought home a different guy every night were degraded as sluts. And what, Susan wondered, was so revolutionary about that? She didn't think romance was all that important, anyway. Her art was what was important, and of the few boyfriends she'd had, none of them had taken her work seriously. Carl, a tall, athletic-looking boy whom she saw on and off during her sophomore year, had shown interest at first, but as time went on Susan saw the real reason for his curiosity: He was hoping she would draw him, even though, as Susan pointed out, she didn't do portraits; she did still lifes and landscapes. She tried explaining to Carl that portraits were tricky, and most of the time the subject was disappointed with the finished product, even when the artist was a pro, which Susan was not. She'd only taken one figure-drawing class, which was required for her major, and then went back to inanimate objects, which were much safer—they didn't argue with you about what they looked like. A portrait artist needed to have that special something to capture a person's essence on canvas, and whatever that special something was, Susan knew she didn't have it.

"Just try," Carl kept insisting despite Susan's protests, and so one day she did, mostly to shut him up. They'd just had an afternoon quickie; Susan had jumped up as soon as it was over and was already dressed, but Carl was still lounging on the single bed in her dorm room, naked, his leather belt looped around the doorknob as a KEEP OUT sign for her roommate, who was due back from her chemistry class any minute. Susan took out her art supplies and tried her best, but even Carl had to admit her sketches weren't very good. When he actually said, "Oh, well, back to the drawing board," Susan knew their affair was over.

There had been a few other boys on and off throughout the rest of her college years, but none of her affairs (calling them relationships would be stretching it) lasted more than three or four months. Susan never had trouble attracting boyfriends—she was of average height and weight with dark-brown hair and eyes, someone a boy wouldn't necessarily notice in a crowd but someone he wouldn't be ashamed to show off to his buddies either. She was the kind of girl a guy would ask out when he didn't have the nerve to approach the girl he really wanted to be with: the curvy blond bombshell who wouldn't give him the time of day unless he was the school's star football player. Susan didn't mind, though. She only dated because she thought it was expected of her. And she didn't want her friends to think there was something wrong with her.

And she liked sex. She liked the things her body did, the way it seemed to rise and expand like a loaf of *challah* baking in the oven before her orgasm exploded, sending little zings of energy everywhere: to her hands, her feet, the nape of her neck, the small of her back, the insides of her thighs. Afterward Susan felt like she sparkled, and she loved to look at herself in the mirror then, to see the red flush spread across her chest and neck all the way up to her cheeks. It was the only time she ever felt truly beautiful. But the truth was, she didn't always come when she was with a boy, though she never had any trouble by herself. By herself it was more intense. She could take her time and not have to worry about what someone else was thinking or what someone else wanted. And best of all, afterward she could just lie in bed naked with the covers pulled up to her chin and smile. She didn't have to wrap her arms around some sweaty, smelly boy and tell him what a wonderful lover he was. She didn't have to dodge the wet spot. She didn't have to wonder when whoever was sharing her bed would leave already so she could get back to her latest painting, waiting patiently for her over in the art building, propped up on its wobbly easel.

Susan got undressed and crawled into her tiny bed, first making sure there were no spiders under the thin cotton blanket. She slept well, not even hearing her roommates come in, until the five o'clock alarm woke her to get ready for work again.

And so the weeks went on: *Pardis* in the morning, *ulpan* in the afternoon, socializing in the evenings. Susan found she enjoyed working in the orange groves. She liked the color her skin was turning: a golden brown similar to the blond oak table in her parents' dining room. She liked the muscles that formed in her upper arms and the backs of her calves. She liked the feeling of accomplishment that came when she got to the end of her row and started up the other side. And she was making slow but steady progress with her Hebrew. She could actually hold a simple conversation about the weather or the time, though she still had trouble reading and writing. She managed to draw a little every day too, though more often than not some boy, either a volunteer or *kibbutznik*, interrupted her, wanting to take her for a walk or, better yet, back to his room. Susan was continuously shocked at the bluntness of these offers, and always declined politely, as she did in the evenings at the canteen, with Madeleine at her side wistfully staring at the "blokes" she fancied, most of whom ignored her.

Summer melded seamlessly into autumn. The days were still hot but not as fiercely so; some nights Susan even had to wear a light sweater to walk back to her room from the canteen. Rosh Hashanah came and went, as did Yom Kippur. Susan was shocked to see that the *kibbutzniks* celebrated the Day of Atonement by having a picnic instead of fasting, and no one even mentioned going to synagogue. There were also field trips for the volunteers on Shabbat, the only day of the week they didn't have to work. Once they went to the Dead Sea, and Susan saw what she'd always heard was true: You could float on your back and read the newspaper; there was so much salt in the water it was impossible to sink. Another time they went to Jerusalem to shop at the *shuk* and visit the Wailing Wall. Susan bought some earrings made of silver and turquoise-colored Elat stones from an Arab who cut the price in half "for your eyes," he said, "your pretty, pretty eyes." She stood at a distance from the Wailing Wall for a long time—watching men and women approach the ancient structure, pushing tiny pieces of paper between its cracks—before she decided what she wanted her "letter to God" to say: *Please keep my parents safe, well, and happy.* Susan, though not exactly happy herself, was not exactly unhappy either. She had grown used to life on the *kibbutz*; she was in a holding pattern, but just as she began to relax into her days everything changed.

It began with the weather. The rainy season arrived, and the words "soaked to the skin" took on a whole new meaning for Susan, who had never experienced such torrential downpours before. The rain came down in absolute sheets, and even when it wasn't raining the air was cold and clammy. The first day the rains began, Susan ran out to the porch to take in a few pieces of laundry she had hung over the railing to dry. When she lifted a navy-blue pullover, a dozen buttons clattered to the porch's wooden floor, making a small, tinny racket. Susan was puzzled: How did all those buttons come loose at once? She knelt to scoop them up and then realized to her horror that they weren't buttons at all; they were hard-shelled black beetles that had holed up for shelter. Susan dropped the sweater with a shriek; it slid over the railing into the mud where it stayed for several months before someone picked it up and took it away.

Working in *Pardis* was out of the question now. First Susan was reassigned to the laundry, which she hated, then she worked briefly in the *kibbutz*'s equivalent of a day care center, but she didn't fare well there either. Susan was intrigued with the way children were raised on the *kibbutz*: From the time they were six months old until they turned eighteen and went into the army, they lived away from their parents in a large building called the children's house. Each section of the children's house had about six kids in it, who grew as close as siblings to each other. Children saw their parents for three hours a day during the week and all day on Shabbat. Susan tried her best, but it was difficult for her to work in the children's house because even though her language skills were slowly improving, she still spoke less Hebrew than a typical four-year-old, making it impossible for her to have any control over her pint-size charges.

That left the kitchen. Madeleine cringed visibly when Susan told her of her new work assignment.

"What's so bad about the kitchen?" Susan asked as she enjoyed what the volunteers considered a special treat: pieces of bread toasted on the metal safety grates of the small kerosene heater that tried in vain to take the dampness and chill out of their room.

"Norit," chorused Madeleine, Yael, and Rona together, pretending to shiver in fright.

"Who's Norit?" Susan asked.

"I'm sure you've seen her, love, sitting by herself in the back of the dining room in khaki trousers and a big white hat?" Madeleine licked butter from the tips of her fingers.

"Tall. Grand. *Gadol,*" Yael said, holding up her arms in a wide circle indicating girth.

"She eats girls like you for breakfast," Rona warned as she knelt in front of the heater to turn her toast with one hand, the other keeping her long, straightened hair out of danger.

"It's because she never married," Madeleine explained. "And she has to be, what? Thirty, thirty-five? She's probably never even had a chap."

"Old maid. No good." Yael tsk-tsked.

"This one girl, Andrea, from Massachusetts?" Rona said. "She told me Norit goes into the chicken house, picks out a bird, cuts its head off with a cleaver, and laughs as the poor headless body runs around the coop."

"Ewww!" Madeleine pretended to gag on her toast.

"Cannot be true," said Yael. She crossed both her hands around her own throat in protection, and then looked at Susan with sympathy. "*Mazel tov,* Shoshana. Good luck."

Susan wasn't too worried about working with "Norit the Nazi," as some of the volunteers called her behind her back (though not within hearing range of the *kibbutzniks,* many of whom were Holocaust survivors). Surely the stories about her were exaggerations, and if Susan just stayed out of her way and did as told she'd be fine.

But it was impossible to stay out of Norit's way. The woman was enormous, and her bulk took up most of the narrow, crowded kitchen where Susan worked, peeling cucumbers, slicing tomatoes, and digging the eyes out of potato after potato. Try as she might, Susan couldn't work fast enough for Norit, who didn't say much, but she didn't have to; a silent scowl was enough to inspire Susan to double her efforts and pick up her pace, even though her arms ached from scraping pounds of carrots against a grater that was in dire need of sharpening.

Norit flew about her domain, barking orders, brandishing knives, reaching for oversize pots and pans that hung on huge hooks above her head and banging them down onto the stove with a clatter. Her hair was a mass of sandy curls; try as she might, they would not stay contained beneath the white chef's hat that stood upright upon her head, adding to her already impressive height and stature. Susan guessed Norit was more than six feet tall and weighed at least 250 pounds. Yet she was all speed and muscle, lifting enormous vats of soup off the stove, pummeling mountains of *challah* dough into submission with her enormous bare hands, hauling in yet another fifty-pound bag of carrots for Susan to peel and grate. Susan was a bit afraid of her, like everyone else—but she was fascinated too, and she couldn't help staring at Norit, though she quickly averted her eyes and went back to work whenever the woman so much as glanced her way. Norit was a mad, whirling dervish of energy. Unlike the other Israeli women, she didn't turn all coy and giggly when a man entered the room. She had no patience for anyone—man, woman, or child—who got in her way or prevented her from completing the job currently at hand. Norit meant business and Susan admired that. Still, did she have to be such a stern taskmaster? By the time they broke for breakfast, Susan was in a sweat; by the time lunch came around, she was beyond exhausted. She noticed no one sat with Norit at either meal. The *kibbutzniks* ate on one side of the dining hall, the volunteers on the other, and Norit just sat in the back at a little folding table, sipping a cup of tea and munching a dry piece of matzo.

Each day after work, Susan went back to her room and drew whatever she found there: Yael's tired, muddy, Van Gogh–like boots slouched against each other in the corner; Rona's ragged stuffed teddy bear lying sideways on her pillow; a still life of

Madeleine's lipstick, compact, and black lace bra. But one day weeks into the rainy season, Susan was seized with cabin fever. There was an hour or so before *ulpan*, and she decided to take a walk. There was actually a break in the rain, though it was far from sunny—it was foggy and misty, almost like Susan was walking through a cloud. She donned a yellow slicker, jammed a pencil and a small sketchpad into her pocket, and started on her way.

She walked down the path to the canteen, around the dining hall, and past the small, square homes of the *kibbutzniks*, each one built exactly alike. Susan didn't have a particular destination in mind; she just wanted to go somewhere she hadn't been before, so she walked wherever her feet decided to take her. After a while, though, she realized she was headed toward something: a sound that was very faint at first but grew louder and stronger with every step. Someone was singing. She couldn't make out the words because they weren't in English, but the melody was lively; Susan could imagine it being sung by a barful of men clinking beer steins and chugging their brew down in one long, uninterrupted swallow—except the person singing the song was a woman, her voice round, lusty, and full. Her song put a bounce in Susan's step and a smile on her face, though she didn't know why. Maybe because Susan herself would never sing a song like that, so lively and full of *joie de vivre*. Susan was curious to see who was singing, even though she imagined the woman wouldn't want to be disturbed, in the same way Susan hated to be bothered when she was sketching. Still, she put one foot in front of the other until she turned a corner and stopped dead in her tracks, unable to believe what she saw.

It was Norit. Enormous, intimidating, gruff, no-nonsense Norit singing at the top of her lungs. And not only that. She was stark-naked, standing underneath an outdoor shower rigged to the side of what must have been her living quarters. Susan knew a decent person would turn and walk away immediately, but she just couldn't move; the sight before her was too mesmerizing. It was as if someone put a spell on Susan, changing her legs into two slim tree trunks rooted into the ground.

Norit, underneath her dirty white uniform smeared with butter, flour, and cooking grease, was magnificent. More than magnificent. Stunning. Ravishing. Gorgeous. Her body was massive, full of curves and crevices, simultaneously hard and soft, sturdy and delicate, completely unlike Susan's body, which had always seemed fine before but now seemed wholly inadequate compared to the work of art that was Norit. As she turned this way and that, soaping herself up, rinsing herself off, and singing all the while, Susan continued to stare at Norit's flesh-covered form, a feast for the eyes, a true masterpiece. How her plump arms shimmered, how her rounded belly curved, how alluring were the two sweet folds of flesh above her waist, how dainty were her tiny feet, how abundant her dimpled thighs! And as if all this weren't enough—*dayenu,* as the Passover song goes—when Norit finally spotted Susan, she didn't shriek and rush to cover herself or yell at Susan to run away. Instead she opened her arms wide and smiled, as if to say, *Look at me. Aren't I fabulous?* and then motioned impatiently for Susan to come join her, as if she'd been waiting for this moment all her life, and what in the world was taking her so long?

And Susan, who had been surprised at everything that had happened to her thus far in this strange yet familiar land, wasn't surprised at all. Finally, she was wide-awake, no longer sleepwalking through what she knew hadn't been much of a life. Finally, the movie of her existence was reaching its climax; at last the director who lived rent-free in her brain was calling for action. And Susan complied: She took off her raincoat, her rain hat, her rubber boots, all the clothing she'd been wearing for weeks in order to stay dry, and dashed into the water. She wanted to be like Norit, drenched, soaked, saturated. The wetter the better. Norit soaped her up, scrubbed her down, singing all the while. Susan felt renewed, rejuvenated, reborn. And for the rest of that afternoon, and many days that followed, Susan at long last learned the subtle nuances of Norit's foreign tongue and discovered just how sweet and tender on the inside a tough, gruff *sabra* could be.

Of course Susan and Norit didn't live happily ever after, though they did live quite happily for the rest of the year, until Susan's time in the holy land drew to a close. Of course there were many tears shed and many promises made, all of which were eventually broken. Susan never did go back to Israel, and Norit never did come to the States for a visit. Their tearful once-a-month phone calls dribbled to an end, and their letters dwindled down to birthday and Chanukah cards. One day a letter Susan had sent to Norit came back stamped "No longer at this address," and that, she concluded, was the end of that.

Until the year that Susan turned forty and, right on schedule, had her midlife crisis. After Susan had returned from Israel (with no boyfriend in tow, much to her parents' dismay) she'd gone back to school for her teaching certificate and made peace with the fact that while she would never be a great artist, she could still have art at the center of her life. She taught drawing and painting at a community college in upstate New York, where she had settled down; she also volunteered her time at a nursing home, helping the residents work with modeling clay, which was good for their gnarled, arthritic hands. She'd had a serious relationship that had lasted the better part of a decade, and though it hadn't worked out in the end, Susan and her ex-lover remained the best of friends. And now she had a new lover, a round, ripe, luscious woman named Beverly who made the short hairs at the back of her neck stand on end every time she walked into the room. Life was good—better than good—but still there was something missing. Susan, on the brink of turning forty, was feeling nostalgic, but nostalgic for what? She didn't have a clue.

As part of entering a new decade of life, she decided to clean out the large shed she built behind the house to use as a studio. She'd recently read a book on the ancient art of feng shui and was intrigued by the notion of creating beauty and peace in one's life by making one's living space and work space as soothing and peaceful as possible. In order to do this, Susan learned, she needed to hold up every object she owned and put it to the test: Did she feel good about the object? Did it reflect who she was today? Did it add to her feeling of well-being or detract from it? Susan was sitting on the floor in the middle of her studio surrounded by piles: things to keep, things to box up and store, things to give away, things she wasn't sure about. She had just come to her old sketchpads from her trip to Israel and was flipping through the pages when there was a knock at the door.

"It's open," Susan called, knowing who it was.

"Want some company?" Beverly poked one foot cautiously into the room. She knew Susan's studio was sacred space and never entered before permission was granted.

Susan looked up and smiled. "C'mon in."

"What are you doing?" Beverly stepped carefully around the piles, knelt beside Susan, and kissed her on the cheek.

"Just sorting through my things. In with the old, out with the new, you know, trying to deal with turning forty."

"The best is yet to come, honey. You'll see." Beverly, having crossed the great divide into middle age several years ago, spoke with authority. "Hey," she looked down at the sketchpad Susan was holding. "I thought you didn't do portraits."

"I don't," Susan said, despite the hard and fast evidence to the contrary spread across her lap. "I just did these as a favor for someone."

"Who's the model?" Beverly squinted her eyes for a better look.

Susan felt her face grow red. "Norit," she whispered softly.

"Wow, she's a looker. Should I be jealous?" Beverly teased.

"No." Susan wasn't in a teasing mood. "You should be grateful. If it wasn't for her I wouldn't be with you."

"Is that so?" Beverly looked from the drawing to Susan.

"She changed my life," Susan said and then told Beverly the story of Norit, hunting up the one photo she had of her.

"Wow," Beverly said when Susan was done. "What a risky thing to do, to seduce you like that. And how brave of you to just dive in."

"Norit said it was *bashert*," Susan said with a faraway look in her eye.

"What does *bashert* mean?" Beverly asked.

"It's hard to translate, but it means fate, kismet, something like that." Susan grew silent for a minute, not telling Beverly that *bashert* had another meaning: Norit had called Susan *bashert* as an endearment, meaning "my destiny," and Susan had called Norit *bashert* as well.

"Wow," Beverly said again, still studying the sketches. "I guess I owe her big-time."

"So do I," Susan said, closing the sketchpad and putting it on top of the "I don't know" pile.

"Were the drawings for her?" Beverly asked, studying the photo of Norit.

Susan nodded. "She liked them a lot, but I don't know. I never did anything with them." Susan shut her eyes for a minute, remembering the endless arguments she'd had with Norit, who, like Carl, had longed to pose for her. First she'd teased her: "Am I not attractive enough for you?" she asked, putting one hand on her hip, the other behind her neck, and then throwing her head back in a fashion model's pose. Susan laughed and tried to explain that it wasn't Norit's lack of beauty; it was her own lack of talent. But Norit didn't buy that. "*Lama lo? Lama lo?* Why not? Why not?" she kept asking, her impatient voice growing louder and louder until one day Susan shrieked, "Because I'm no damn good!" and then to her horror, burst into tears. Norit had held her and stroked her and then abruptly pushed her away. She disappeared into the bathroom for a moment and then returned without a stitch of clothing on. Susan reached up to undo the top button of her own blouse, but Norit didn't want to make love. She wanted Susan to draw her and demanded she do so in a voice that would not take no for an answer. Susan dried her eyes, glared at Norit, and drew.

"*Tov. Yoffi.* Good. Pretty." Norit had been pleased, but Susan, always the perfectionist, saw only the flaws in her sketches. She put them away and, though Norit continued to ask, plead, and demand, never drew her again.

"I know how you can pay her back." Beverly's words cut through Susan's thoughts. "May I?" She reached for the pad after Susan nodded. "You can work on these."

"What do you mean?"

"I mean, these are stunning. Look at the lines, the shapes, the shadows. These drawings have something those don't." Beverly waved a plump arm at the studies of fruit and furniture hanging on the wall. "I may be going out on a limb here, Susan, but these drawings have...I don't know...heart. They have your heart. And soul. They're alive. Your other paintings...I mean, they're good and everything, but they don't...they don't move me like these do. Even unfinished, these sketches have a life to them your other work doesn't have. Oh, God." Beverly looked down at her hands. "Me and my big mouth. Did I go too far? Are you going to break up with me?"

"No," Susan said slowly, looking from the sketchpad to the

wall and back again. "Only because I know you're right. But I don't know if I can do it."

"Why not?"

"I don't know." Susan flipped through the sketches. "They're so…so out there. I'm afraid of exposing Norit like that."

"I think," Beverly stayed Susan's hand with her own, "you're afraid of exposing *yourself* like that."

"But all I have are these sketches and this one photo," Susan whined. Knowing she'd been found out, she looked for any excuse. "You know I need to have something in front of me in order to draw it."

Beverly threw Susan a look that said, *I'll love you whether you rise to the occasion or not, but both of us know what's really going on here,* and then got to her feet. "I'll come by later, OK?" she said. Then she tiptoed out of the studio, shutting the door behind her.

For the rest of that afternoon Susan drew. She drew from memory, she drew from experience, she drew from deep inside her. And when Beverly came back later that evening with take-out Chinese to share, she didn't have to say what Susan already knew: That afternoon's work was the best she'd ever done.

Susan hadn't submitted her work to galleries for years, but with Beverly's coaxing, which grew into insistence ("It's not for nothing you're dating a pushy broad"), she took slides of her work and sent them out. First she was accepted to group exhibits, then she sold a painting or two, and at last a New York gallery offered her a one-woman show. When the letter came, Beverly grabbed Susan's hands and whirled her around the room. "You did it!" she shrieked, engulfing her lover in a big bear hug.

"You mean *we* did it. I never would've done those paintings if it weren't for you," Susan pointed out, eager to share the glory.

"I didn't do anything," Beverly shot back. "It was *bashert.* Meant to be."

❀

Susan looked up at her paintings, framed so elegantly and hung so expertly on the gallery's walls. She'd obscured Norit's face for the most part, with a raised arm or a turn of the head, just to be on the safe side, even though twenty years had passed and she was sure that Norit, like herself, had changed over time. Still, Susan wanted to be sure that Norit remained unrecognizable. It was a small world, and one never knew—perhaps somehow, someday Norit would stumble across her paintings. Susan wondered what Norit would think of them. The woman had no shame when it came to her body, and Susan imagined she'd be flattered, proud, pleased. At least she hoped so. She closed her eyes for a moment and whispered to Norit, *Toda raba,* thank you so much. For everything. For teaching me to love you and therefore love myself. For holding me tight and letting me go. For inspiring me and believing in me. For this moment that I've waited for all my life. And even though the room was noisy with the oohs and aahs of the crowd, Susan could swear she heard Norit's voice close to her ear, whispering *Bashert, b'vakasha.* My destiny, you're welcome.

Girls Will Be Boys

It all started with a dare. And ended with a dare. They said we were a daring couple, Sheila and me. Or maybe they said we were a darling couple. I don't know. I do know, however, that one little letter can make a very big difference. The difference between lighting and lightning. Pride and prude. Pal and gal. She and he.

❀

But it all started long before I even knew Sheila, in the biblical sense or otherwise. It started back in the early seventies, when I was about eight years old. My mother, my sister, and I were gathered around the television to watch *Peter Pan.* My mother was more excited than we were. "Wait, you'll see," she said when it was clear my sister and I thought the Darlings with their bumbling pooch Nana were just plain silly. "Wait," said my mother again. "They're going to fly." Lily, who was barely a year older than me, spread her arms wide and ran around the room during the commercials. "I'm flying! I'm flying!" she yelled, running up and down the couch and chairs, her white Wendy-like nightgown flowing behind her. But I couldn't care less about flying. My eyes were glued to the set as I waited for Mary Martin to return and prove to me what I had known in my tiny bones all along: Most girls grew up and became women, but some girls were lucky enough to grow up and turn into boys.

❀

That summer I was out in the backyard with the boys from next door, Tommy and Ben, building a fort out of my mom's old blankets, a crate we'd dragged up from the basement, and a bunch of sticks. The sun was high and bright in the sky, and we were practically baking inside that rickety structure of wood and wool. Tommy and Ben took their shirts off; without thinking, I did too. We continued to play until I ran in the back door and asked my mom for some lemonade.

"Where's your shirt?" she asked, taking three paper cups from the cupboard.

"In the fort." I grabbed. the cups, eager to get back to my friends.

"Go upstairs and put something on," my mother said, a pitcher of lemonade in her hand.

"Why?" I reached for the blue Tupperware pitcher, but she held it high out of reach.

"Because it isn't ladylike," she answered, stretching out the word like I was still a baby.

"But I'm not a lady," I pointed out.

"Not yet, but someday you will be. And in the meantime, you're a girl."

I am not, I wanted to cry, but that wasn't exactly true. I was a girl; I just didn't feel like a girl. I decided to try a different tactic. "But Tommy and Ben have their shirts off. That's not fair."

"A lot of things aren't fair, Jacqueline. You'll learn that as you get older."

I won't grow up, I won't grow up. I sang Peter Pan's theme song under my breath as I ran upstairs to obey my mother.

❀

It all comes down to the movies. Who did you want to be, Romeo or Juliet? Rhett or Scarlett? Who did you lust after, Elizabeth Taylor or Richard Burton? James Dean or Natalie Wood? Did you want to be the girl or get the girl? I knew what I wanted, beyond a Tinkerbell of a doubt. And just as surely, I knew I had to keep it to myself.

❀

For a long time I could fool myself into thinking I would stay just as I was. A tomboy—or a girlboy, as I thought of myself. I kept my hair short, my chest remained flat, and though I didn't have a penis, no one but me had to know that. Besides, maybe one would grow. Other things were starting to grow. Hair, for example, was sprouting in weird places. Under my arms. Between my legs. Maybe I'd start growing a mustache too. You never knew.

But time was ticking away like that clock inside the alligator that was after Captain Hook. One day when I was fourteen, disaster struck. Blood. Down there. I knew what it was. Lily had gotten her period when she was only twelve, and my mother had sat us down for "the talk." Showed us how to use sanitary napkins. Told us how babies were made. We couldn't imagine it. Since we didn't have a father, we never really thought about how we came to be. We knew we'd lived in our mother's stomach once upon a time, but that seemed as unbelievable as the other things my mother said were surely going to happen to us in the not-so-distant future.

I didn't want to tell. Saying it out loud would make it real.

Besides, maybe I had hurt myself on my bike. Maybe it would go away. But Lily found the pads in the garbage pail, rolled up in yards and yards of toilet paper like miniature mummies. That night at supper, she glanced sideways at me and then singsonged, "Someone has her period. Someone has her period." My mother looked up from her pot roast, but I refused to catch her eye. My burning cheeks told her everything she wanted to know.

Later I stole some tampons from my mother (she said we couldn't use them until we were older) and tried to figure out which end was up inside my underpants. Accidentally I touched something that made me jump. What was that? I touched it again. And again and again and again. My mother had never mentioned this during "the talk." She told Lily and me about eggs and sperm and tubes and wombs. But she'd never said anything about what I later learned was called a clitoris. And she certainly didn't say anything about pleasure.

❀

Even Pinocchio managed to become a real live boy eventually. If that naughty, lying, long-nosed, clumsy contraption of wood and string could figure it out, Jiminy Cricket, why couldn't I?

❀

If there really is a hell, I imagine it to be just like high school. Boring classes. Barf-like food. And worst of all, kids. I didn't fit in anywhere. Tommy and Ben, my former friends, wanted nothing to do with me. That had started back in junior high when they'd been teased for losing a game of running bases to a girl. In fact, none of the boys wanted anything to do with me. They weren't interested in me *that way,* which is all they thought girls were good for. And the girls all thought I was a freak because I refused to wear dresses or makeup and I wasn't interested in how many calories were in a school-size serving of macaroni and cheese.

I had one friend, a new girl whom no one liked either, simply because she was fat and had red hair. Frizzy red hair. I mean, big deal, right? But that's how shallow the kids in my school were. Risa wasn't like them. She was actually nice. She wanted to be an artist, and she was really good with her charcoal and pencils. We'd take walks in the woods until we came to a cozy spot, and then I'd sprawl on my back and watch the clouds float by while she drew whatever she saw: mountains, trees, once a salamander sunning on a rock. Risa could talk as she worked, and we'd discuss our plans for the future. Neither of us wanted to get married or have kids. Risa wanted to be a famous artist or at least an art teacher at a fancy college. I didn't know what I wanted to be, just what I didn't want to be: a wife and mother. Risa was the first person to understand that.

"I don't really like babies very much," she said. "I like animals better."

"Me too," I said. "I've always wanted a puppy, but my mom won't let me get one. She thinks I'm not responsible enough. She says if I can't even keep my room clean, how can she trust me to take care of a dog? I don't know what one thing has to do with the other."

"Me neither," Risa agreed. "Let's live in a big farmhouse when we get out of high school and have dogs and cats and goats—"

"And a horse," I said. It sounded like heaven. Risa could draw and paint all she wanted, and I could just take care of things. Even though I knew even as we said the words that it was a fantasy, it still gave me something to dream about, something to get me through the endless days before the freedom that graduation would bring.

Of course the kids at my school couldn't leave well enough alone. Were we hurting them by being friends? What the hell is wrong with adolescent boys anyway? Risa and I were walking up the hill toward town after one of our lazy afternoons when some kids on their bikes spotted us. "Ooooh," they crooned in triumph. "We know what you've been doing."

"What?" Risa asked, sounding genuinely curious. She hadn't known these boys since childhood, didn't know how mean they could be.

"Kissy, kissy, kissy," one of them chanted, and then the others started smacking their lips together. "Ooh, Risa, ooh baby, baby—"

"Shut up," I said, but my red face betrayed me. I don't think I realized until that moment that I did want to kiss Risa.

"Ooooh," they chorused again. "Jackie's got a girlfriend, Jackie's got a girlfriend."

"Shut *up,*" I said again, but of course they didn't.

"Jackie is a lezzie. Jackie is a lezzie."

I couldn't just stand there and let them say that, even though I knew all at once that it was true.

"C'mon, Jackie," Risa pulled at my arm. "Just ignore them. They're idiots."

I shook her off and balled my fists. I didn't know which one I wanted to hit first. There were three of them and one of me. I knew Risa wouldn't fight, and I didn't want her to. "Go home," I hissed at her.

"Jackie—"

"Just go," I said, and started swinging. By the time the fight was over, I had a bloody lip and a black eye. But I'd given out worse than I'd gotten. I had years of pent-up anger on my side. Plus, though they wouldn't admit it, I knew my classmates had mixed feelings about hitting a girl, even a girl who could beat them all with one hand tied behind her back.

Jackie is a lezzie. Jackie is a lezzie. At least now I had a name for what I was.

❀

My mother thought it was all her fault. Maybe because I didn't have a father and I was the oldest, I thought I had to be the man of the house. I didn't know what fathers or men had to do with it. I didn't really want to be either of those things. I just wanted to be myself.

❀

Lily got married the week after she graduated. Not because she wanted to be a June bride but because she had a bun in the oven. She was barely eighteen, and her boyfriend wasn't much older. My mother was extremely unhappy about becoming a grandmother at the tender age of thirty-seven. But it was more than that. I think she was really upset that Lily was "ruining her life" as she yelled one night after supper during one of their nastier fights.

"Like you ruined yours?" Lily yelled back, referring to the fact that my mother had also gotten pregnant in high school. A long silence followed. What could my mother say? Could she admit that Lily and I had ruined her life? And more important, *had* we?

I tried to stay out of my mother's way that June and not cause her any more trouble, but the day finally came when she realized I had to wear something to the wedding. Lily's best friend was going to be her maid of honor, so I was off the hook for that. But still, I was the sister of the bride. I had to look halfway decent. And to my mother's mind, that meant a dress.

Need I say how ridiculous I looked in that sky-blue, empire-waisted, spaghetti-strapped taffeta? I stepped out of the dressing room, and my mother winced, like someone who had just seen a particularly gruesome disaster on the evening news. Even the saleswoman who had oohed and aahed in a voice full of envy over my supermodel-like shape didn't know what to say. What were they going to do with me?

"Can't I just wear pants?" I asked for the seven-millionth time. My mother just looked at me and sighed. She sighed a lot that summer.

"I do have one outfit that might be appropriate." The saleswoman, whom I'd never have pegged for a friend, actually saved the day by handing my mother a mock tuxedo, cut for a feminine figure.

"I don't know..." My mother's dreams were disappearing slowly but surely, like a balloon full of helium that had come untied from a little kid's wrist. Her older daughter wasn't going to go to college, and her younger daughter sure wasn't going to be the belle of the ball.

"I'll just try it on," I said, before my mother could say no, and into the dressing room I went. The getup wasn't exactly my cup of tea, but I knew it was the best I could do. It was a black-and-white jumpsuit, the bottom black and the top white, complete with a little black jacket, double-breasted with fake tails in the back. I thought I actually looked quite sharp in it. *Dapper* was the word that came to mind. And even my mother had to admit it was a hundred times better than any dress I had tried on.

"Oh, she looks precious," the saleswoman said, clasping her hands to her chest. This time I winced. Precious? Handsome was more like it. But I didn't care, as long as my mother whipped out her checkbook.

❀

Senior year passed in a blur. The best part of it was getting my driver's license. My mom couldn't afford to buy me a car like some of my classmates' parents, but she did let me drive her to work so I could use the station wagon during the day. The only hitch was I had to pick her up on time and keep the gas tank filled. I was running late, but I knew better than to show up at my mother's office with the little red arrow pointing to empty.

"Yes, sir?" An attendant appeared at my window.

"Fill 'er up," I choked out, making my voice as deep as possible, like a radio DJ. *Sir.* My whole body thrilled at the sound of it. Such a little word, but it packed a big punch. *Sir.* A word of respect, unlike *ma'am,* which made my mother cringe when it was directed at her. *Anything else, sir? Here's your change, sir. Have a nice day, sir.* Yessirree.

❀

"Mommy, is that a boy or a girl?" On the street, in the library, at the post office, in the grocery store. I didn't even bother looking up anymore.

❀

College was my ticket out. I'd kept my grades up, so getting financial aid and even a tiny scholarship wasn't a problem. I went as far as my mother would send me, to an East Coast liberal arts college that had more than 100 school clubs, including a gay-lesbian-straight alliance. With my heart in my hands, I stood before the door, staring at the enormous upside-down pink triangle on it as if it were a mirror. I had a feeling that once I walked through that door, my life would never be the same. You'd think that feeling would have propelled me inside at once, since my life wasn't so great as it was, but instead I stood frozen to the spot. I might have stayed there forever, or turned and ran down the steps of the student union, if the door hadn't opened, as if of its own accord. "I'll see you Tuesday," the person whose hand held the doorknob called into the room. And then to me: "Oh, hi." And then to no one in particular, "Bye."

"Hi. Bye," I said and then, having no choice, I walked into the office. The room was tiny as a closet and was completely packed with books, pamphlets, buttons, bumper stickers, and a cluttered desk upon which stood a computer with the word QUEER running across it continuously in bold black letters.

"Hi, I'm Brian. Can I help you?" A boy with dirty-blond hair falling over one eye looked up from a notepad he was writing on.

"Um…um…" was the most I could muster.

"Are you here for information about Tuesday night?" he asked.

That sounded good; I nodded.

"Here's the info. We'll meet here at 7:30. I'm hoping to find a bigger space between now and then. If I do, there'll be a note on the door."

"OK. Thanks." I took the flyer and backed out the door, relief flooding my veins. *I'm out of the closet!* I thought, laughing at my own joke as I hurried down the steps. I folded the paper in half, quarters, eighths, and then jammed it into my back pocket. Only in the privacy of my tiny single room (again, no bigger than a closet) did I feel safe enough to unfold the piece of paper and see what Tuesday night would bring.

Fag Sissy Mama's Boy Queer

Are you gay? Do you think you might be?

Come to a rap group and hear what others have to say.

All males welcome regardless of experience or how you identify.

Tuesday, 7:30 P.M. You may be straight, but don't be late.

I stared at the paper in my hand for a good twenty minutes, trying to sort it all out. Brian thought I was a guy? A gay guy? Even my own people didn't know what to make of me. I took a long, hard look at myself in the full-length mirror on the back of my door. If I didn't know, what would I think? My hair was short and sand-colored, cut to leave the back of my neck and my ears blowing in the breeze. I wore no makeup or jewelry except for a watch with a plain brown leather band. My clothes were simple: a baggy green T-shirt and even baggier jeans. Sneakers covered my feet. I suppose I could be either sex. Or both. Or neither. I hadn't kissed anyone yet—even *I* knew practicing on the soft flesh inside my upper arm didn't count. Maybe I was sexless, like a dog who'd been fixed. But thanks to my tampon experimentation, I knew that wasn't true. I touched myself and fantasized about blond bombshells like Madonna more often than I would ever admit or even thought was healthy.

So what should I do? Go to Tuesday night's meeting and shock them all? Hardly. I couldn't even bring myself to go back to the office of the alliance and ask them if they had a rap group for lesbians. What if all the other women there hated me? What if they told me to get out? Where would I go? Clearly this was something I had to deal with myself.

❀

Which brings me to the dare. Which I didn't know about at first. All I knew was I was lonely. Incredibly lonely. Ache-in-the-chest, cry-myself-to-sleep, howl-like-an-old-dog-left-to-die lonely. I had no friends on campus. Kept to myself. Went to my classes, did my homework, sat alone in the snack bar at the student union smoking cigarette after cigarette while I nursed a bottomless cup of coffee. This was how it went for several semesters. And then something happened in the next town over. A gay bar opened up. Everyone on campus was talking about it. The weekly alternative newspaper even did a feature article on it, complete with an interview of the owner. He named the bar "Wilde" with an "e" on the end, for Oscar Wilde, who I guess was this famous gay person. A writer who went to jail because of it and everything. That didn't make me feel too confident. Sure, this was the next-to-last decade of the twentieth century, and I guess we've made some progress, but people can still be pretty damn mean. More than mean. Downright ugly. The owner said he hoped the name would be a code, like you could say to someone, "Wanna go Wilde tonight?" and they would know what you meant. But now that he'd said that in the paper—I mean, how stupid can you get?—the cat was out of the bag.

The bar was all I could think about. I was like a magnet, attracted and repelled at the same time, depending on which way I was pointed. Toward what I knew what I wanted, or away from what could turn out to be just another big disappointment. What if people laughed at me? I didn't know how to dance. At this point I didn't even know if I remembered how to talk outside a classroom. But what if the big if? What if I met someone? What if I got to hold a girl close, maybe kiss the top of her head as she melted against me while we swayed to the music with the lights turned down low? My arms ached with emptiness. My heart throbbed with hope. It was as if my body just took over and left me with no choice.

I found the place with no trouble, even though it was out in the middle of nowhere. Drove the old used Chevy I'd managed to save up for and parked it way in the back of the lot. Wilde was a tiny place, a square, shack-like structure that looked as shaky as the forts Tommy, Ben, and I had built years ago. I walked in on trembling legs and headed right for the bar, my eyes looking down at my feet the whole time. It was only after I ordered a beer, sat down on a stool, and lit a cigarette that I gathered up the courage to lift my head and take a look around.

It was dark and smoky, and at first I couldn't see much. Couldn't hear much either except for loud pumping music and an occasional *clack* as someone started a new game of pool on the table in the corner. I felt pretty invisible, which was fine by me. It was what I was used to.

Once my eyes adjusted, I studied the crowd. There were girls and there were guys, and most of them seemed older than me. It didn't seem like a college crowd. It's hard to explain, but the people I saw looked like they had more important things on their minds than whether they were going to ace their next exam. They seemed, I don't know, worldly maybe. Like they'd been around the block. Like they'd known trouble, but they also knew how to have a good time. No one bothered me except one guy who asked to bum a cigarette. I gave him two, and he gave me a big smile, started to sit next to me, but then for some reason changed his mind and walked away.

Then just when I was starting on my third beer, the door swung open and trouble arrived. I knew they were trouble from the minute they walked in; I just didn't know what kind of trouble. They were loud, for one thing. And half in the bag. Everyone turned around to stare at them and then turned away. It was like we were all thinking the same thing: *If we ignore them, maybe they'll go away.*

There were a bunch of them, maybe six or seven. All girls. Young. With long hair and tight jeans. Clunky shoes and shoulder bags. One of them was wearing a halter-top, and when she had her back to me it looked like she had nothing on from the waist up. My fingers itched at the sight of all that smooth, flawless flesh.

It must have been obvious that I was staring, because pretty soon Miss Bareback came over to me. "Hey," she said softly, and that one word was all it took to break my heart.

"Hey, yourself." I somehow found my voice to answer.

"Got an extra cigarette?" She nodded toward my pack on the bar.

I didn't say anything, just got one out for her. She put it in her mouth and waited. I flicked my lighter, and as I cupped my palms around the flame and brought my hands close to her lips, my stomach dropped 10,000 feet. I felt like a movie star, like the hero of my own life. This was the moment I had been waiting for, and it was even better than I'd expected.

But there was more to come. She propped one hip up on the stool next to me, pressed her leg against mine, and, putting her hand on my thigh, said, "I'm Sheila. What's your name?"

"Jacq."

"Hey, Jack."

"It's J-a-c-q," I explained, in case she thought that was weird, me having a guy's name.

"J-a-c-q," she repeated, like she wanted to remember it. Then she leaned in real close and asked in a husky whisper, "And what comes after the 'q'?"

"You," I said, and then, full of liquid courage, I kissed her, right on the mouth. Her lips were the sweetest thing I'd ever tasted. I felt I could die right then and there with no regrets and my life would be complete.

"Wow," she said, breaking away and taking a drag off her cigarette.

"I'm sorry," I said, even though I wasn't.

"Hey, Jacq," was all she said, a little smile on her lips. And then, "Let's dance."

We danced a bit to a few fast numbers, and then she brought me over to meet her friends. I felt like a prize.

"Leave it to Sheila," one of them said. Another one wouldn't even look up. A third was impatient to leave. "OK, you've had your fun," she said. "Can we go?"

"What's wrong with them?" I asked, as Sheila pulled me aside.

"Don't mind my stupid friends," she said, loud enough for them to hear. Then, soft enough so they wouldn't, "Give me your phone number."

We had to go back to the bar for a pen and a napkin. By the time I wrote down my number Sheila's friends were waiting for her out in the parking lot. A slow song came on, and I begged her to stay. "I'll drive you home," I said.

"I'll call you," she answered, and without so much as another kiss she was gone.

❀

I sat by the phone for hours, days. Didn't go to class. Barely went to the bathroom. Dashed down to the dining hall, grabbed some food, and ran back up to wolf it down in my room. Couldn't risk missing her call. For the first time in my life I felt like a girl.

❀

"Jacq?" Friday night, her voice warm and breathy in my ear.

"Yeah?" was all I could squeak out.

"Wanna go Wilde tomorrow night?"

"Yeah." This time the word wasn't a question.

❀

It was a hot Saturday night. Hot and humid. I took a long, hot shower. Wore a brand-new undershirt under my best white button-down. Ironed my jeans. Didn't know what to expect. Didn't let on even to myself how much I cared.

She was there, with only two other friends this time. Came right up to me and took my hand. Led me onto the dance floor and whirled circles around me. She was wearing a dress, short and twirly, with little puffy sleeves that showed off her collarbones and shoulders. She smiled a lot. I did too.

Finally, a slow number. Finally, my arms full of soft, warm girl. Finally, a real, live, honest-to-goodness female pressed up to my chest, her strawberry shampoo filling my nostrils, making my heart turn over deep inside. I backed us up into a corner and leaned down to kiss that warm, sweet mouth. She pressed up against me for all she was worth. We stayed there until the song was over and two more had played. No one bothered us. She didn't even notice when her friends left. I guess she knew she was in good hands. I'd see her home safe and sound.

We danced some more and drank a bit. Then went outside to neck in my car. The top of her dress slid down easily, and she wasn't wearing a bra. Her breasts were round and full as the moon that shone brightly through the window like a spotlight, but I didn't care. I had finally figured out what I'd been born to do. Love a woman with my heart and soul, my flesh and bones. And Sheila was quite a woman. The way she moved, the sounds she made…

She took my hand and put it between her legs, pressing, until there was no question about what she wanted me to do. And I did as I was told, amazed at the gift she was giving me, awed by how powerful her body was between my trembling hands. Afterward we sat side by side, my arm around her shoulder, smoking cigarettes. She was the first to speak.

"Jacq, I really like you," she said, and I swear, my eyes filled with tears. "You know, most guys just want to stick it in. They just want to make themselves feel good, you know. They don't care what the girl wants. But you're not like other guys. You're different."

I'm different, all right, I thought to myself. But damn if I would tell her.

❀

Boy meets girl. Boy gets girl. Boy is girl. Boy oh boy oh boy.

❀

What was I thinking? I wasn't thinking. I was feeling. I was feeling my oats, feeling her oats, feeling mighty fine. Sheila and I became quite an item. I didn't have any friends, so there was no one to blow my cover. And her friends didn't want much to do with us. My guess was they thought I was trash and Sheila shouldn't be hanging out with the likes of me in a bar like that. Like I cared. I wasn't dating them. I was dating her. If you could call it dating. We'd meet at the bar every Saturday night, to the delight of the old-timers, who lit up at the sight of us. "Ah, young love," someone would inevitably sigh in a voice full of longing and regret. Often someone would send us a round of drinks. The bartender referred to us as the "little darlings." I wanted to take Sheila someplace fancy, maybe dinner and a movie, but I didn't really have the money, and she didn't seem to mind the way we spent our time: drinking, dancing, and getting down and dirty in my car. I never even saw her in daylight. Not that I was complaining. I lived for those Saturday nights, so different than the rest of my week when I was the oddball, the loner, the bookworm. I was like Clark Kent, meek and mild six days of the week and then on Saturday night I turned into Superman.

But did I really think my ruse could last forever? Like I told you, I wasn't thinking. I was too busy being happy. But after a few weeks went by, Sheila said she wasn't happy. She wasn't satisfied. She certainly sounded satisfied, what with all the noise she had just made in the back of my car. But she wanted to go "all the way." At first she thought it was wonderful that I didn't put pressure on her, that all I cared about was her pleasure. But she cared about my pleasure too, she said. She wanted to make me feel good.

"You do make me feel good," I said, pressing the balled-up sock I now wore inside my underpants on Saturday nights against her leg for emphasis.

"But I want to make you feel better," she said, reaching for my crotch.

I playfully slapped her hand away. "I couldn't feel any better than this," I said. "Trust me." And I tried to divert her attention with a kiss, but she struggled to sit up.

"Jacq," she said, a new sternness in her voice. "Maybe my friends are right."

"Why? What did they say?" I tried to hide the panic in my voice.

"They say you're gay. That I'm wasting my time with you. Oh, God." She turned away from me and muttered out the car window. "I shouldn't tell you this."

"Tell me," I said, wanting and not wanting to hear it.

"No, you'll hate me."

"I could never hate you. Sheila, look at me." I put my hand under her chin and turned her face toward me. "I could never hate you," I repeated, looking deeply into her eyes. "I love you."

"Oh, Jacq." My words seemed to make Sheila sad, not happy. "Jacq," she said again. "The thing is…" She hesitated and then spilled it all out in a rush. "The first night I met you, I was there on a dare. You know how girls are, we were all sitting around drinking and playing that obnoxious game truth or dare. Well, I've always been a little, I don't know, out there I guess, so they knew they could push me. They dared me to go to Wilde and ask a gay guy to dance. I said OK, but they all had to come with me. I thought that would be the end of it, but the next week we played truth, dare, or double-dare, and they said I had to go back to the bar and have sex with a gay guy to see if I could turn him straight. So I called you. And I did my double-dare, but that wasn't the end of it because I started to like you. I mean, really like you. You know how I feel about you, Jacq. It isn't a game anymore. But why won't you go all the way with me? *Are* you gay?"

My head was spinning around so fast from everything she said, all I could do was tell her the truth. "Yes," I said, my voice barely a whisper. "Yes, I am."

❀

It started with a dare, and it ended with a dare. I told Sheila everything and dared her to love me for who I was. But she couldn't. I tried to reason with her: Wasn't I still the same person she'd been kissing five minutes ago, before she knew? I tried pleading with her, telling her over and over how much I loved her, how I'd do anything for her, but she wasn't the least bit moved. I finally got mad at her, yelled that she had no right to play games in a gay bar like that and that she got what she deserved. That did it. She leaped out of the car in a big huff, slammed the door, and disappeared into the night without a word.

I never went back to the bar. What would be the point? I knew Sheila wouldn't be there. I knew my heart was broken. And I knew I was back where I started. Between a rock and a hard place. Between fury and despair. Between boy and girl.

Lots of years have passed between then and now. I've had my share of ups and downs, like everyone else. I could tell you more stories. Stories of being stared at by women in department store dressing rooms. Stories of taking my life in my hands and using men's restrooms when I got tired of women freaking out as I walked through the door marked LADIES. Stories of being scowled at by lesbians in women's studies classes, women's music festivals, women's dances, women's bars. But it hasn't all been doom and gloom. Plenty of lovers have come and gone, though mostly gone, unable to handle who I am and what I've become. Which is to say, myself.

I started transitioning a couple of years ago. It's a long process. First I had to see a shrink. Took a while before I got the thumbs-up to start hormones. Once that got going I had to scrimp and save to afford both operations: one to remove my breasts, the other to take out my plumbing. I don't miss having my period, that's for sure. I don't know if I'm going to go any further. That is to say, I don't think I want a penis, not that it's any of your business. I don't like guys for the most part; I don't really want to be a man. Like I've always said, I just want to be myself. A girl with chest hair. A guy with a clit. A he/she, a shemale, a drag king, a genderfuck. A boydyke, girlfag, manwoman, womanman. I'm not either/or. It doesn't always come down to black or white. I don't fit neatly into a little box like most people want me to.

Why is it so important, anyway? I see you staring, wondering if I'm one or the other. *Is that a boy or a girl?* I've heard that question all my life. Well, here's my final answer: I'm both. And neither. I'm your worst nightmare and your best fantasy. I'm the one you long for and the one you fear. I define morbid fascination. ("Take a picture, it lasts longer.") I'm something old, something new, something borrowed, and sometimes blue. Like Popeye would say, I yam what I yam. Like it or lump it.

Mothers of Invention

"Hi honey, I'm homo." I flung open the back door and tossed my usual and, in my opinion, extremely clever greeting into the empty kitchen, where it was met with an unusual and not nearly as clever silence.

"Phoebe?" I called again. It wasn't like her not to answer. I threw my keys down on the mail-strewn table and poked around the living room, dining room and bedroom, but there was no Phoebe to be found. Where was she? There weren't that many hiding places in the tiny house we had somehow managed to buy a little over two years ago. Maybe she was waiting for me in her walk-in closet wearing nothing but a few feet of Saran Wrap and her favorite red fuck-me pumps. That would be just like Phoebe, who liked to start the weekend off with a bang. Last Friday I dragged my weary ass home from another day at the salt mines only to find my beloved standing at the stove calmly stirring a stainless-steel pot of homemade tomato sauce with a long wooden spoon, adorned in nothing but a yellow-and-white checkered apron tied loosely at the waist, her luscious butt bared for all the world to see. That's my Phoebe. She sure likes to keep me guessing. And God bless her, she makes it a point to keep our sex life hopping. Phoebe sets the rules around here, and luckily they're pretty simple: She insists we do the hokey-pokey at least twice a week "whether we want to or not."

I cracked open a beer, plopped myself down on the couch, and called half-heartedly, "Come out, come out, wherever you are," knowing my plea was useless. Phoebe would come out when she was good and ready. But when I finished my brew and there was still no sign of her, I began to worry. I knew she was home—her maroon Saturn was hogging the driveway—so where was she? I was just about to get up and conduct a more thorough search of the premises when I heard the bathroom door open. Quick as a wink I wiped my mouth with the back of my hand and rose to give my girl a proper greeting.

"Hi, baby," I said, but to my surprise Phoebe didn't head right into my open arms and nestle her head against my waiting chest. Instead she pushed me away and burst into tears.

"Baby, what's wrong?"

"Don't call me baby," she wailed, sobbing in earnest, with her shoulders shuddering and snot running from her nose like, well, like a baby. And only then, idiot that I am, did I remember.

"Oh, no. Did you get your period?"

"Yes." Phoebe's voice broke into a sad little gulp of a hiccup as she finally melted against me and let me hold her.

I stroked her auburn curls and offered inadequate words of comfort. "Poor you," I murmured. "Poor Phoebe. Poor baby."

And by the time I realized what I said, Phoebe had run back into the bathroom, slamming the door behind her.

When Phoebe's upset she likes to be alone, so I grabbed another beer and headed out the way I came. There was a rickety lounge chair on our back porch with my name on it, so I parked myself, took a swig, and swallowed. The summer sun wouldn't be setting for at least an hour so that gave me plenty of time to think. Of course my thoughts turned to Phoebe. And while my heart ached for her, my sympathy was tinged with a good, healthy dose of relief too. It was no secret I felt ambivalent about having a baby.

I've never really wanted one, though I've never really not wanted one either. I simply didn't think about it. It's not like I was ever going to fall into bed with someone and wake up the next morning big with child. I knew I liked girls from the time I was a young pup—maybe fifteen or so—and I've never even kissed a guy, let alone done something that would result in me winding up a mother-to-be. I suppose I always knew there was the possibility I'd fall in love with a "late-bloomer" who hadn't realized she was a lesbo until after she'd married some guy and had a couple of kids. But that never happened, even though it easily could have. I've always been a sucker for older women.

So I thought all that was settled, and then along came the "gayby boom." It seemed like a million dykes woke up one morning and heard the same sound: the nearly deafening roar of their collective biological clocks tick-tocking away. Overnight support groups were formed, hotlines for sperm-runners were set up, and before you could even say "turkey baster," gay pride was overrun with dyke-style nuclear families: two women pushing a baby carriage, a dog on a lavender leash trailing behind them.

Now the dog part I can understand. I've always wanted a dog. And not some wimpy, yappy little thing like a poodle or a Chihuahua either. I want a dog's dog. A chocolate lab, a blue-eyed husky. A dog you don't have to bend over to pet. A dog that can rest its mighty head against your thigh. But our house remains a pooch-free palace because Phoebe, who is perfect in nearly every other way, is just not an animal person. She doesn't want some big galoof of a mutt tracking mud all over our nice, clean floors and shedding its smelly wet fur on our nice, clean (secondhand) furniture. Come to think of it, I haven't brought up the canine question in quite a while. Now I kind of wish I'd gotten a puppy before I met Phoebe. Then she wouldn't have had a choice—we would have been a package deal. But I didn't think it was fair to have a dog when I was living solo.

The poor thing would have been all by its little lonesome from nine to five and sometimes longer, since there were many a night when, Don Juan that I used to be, I never made it back to my apartment. Then when I moved into Phoebe's place, between all my stuff and all her stuff, things were so cramped there was hardly room to add a hamster, let alone fifty pounds of bark and fur.

I thought when we finally bought our house the time would be right. But I found out that buying a house—especially a fixer-upper like ours—is like getting a full-time job. Which would have been fine except I already had a full-time job. Now instead of coming home and putting my feet up (and maybe convincing Phoebe to give them a little massage), I need to get busy and do something useful like tear up the kitchen floor, mend the back steps, or rescreen a window on the front porch—there's always something that needs to be done. And Phoebe's been pretty busy too, planting the garden, sewing curtains for the windows, buying little rugs for the hallway—you know, adding a woman's touch to the place so it feels all warm and cozy. Like a love nest. I should've known it was only a question of time before Phoebe started talking about a baby. After all, what's the use of a nest without any eggs in it?

Way back when we first started dating, Phoebe told me that someday she wanted to have a baby, but I didn't pay too much attention to what she was saying. First of all, she said she wasn't planning on getting pregnant for a "really, really, *really* long time," and second of all, I was so knocked out by her she could have said, "Someday I'm going to be a cloistered nun," and I would've paid her no mind. Neither of us paid the other much mind, come to think of it. It was all just pillow talk. We'd live happily ever after someday with her baby and my dog, and we'd take a year off and sail around the world, maybe live in Alaska for a while (something I've always wanted to do) or gay Paris (something she's always wanted to do). You know how lovers talk.

And besides, smitten as I was, I had no idea we'd actually stay together this long (six years and counting). It's not like either of us had a stellar reputation in the longevity department. And we didn't plan any of this. It all just sort of happened in typical lesbo fashion. After we'd gone out for a while and Phoebe finally let me into her pants, I began spending every night at her apartment. After a few months of that, I realized how stupid it was to be paying all that extra rent just for a place to hang my clothes, so I moved in with her. Then, after we'd lived together a while, both of us decided it made no sense for us to be shelling out so much dough to a landlord when for just a little more money we could be investing in a place of our very own. So, with the money Phoebe's mom left her after she died, we bought the house.

Not that I'm complaining about any of this. There's no one I'd rather be with than Phoebe, and I should know since I've been with plenty. It's not like I was the playgirl of the Western world or anything. I was the playgirl of the Western, Eastern, Northern, and Southern world. Think I'm exaggerating? Entire softball teams could be formed by my ex-lovers. Entire softball *leagues*. What can I say? I've been with tall amazons and short goddesses. Plump beauties and hipless cuties. Femme tops, femme bots, lipstick lesbians, and glamazons. Androgens, kikis, jocks, and, though I hate to admit it, in moments of sheer desperation, even a butch or two. Lesbians, hasbians, bisexuals, bi-lesbians. Girls who were straight but not narrow, girls who were narrow but not straight. Rude girls, crude girls, shrewd girls, and lewd girls. Shy girls, sly girls, dry girls, and fly girls. I've had lovers, fuck buddies, sweethearts, and pain-in-the-butts (sometimes all at the same time). I've had a main squeeze, a honey, a girlfriend, and a partner. I'd thought I'd been with just about every type of woman under the sun.

And then I met Phoebe.

Phoebe is all of the above and none of the above. Phoebe is

adamant about not calling herself a lesbian, but as I pointed out one lazy Sunday afternoon when I had four fingers deep inside her, she isn't exactly straight either. Phoebe replied, between grunts and groans, that the only labels she wore were on the inside of her size-12 jeans, a pair of which, at that moment, were balled up in a heap on my living room floor. Phoebe has told me over and over that she thinks labels are limiting, and she likes to be open to all possibilities. From the start she was an enigma to me, the original diehard dyke. She once told me her name literally means "personification of the moon." And what could be more mysterious than the moon? One night it's so high and brilliant in the sky you feel a sudden kinship with your pagan ancestors and find yourself howling with awe and delight. Another night it's a snippet, no bigger or more significant than the white part of your little left pinkie nail. Then it's gone altogether and then it reappears more magnificent and luminous than ever. And that just about describes my Phoebe.

We met on a warm summer night, not all that different than this one, at a mutual friend's graduation party. I was on the prowl, as usual, and she was on the rebound, though she wouldn't tell me if her last lover was a guy or a gal. I'd had a few drinks and made some comment about her being a Phoebe and me being a Robin and us being birds of a feather or something like that. I think I might have said I wanted to tweak her beak too.

"Another time, birdbrain."

"Sorry I ruffled your feathers," I slung at her back as she turned to walk away in a huff. But even half-looped as I was, I couldn't help noticing her ass. Phoebe's ass happens to be the eighth wonder of the world. And she knows it. And works it too, in those so-tight-they-look-like-she's-been-sewn-into-them size-12 jeans of hers. That night her jeans were white and I could have howled at her caboose, round and mesmerizing as a full moon. But thank God I did no such thing. I merely muttered, "Wish I had a swing like that in my backyard," just loud enough for her to hear.

"You should be so lucky," she shot back over her shoulder before disappearing into the crowd.

Flighty bitch, I thought, but of course I knew a challenge when I heard one. And Phoebe knew I knew. Knew I'd call, even though she didn't say another word to me all evening, let alone give me her phone number. Knew I'd get it from our host, along with a warning: "Now, Robin, Phoebe's not like other girls. Don't fuck with her." Whatever that meant. Knew enough to be busy the first *and* second Saturday night I called to see if I could take her to dinner. Knew unavailability is the most potent aphrodisiac known to womankind. And knew, I'm proud to say—though she sure didn't act it—that she wanted me *bad,* from the moment she first laid eyes on me. And thank God, Phoebe knew just how to clip my wings too.

She wouldn't sleep with me for months after we started dating. Wanted me to court her. Wanted me to woo her. Said she needed me to prove I was worthy of getting the goods before she handed them over. You'd think I'd just tell a snotty bitch like that to stick it where the sun don't shine, but Phoebe's attitude had the opposite effect on me. I wanted to win her over. I wanted to clean up my act. I stopped flirting, cut down on my drinking, and even learned how to shine my shoes and iron my pants. I felt like a teenage boy—with blue balls and a perpetual hard-on. Which isn't a bad way to feel. I was in a constant state of expectant ecstasy: Would tonight be the night? Phoebe gave me just enough—plenty of kisses and a little tit now and then—to keep me coming around. "Less is more" is her philosophy. And it worked like a charm.

Phoebe's no dummy. She knew I'd been around the block and then some. Knew I was the love 'em and leave 'em type, and she wasn't having any of *that.* No, Phoebe had turned a corner in her own life, unbeknownst to me, and decided it was time to settle down. At least for a while. And so she cast a spell on me, stealing my heart before I even knew it was missing, like a magician who shows you your wedding ring in the palm of his hand before you realize it's gone from your finger. I was caught hook, line, and sinker. Before I had a chance to bid my bachelor days *adieu,* they were gone.

No one believed that two wild things like us had a chance in hell of making it, but we figured we'd show them. This was different. I didn't know Phoebe before I met her (obviously), but I knew myself and I sure felt different. Me, the butch who'd rather be committed than make a commitment, now actually liked calling Phoebe every day from work to see if I was going over to her house or she was coming over to mine. I liked moving in together, lining up my loafers, sneakers, and workboots with her flats, slingbacks, and slides. And even though it was scary as hell, the day we signed the mortgage papers was the happiest day of my life.

Phoebe likes to say she tamed me. According to her, before we started dating, I probably thought she was "just a girl. A pretty girl, maybe, a curvy girl definitely, but still, just a girl like any other girl." The difference is, now that we've been together all this time, Phoebe is *my* girl. Now I could walk into a room of a hundred girls just her height, weight, and coloring, and I'd pick her out in a heartbeat. Even if I just saw her from behind, because I've memorized the shape of her behind. Even if I was blind, because I know her smell by heart. Even if I couldn't see her or smell her or hear her voice, I'd know her by the touch of her hand. It's amazing; I don't even look at other women anymore. Who could compare to my Phoebe, whose blue eyes I've looked into a thousand times (the right one is slightly larger than the left); whose breasts I've fondled a million times (the left one is slightly higher than the right); who sometimes whistles through her nose when she sleeps; who has a birthmark shaped like the Statue of Liberty on her belly; whose lovely face is even more familiar to me than my own.

I was amazed at how well married life agreed with me. Well,

not married life in the legal sense of the word, of course. And even if we could get married, I wouldn't want some flimsy little certificate holding us together anyway. That's the beauty of being a lesbian: We don't have to fill out the paperwork. I can hoof it any time I want to. But I don't want to. Imagine that. I'm like a feral cat who finally allowed herself to be coaxed in out of the cold and the rain to sit on a nice, comfy couch in front of a warm, cozy fire. *What did I think would be so bad about all this?* I wondered night after night as Phoebe and I snuggled under the blankets together, hugging and kissing and going to town. I kept waiting for the shoe to drop, the bickering to start, the lesbian bed death to set in. I knew it was inevitable. Every couple has problems, right? No relationship is perfect. It took a long time, but finally the shoe did drop. Only it wasn't a shoe. It was a tiny yellow bootie.

Phoebe—who gets up with the birds, with the phoebes in fact who call her name over and over right outside our bedroom window, starting at five o'clock in the morning—had gone off in search of tag sales, a Saturday morning ritual I never did understand. As far as I'm concerned, Saturday mornings are for sleeping in, making love, and falling back to sleep again. But according to Phoebe, the early bird catches the worm, so off she went, leaving me deep in dreamland. But it's a funny thing: Our bed just isn't a fun place to be when Phoebe's not in it. So after a while I got up, helped myself to the coffee that Phoebe had left in the pot on the stove, and decided to do something industrious. Phoebe had been bugging me to paint the bathroom, so I decided to get to work. I was up to my eyeballs in peach-colored paint when she came flouncing into the tiny room.

"Robin and Phoebe, sitting in a tree. K-I-S-S-I-N-G." She laid a nice, fat, wet one on my lips before I could even put my paint roller down.

"You're in a frisky mood," I said when she finally let me up for air.

"First comes love, then comes marriage, then comes Phoebe

with the baby carriage." She finished her little ditty and held up two tiny yellow booties, waving them around like flags.

I guess I'm pretty thick, because I still didn't see what she was getting at. Or maybe I didn't want to see. "Earrings?" I asked.

"Robin!" Phoebe lifted her foot to stamp it in exasperation, but then changed her mind and her tune. "Aren't they adorable?" she crooned, holding them closer for me to inspect. "I got a matching hat too. This woman over on Union Street is some knitter. She had all these cute little sweaters too. Maybe after breakfast we can go back and look at them."

"Wait a minute." I left my roller in its paint-filled aluminum tray and led Phoebe out of the bathroom into the kitchen. The little yellow hat she had bought to match the booties was spilled across the table. "Are we having a baby now?" I asked Phoebe. "What's going on?"

"Robin, you know I want a baby. And I'm thirty-seven. And a half. The time is now."

For some reason that reminded me of an art installation an old lover of mine had dragged me to once, full of this avant-garde garbage I didn't understand. One thing kind of tickled me, though: Someone had hung up a clock but removed the hour hand and the minute hand, leaving only the second hand sweeping around the clock face. The artist had called it "The Clock of Eternity." She could just as well have called it "The Time Is Now." Or "The Jig Is Up."

Still, I thought I'd try the rational approach. "Phoebe," I said, "you haven't talked about having a baby for a long time. Why are you bringing it up today? Babies are expensive, and we're still catching our breath from becoming home-owners. Can't this wait a year?" *Or a lifetime,* I wanted to add. But I knew that would be futile. Once Phoebe makes up her mind about something, it's no use arguing with her.

"It's not like this is a surprise, Robin. I told you from the start I wanted a baby."

And I told you from the start I wanted a dog, shot through my mind, but I knew this wasn't the moment to bring that topic up. Instead I said, "And I told you from the start I didn't know if I wanted to be a parent or not."

"And I told you from the start I really didn't care."

Which was true. Phoebe had made it clear that my feelings didn't much matter one way or the other. She got all high and mighty about it, launching into a speech about how each woman's body was her own to do with as she pleased, and every woman has the right to reproduce or not, no matter what anyone else feels or says about it. In other words, she was going to have a baby. With me or without me. Whether I wanted to participate or not.

Phoebe didn't say anything more about the baby for a few months, but she didn't have to. As they say, actions speak louder than words. Like, take the morning when, after a particularly acrobatic and mutually satisfying horizontal tango, I got up, pulled on some boxer shorts, and made us a big breakfast of bacon, eggs, and home fries. Phoebe entered the kitchen wearing a short red nightie I bought her one year for Valentine's Day, and sat at the table waiting to be served. I set her plate down but before she had taken her first bite, she jumped up to turn the frying pan so its handle wasn't pointing outward, reminding me, without a word, not to endanger the life of our future child who could have grabbed the tempting handle, pulled down the hot, grease-filled pan, and done permanent damage too scary to even think about. Another day I came home and found that she had moved our potentially poisonous cleaning supplies—the Windex, bleach, Mop 'n Glo, etc.—from under the sink, where they were within easy grasp, to a cabinet above the refrigerator where even I, never mind a child, couldn't reach them without a stepladder.

And then came the toilet bowl clamp. Phoebe had read some tear-jerking article in one of those parenting magazines she kept bringing home about a poor woman whose toddler had fallen headfirst into the toilet bowl and drowned. Phoebe had gone out that day to buy the clamp, ensuring that we would never have a chance to be visited by that particular heartbreaking tragedy.

"Phoebe, get real," I said, studying the white plastic thingamajig she was trying to fasten around the toilet seat cover.

"Robin, I am getting real," she said. "This is it. Next month I'm going to inseminate."

Call me the world's biggest sucker, but given the options—life without Phoebe or life with Phoebe and a miniature Phoebe—what choice did I have? I couldn't figure out how it happened, but somehow over the years life *sans* Phoebe had become unimaginable. Me, the lesbian formally known as Bachelor #1, had finally met her match, and I wasn't going to do something as stupid as lose the girl of my dreams over something as tiny as a newborn. A little angel with clear blue eyes like my Phoebe's and a mop of curls the color of an Irish setter. At least that's how I pictured the kid: an exact replica of Phoebe, complete with a smattering of freckles across her nose, a dimple in her left cheek, and a beauty mark on her right. I never even considered that the little she might be a little he, or look like our donor—not that we'd ever know, since he was to remain forever anonymous. At least Phoebe and I agreed on that, once I reluctantly copped to the fact that this was actually happening. Neither of us wanted some dewy-eyed dad knocking on our door six days, months, or years down the road, wanting to claim the carrier of his gene pool. And since money was an issue, we decided to do things the old-fashioned dyke way, outside the system.

Leave it to the girls. We had it all figured out. One dyke would get the sperm from any number of guys whose only requirements were that they could prove that they'd tested negative for AIDS and that they had no interest whatsoever in what happened to their precious goo once it was deposited in a clean baby food jar. Dyke A would collect the sperm and hand the jar to Dyke B, not telling her from whom it had come. Dyke B would give the jar to us, but not tell Dyke A which one of her potential breeders was receiving the goods. Anonymity assured, and all for a fraction of what the clinic route would cost. (Believe it or not, sperm can cost as much three hundred bucks a pop.)

It all seemed easy as pie. Phoebe started trying to pin down her ovulation by charting her periods, which were pretty regular. She took her temperature first thing every morning—she wouldn't even talk to me before she read her thermometer. And she spent hours in the bathroom inspecting her mucus like it was the most fascinating thing in the world. When Phoebe thought she was in the time zone when she could become pregnant—a couple of days before ovulation until the day after—she'd call our faithful sperm runner, who, after getting some guy to whack off for us (an image I tried not to think about), would show up at our door, baby food jar in hand. My job was to help Phoebe insert the sperm—which smelled to high heaven, thank you very much—then sit with her while she lay on our bed with her feet propped up on the wall and her legs sticking up straight, the better to let gravity help nature take its course.

"Robin, you're being really good about all this," Phoebe said, her face radiant at the mere thought of being pregnant.

I shrugged off the undeserved compliment. "Hey, if Mama ain't happy, ain't nobody happy," I told her, quoting a T-shirt I'd seen in one of the millions of maternity catalogs that were clogging up our mailbox on a daily basis.

But Mama wasn't happy, because Mama was having a hard time becoming a mama. The sperm didn't take the first time, the second time, the seventh time, the twelfth time. Phoebe got very discouraged. Every month she'd get all hopeful, lying there with her legs up in the air and me sitting beside her reading aloud a kid's book she was especially fond of, like *Winnie the Pooh* or *The Cat in the Hat.* Then after an hour or two, I'd take her out for ice cream. Phoebe figured it was never too early to start eating for two, but I think that was just an excuse for her to indulge in her favorite treat: a gooey banana split made with chocolate chip, pistachio, and strawberry ice cream.

Phoebe would try not to think about it, but each and every month she was sure the insemination was successful, and each and every month it got harder and harder for her when reality arrived in the form of blood stains on her pink satin underwear. I tried to convince her not to take it so hard every time, but she waved away my attempts to console her.

"You don't understand, Robin. You've never wanted anything this badly," she said, her words hurting my feelings for reasons I didn't fully understand. Probably because they were right.

Finally, Phoebe went to the doctor and had a million tests done, but they couldn't find anything wrong with her. Except maybe that her eggs were getting old. So she convinced herself that there was a problem with our donor, but our sperm-runner told us that for the past several months she had been using several guys who had each successfully sired a child. That really got Phoebe down. The next thing to discuss was fertility drugs, but my girl won't even take aspirin. She was scared to put all those chemicals in her body, and I didn't blame her. Besides, neither of us was crazy about the idea of having twins or triplets, which was a good possibility if she went on the drugs. The thought of adding just one human being to our family was overwhelming enough. The day we had that discussion was the day I found out something I didn't know about Phoebe: My "feminism is not a dirty word" girlfriend didn't believe in abortion.

"What happened to 'each woman's body is her own'?" I couldn't help asking as we sat in Friendly's, Phoebe having one of her post-insemination banana splits and me sipping a mug of lukewarm coffee.

"I didn't say I didn't believe in it for other women," Phoebe defended herself. "I just know *I* couldn't do it. Like, remember that woman who had a litter of seven kids because she couldn't tell her doctor to abort some of the fetuses even though that would give the ones that remained a better chance of survival?" I nodded; the woman had been all over the news. "I'd be the same way." Phoebe paused to think while she licked some green ice cream off her spoon. "I don't get it. I'm not even forty yet, my periods are regular…why am I having so much trouble?"

"Maybe you're too tense about it," I said, as if I really knew anything. "Didn't the doctor say it was important to relax?"

"Yeah, but that's so much easier for straight people. They just throw out their condoms and birth control pills, go at it like bunnies, and don't even think about it. So even if nothing happens, at least they have a good time."

I don't think Phoebe meant to take my heart out of my chest, put it on the table, and smash it to bits with the side of her fist, but that's the effect her words had on me. "Phoebe," I said, after a few minutes, when I found my voice. "The door's open. You're not a lesbian, as you've so often informed me. You can walk out the door and do this the good old-fashioned way any time."

"Oh, my God. Robin, I didn't mean it like that." Phoebe got up and came around to sit next to me in the booth. I couldn't look at her. "Robin." She tried to turn my face toward her, but I wouldn't give an inch. She sighed and took my hand, which flopped in her palm like a dead fish. "Robin," Phoebe said, "if this is meant to happen, it will. And if it's not meant to happen, it won't. That's all there is to it. And besides, I've made a decision."

"What?" I asked, finally turning to her.

"If I'm not pregnant this time, I'm going to take a break. I can't take it anymore," she said, and then she started to cry.

"Hey, hey, wait a minute, Phoebe." I put my arm around her and kissed her forehead. "No use crying until you know for sure. For all you know, you could be pregnant this very minute. C'mon now. Don't throw out the baby with the bathwater." She didn't even smile.

Well, Phoebe wasn't pregnant, and true to her word, she did take a break from inseminating. And little by little, our lives got back to normal. I could roll over and give my girl a kiss in the morning without almost putting my eye out with the thermometer that was stuck in her mouth. We could have wine with dinner again. We could even go to the mall and walk by Gap Kids without her having a meltdown. As the months went by I, being the Queen of Denial, thought the issue was closed and Phoebe had made peace with her non-mommyhood status. But I was wrong. A few weeks ago, out of the blue, Phoebe announced she was ready to try again.

Which brings us to today.

I sighed, raised my carcass off the chair, and headed inside, my empty beer bottle in hand. To my surprise, Phoebe was in the kitchen, mixing up the ingredients for one of my favorite dinners, macaroni and cheese with her special killer crust. Ani DiFranco was singing on the stereo and Phoebe had put on lipstick and some kind of makeup that tried but failed to hide the puffiness around her eyes. She greeted me with a smile I hardly deserved. *My brave little soldier,* I thought, but I didn't say anything. It was hard to read her, and I knew enough to wait for her to make the first move.

"You hungry?" she asked, like nothing had happened. I nodded and made myself busy tossing a salad together and pouring our drinks. We sat and ate, mostly in silence but not that easy, comfortable silence we often share, when both of us have had a hard day at work and neither of us feels much like talking. No, this silence, full of so much that's unsaid, felt like the quiet that has settled over two people on a first date, both of whom know there's no chemistry between them, but neither knowing how to get themselves out of an awkward-as-hell situation. Phoebe's macaroni and cheese stuck in my throat and tasted like wallpaper paste.

Finally I couldn't stand it anymore. "Phoebe," I started, but she cut me right off.

"I don't want to talk about it," she said, jumping up to clear our plates. "It's over. I'm done."

"But—"

"No buts." Phoebe was at the sink with her back to me, but I'd have bet the rest of our mortgage she'd begun to cry.

Over the next couple of weeks Phoebe pulled herself together and acted like there was nothing on her mind. Well, maybe that's that, I thought, cautiously. Phoebe never was one to hold a grudge. Maybe she wasn't one to hang onto a plan gone awry either. She put away all the baby things she had collected, the clothes, the books, the toys, hoping maybe the old "out of sight, out of mind" thing really did work. And maybe it did, because weeks went by and she never brought up the topic again.

But the funny thing was, now *I* was thinking about it. Constantly. I even tiptoed toward bringing the subject up with her, but each time I came close I wound up chickening out. I wondered why Phoebe had never mentioned adoption. I knew it was an expensive way to go, but money would never have stopped Phoebe. The only conclusion I could come to was that my beloved wasn't ready to open herself up to the possibility of more heartache. Which certainly was possible if you went the adoption route. We knew one lesbian couple who went through the whole process—the application, interviews, home visits—but in the end they weren't approved. Another couple Phoebe knew had been approved, but they'd had to wait more than two years to get a child. No, maybe, as Phoebe had said and now obviously believed, it just wasn't meant to be.

You'd think this turn of events would make me happy, and while part of me felt an enormous sense of relief, another part of me felt something else, something that kept me from turning cartwheels and jumping for joy. I couldn't put my finger on it at first. I just felt empty. Like there was a hole inside. Kind of how you feel when you miss someone. This really puzzled me: How could I miss a baby who never existed, a baby I never even wanted in the first place? Then one night at dinner, I realized I didn't miss the baby. I missed Phoebe.

It was an unusually warm mid-September evening, and we were sitting at the picnic table in the backyard eating a simple supper of hamburgers I had cooked up on the grill. The sun was setting, and the whole sky looked like a lovely watercolor painting of yellows, golds, and oranges, the same colors as the late blooms in Phoebe's flower garden.

"Look, Phoebe," I said, pointing to the sky with my forkful of potato salad. "You and God must be in cahoots." I nodded my chin toward her chrysanthemums.

"Yeah, right," she muttered—so unlike my Phoebe—and then she turned away so I wouldn't see the tears in her eyes. A minute later she recovered. "Red sky at night, sailor's delight," she said brightly. "If the weather holds, maybe we could go for a hike tomorrow."

"OK," I said, pretending not to hear the false cheer in her voice. And then all at once it hit me—Phoebe's voice had been full of that phony, rah-rah, everything's OK tone for the past several weeks. And I hadn't been with it enough to notice. Or to see that the light that usually glittered in her eyes was gone. As was she. Oh, she was there all right, pouring me a cup of coffee, then sitting beside me, leaning her head on my shoulder and stroking my hand. But her core was gone. Her essence. The Phoebe-ness of her had taken flight. And for the first time in my life, I wanted something as much as Phoebe had wanted to have that baby. I wanted my baby back.

Like I said, I'm a go-with-the-flow kind of gal and I don't really plan things. What I've learned is, when you don't plan things, life plans things for you. Without you even knowing. One fall weekend, when Phoebe was away visiting a friend, I found myself alone and totally bored. I picked up a lesbian magazine we'd gotten as a free promo in the mail, and I happened upon an article about a dyke whose girlfriend was deathly ill. She'd had diabetes since early childhood, and her time was running out. She needed a kidney transplant, and she needed it fast. And the dyke, without a moment's hesitation, had volunteered to donate her flesh and blood. Furthermore, she didn't even see what the big deal was. "I love her," she said in a boxed quote. "I never even thought about not doing it. What's mine is hers and what's hers is mine."

Now, I don't usually read these kind of articles—they're more Phoebe's cup of tea than mine—but for some reason I read the whole story from beginning to end, and by the time I was finished I had more than a glimmer of tears in my eyes. I put the magazine down, wiped my soggy cheeks, and suddenly, just as I blew my nose, a light bulb appeared above my head, shining as brightly as the light that used to shine in Phoebe's eyes.

What's mine is hers and what's hers is mine, I thought as I ran up to the attic. It didn't take long to find what I was looking for: the box full of how-to-get-pregnant books and pamphlets Phoebe had collected during Operation Baby. I read everything I could that night and picked up where I left off the following morning. It all seemed easy enough. My periods were totally regular—you could set your clock by them. They arrived every 28 days at 10:10 A.M. Really. It was some sort of phenomenon, I guess, though I'd never really thought about it much. Until now.

The trick was, according to what I'd read, you don't ovulate fourteen days after you get your period; you ovulate fourteen days before you get your next period. Which makes it harder to pin down. But since I'm so regular, I just calculated when my next period was supposed to start and counted back fourteen days. Then I looked up our trusty sperm-runner, who seemed surprised to hear from me since Phoebe was always the one who had called. I told her Phoebe had gotten too emotional about the whole thing, and I would be the one to handle all the details from now on. And I would be the one to meet her at the door.

On D-Day, which fell during the week, thank God, I took the day off from work so Phoebe wouldn't know what was happening. I locked the door after the sperm-runner left and snuck the jar she'd handed me down the hallway into our bedroom like it was full of drugs or stolen goods. Then I stripped off my jeans and BVDs and thought, *Well, here goes nothing,* as I inserted the sperm with a syringe. That done, I lay on my back and walked my feet up the wall until my body was shaped like a giant L. How long did it take to get pregnant? A second, a minute, an hour? I wished I hadn't slept through high school biology, but it was a little late for that. And it was a little late to wonder about what I had just done to myself. As Phoebe said during one of those rough periods she hit when she was still trying to become preggo: *If this is meant to happen, it will. And if it's not meant to happen, it won't.* Only time would tell.

I figured I had a good half hour to kill, so I set the timer and shut my eyes to catch forty winks, but my position wasn't exactly conducive to slumber. And even if it was, my brain was spinning like a merry-go-round. My mother's voice, of all things, echoed loud and clear in the memory chambers of my mind: "Every woman in our family has a back-tipped uterus," she'd told me long ago, during our one and only mother-daughter talk. "That means you can get pregnant just by looking at a boy." She'd laughed at the expression on my face, realizing I was so young and naïve there was actually a chance I was taking her words literally. "What I mean is," she explained, "you come from a long line of fertile women. Both your grandmother and I got pregnant the very first time. So be careful." And that was the end of our discussion.

I guess it made sense for me to think about my own mother at a time like this, but that didn't mean I had to be happy about it. If I did get pregnant, giving birth would be just about the only thing I'd have in common with the woman who spread her legs and released me to the world. Weird to think that at one time we were so close we took up the exact same space, and now we were so far apart we probably wouldn't recognize each other if we passed on the street. No, in fact the last time I saw my mother she didn't know me at all. But in some ways that turned out to be a good thing.

My mother has Alzheimer's. She resides in a nursing home but lives in a fantasy world. I fly across the country to see her only every other year or so, and I'm not sure why I even do that. Out of guilt, I suppose, but what should I feel guilty for? Sure, I'm a lousy daughter, but she's a lousier mother. She's the one who abandoned me, not the other way around, which is what she thinks, since I stopped visiting her long before she lost her mind. We were never very close, but through most of my childhood we at least pretended to have something of a relationship. Until the day I sent my parents a coming-out letter. My mother, who never even showed the letter to my father, sent me a letter back in which she called me "sick, perverted, and disgusting," among other things. At least she didn't disown me, but what she did was in some ways worse—she acted like I'd never even told her.

"How's Jonathan?" she asked whenever we spoke on the phone. Jonathan was the boy I hung out with in high school, who my mother hoped I would marry, and who of course turned out to be as queer as yours truly.

"He's fine, Ma. Hey, listen, did you read the article I sent you about the gay youth center I'm volunteering at?"

"No, dear."

"Why not?"

"Robin, I don't know. I just haven't had time. So how's that boy Douglas? It's so nice you two wound up at the same school. Do you see him anymore?"

"No, Ma." Douglas was an asshole who tried to feel me up once during a high school field trip, but my mother knew his mother from around the neighborhood, so of course she thought he was nice. "Did you get the PFLAG pamphlets I sent you?"

"I don't know, Robin. Maybe they're around here somewhere."

"Well, will you look at them?"

"I can't promise. Your father and I are very busy. How's the weather up there? Cold?"

And it was just as bad in person. Whenever I tried to talk about my life, she would change the subject. And my father wasn't much better. He was hardly ever home; since we always needed money, he worked extra shifts whenever he could. When he did remember he had a family and actually spent some time in the house, he didn't bother with us much; he always headed straight for the living room before the rest of us were done eating supper, to turn on the TV and watch a baseball game, a boxing match, or whatever sports event happened to be on.

The only reason I did bother coming home from school was to see Max, the dog I grew up with. That cocker spaniel was my only friend from the time I was twelve until the day I left for college. He died when I was twenty-four—I still can't look at his picture without bawling—and after that it was just too unbearable to set foot in my parents' house anymore. So I stopped visiting, and my calls home dwindled down to once a month, once every other month, and then not even that. It got to the point where I spoke to my parents two or three times a year, which seemed to be just fine with both them and me.

The last time I went to see my mother I tried, I really did. There wasn't much I could do about the crew cut I was sporting, and I sure wasn't going to put on a dress, but I cleaned up the best I could. Phoebe offered to come with me, but some things you just have to do alone. And besides, why waste money on an extra plane ticket unless we were going somewhere fun? Phoebe thought we could make a vacation out of it, but when I go to see my mother I don't like to stick around. I'm in, I'm out. Hello, goodbye.

At least that's the way it usually is. But this time my mother jumped to her feet and lit up like the sun when I strolled into her room at the nursing home. "Hel-*lo,*" she said, as though she'd been waiting for me, her voice full of joy and her arms open wide.

I took a few more cautious steps into the room and dropped the box of chocolates I had brought onto the bed. "Hi," I said, stopping a few feet from her. I hadn't physically touched my mother in a long time. "How are you?"

"Fine, fine," she said, dismissing my question. "Aren't you going to give your own mother a hug?"

"Sure," I said, hoping my tone wasn't giving away my surprise. I took the tentative final steps that closed the gap between us and let her embrace me. She's a big-boned woman, and tall besides, and her arms, though doughy, were strong. I didn't dare breathe, because I knew if I did I would break down and cry and I sure didn't want that to happen. Why ruin our one good moment in fifteen years? But not to worry—I didn't ruin it. My mother ruined it.

"Let me look at you." She finally released me and took a step back to eye me up and down, with a mixture of shyness and pride. "You look good," she said, finally passing judgment. "The girls must be climbing all over themselves just to get a glimpse of you."

This was too much. This couldn't be my mother. "Ma?" I asked, puzzled. Was she on some new medication with an anti-homophobic serum built into it?

"Sure." She plopped herself down on the only chair in the room and motioned for me to sit on the bed. "So tell me, is there someone special in your life?"

"As a matter of fact, there is," I said, thinking, *If some queer-friendly alien has taken over my mother's body, I might as well enjoy myself.* "Her name's Phoebe. You'd like her, Ma. She's really pretty and she's really—"

"Phoebe?" My mother cut me off. "What happened to Gloria?"

"Gloria?" I'd never dated anyone named Gloria. At least that I could remember.

"Yeah, you know. Gloria. You brought her to the house just the other night. Remember, she loved that strawberry rhubarb pie I picked up at the bakery, had two big helpings, a skinny girl like that, wonder where she puts it. She's a nice girl, that Gloria, you should hold onto a girl like that..."

Oh, my God. Gloria. Gloria was my older brother's girlfriend. *When he was in high school.* The night my mother was reminiscing about took place more than twenty years ago. And she hadn't seen my brother in almost as long, except for the day of my father's funeral. No, I was the one who made sure, despite everything, that she was taken care of when my aunt, the only one who'd kept in sporadic touch with me, called to tell me my mother was wearing her nightgown with nothing underneath it to the grocery store. My mother was putting on water for tea and forgetting about it until she almost burned down the house. My mother was wandering around strange neighborhoods at night, ringing doorbells and asking for a cup of hot chocolate. My mother needed to be taken care of, and I took care of her. No, I didn't have her move in with me, but still, I did the best I could.

And for that, this was the thanks I got. Her look of delight wasn't for me, her darling, dutiful daughter. No, with my short hair, pullover sweater, and pressed jeans, she thought I was Kevin, her firstborn, her son, the child who could do no wrong even though he'd deserted the family long ago, first to become a Hare Krishna, then a Jehovah's Witness, and last I heard some kind of Jesus freak. The only one who ever heard from Kevin was my aunt, and that was only when he needed money, which of course he never bothered to pay back. But still my aunt would send him a check without a moment's hesitation, just as I'm sure—as my mother so clearly proved—that Kevin could walk in here, even after all these years, and be clasped to her heaving bosom, no questions asked.

I realized by the silence in the room that my mother had just asked me a question and was waiting for an answer, but I had none to give. I'd already gotten more than I'd bargained for: a hug—meant for my brother, but a hug nevertheless—so I bade her a fond farewell and headed out the door, straight for the airport.

When the timer rang, I shook my head like a wet puppy, hoping to clear my mind, and swung my legs down from the wall before my brain decided to take any more trips down memory lane. I figured the half hour I'd spent flat on my back was enough time to seal my fate, so I pulled on my clothes and headed into the kitchen for what could turn out to be my last beer for a very long time. I wondered if I'd follow in my mother's and grandmother's footsteps and become pregnant on the first try. First and *last* try, since I seriously doubted I'd ever do this again. I was already half regretting my noble deed and fully hoping it would all come to naught. That way I could tell Phoebe what I'd done (I had the empty jar for proof), score some big Brownie points, and have our lives continue just as they had before.

But just my luck; for once in her life my mother was right. That night, at exactly 4:37, with Phoebe slumbering and unsuspecting beside me, I woke up in a total sweat, my tits all swollen, tender, and hard. And I mean *hard.* Like steel or granite. Clearly this was no ordinary case of PMS. Unless PMS now stood for Pre-Mommy Syndrome.

Still, it was no use telling Phoebe until I was absolutely sure, so I kept my little secret a few more weeks, just in case it was a false alarm. Old Faithful (Phoebe's nickname for my period) didn't arrive the day it was supposed to, but still I kept mum, waiting for just the right time to tell her, whenever that would be. I tried to act normal, despite feeling completely nauseous every morning after about the first week and a half. I found if I just lay in bed completely still for a while it would pass, but of course Phoebe knew something weird was going on.

"Are you all right?" One Tuesday when I was still under the covers even though the snooze button had gone off three times, Phoebe, who'd been up for hours, came around to my side of the bed and perched on the edge of the mattress. "What's up?" she asked, stroking my damp forehead. "You're all sweaty. Are you sick? Do you think you have a fever?"

"No, I'm fine," I said, thinking, *If she keeps rocking the bed like that, I'm going to puke all over her for sure.*

"Want pancakes for breakfast?"

"OK," I mumbled, knowing she'd really be suspicious if I refused such a generous offer. I waited until she was busy in the kitchen, and then I dashed into the bathroom, ran the water hard, and barfed my brains out. Afterward, I felt better and came to sit at the table.

"You don't look so good," Phoebe remarked as she put a plate in front of me. Just the sight of those steaming hotcakes was enough to make me upchuck all over again. "In fact, you haven't looked good in over a week."

"Thanks a lot," I said, picking up my fork. "Am I losing my good looks? Is it all over for me at thirty-three?"

Phoebe wasn't in a joking mood. "Can I ask you something?" She sat down across from me.

"Sure," I said casually, trying not to panic. Could she possibly know? How? For some reason, I still wasn't ready to tell her. Maybe because that would make it real, and I wasn't sure I was ready to face that yet.

"Robin, there's no easy way to ask this, so I'll just say it." Phoebe kept her eyes down, studying her place mat, and my heart started banging around in my chest. "Robin, are you having an affair?"

"What?" I burst out laughing, which I'm sure was not the reaction Phoebe had expected. Maybe my hormones were already going to my head, because I laughed and laughed until the tears ran down my face. Phoebe just looked at me like I was someone she had never seen before. I kept trying to calm down and speak, but every time I started talking my words grew all shaky and I broke out laughing again.

"Shall I take that as a no?" Phoebe couldn't help smiling after a while, probably at how ridiculous I was acting. "It's just that you've been awfully quiet lately, and we haven't, you know, in kind of a while."

"It hasn't been that long, Phoebe," I said, though the truth was I couldn't remember the last time we had done the nasty. For reasons unknown to Phoebe, I hadn't been feeling as arduous as usual lately. "Hey," I tried to catch her eye, "I thought we were nonmonagamous anyway."

"In theory," Phoebe the label-avoider reminded me, finally

looking up. "Not in practice." She studied me closely. "So answer me. Are you having an affair? Or just losing interest in me?"

"None of the above." I reached across the table for her hand. "But I have been keeping a secret from you." *The time is now,* I thought as Phoebe's face changed. *The jig is up.*

"Is it a surprise?" she asked. Phoebe loves surprises.

"Yes."

"Let's see. Is it bigger than a bread box?"

"Not yet."

"Not yet?" Phoebe's brow furrowed. "So it's something that grows. A plant?"

"No."

"Hmm. Is it in the house?"

"Yep."

"Is it in this room?"

"Yep again."

Phoebe got up and looked around the kitchen. She opened cupboards and poked around but didn't find a thing. She ransacked the oven, the broom closet, and the silverware drawer. Finally, she searched my face but couldn't read it.

"I give up," she said, sitting down again.

"Phoebe." This time I kept my gaze down and studied my place mat. "There's no easy way to tell you this, so I'll just say it." I looked up into my girlfriend's eyes, hoping my words would bring their spark back. "I'm pregnant."

"What?" Phoebe's features scrambled all over her face trying to settle into one emotion, but shock, disbelief, joy, and grief were all vying for attention. "Robin?" She said my name like a question and so I answered it. I showed her the article about the dyke with the diabetic girlfriend and told her what I'd been up to the past few weeks. Phoebe just stared at me as I spoke, shaking her head and making these sounds that were somewhere between a laugh and a cry. When I was through with my story, she got up, and without saying a word hugged me so hard I thought she'd break my bones. And that night we had the best sex we'd ever had (and we've had some absolutely transformational episodes, let me tell you). *So, if nothing else, at least we're back to making whoopee,* I thought the next morning as I bent over the toilet bowl and gagged up my breakfast.

Phoebe was all sympathy. She fed me soda crackers, made me tea, insisted I put my feet up and not lift a thing. I thought maybe she'd be resentful that I was the one who was pregnant, who got to experience all the joys (ha!) of the condition. Believe me, with the way I was feeling I'd have traded places with her in a heartbeat. But Phoebe bore me no grudge. If anything, she felt bad that I was feeling so awful and there was nothing she could do about it. She even offered to throw up every time I did—Phoebe had been bulimic all through college, so she was a pro—but I declined her generous offer. She kept asking what she could do for me, she was so knocked out over what I was doing for her (as was I). If she had any feelings of envy, she kept them to herself. And then, not to be outdone, my Phoebe came home one day with a little secret of her own.

"I've got a surprise for you, Robin," she said, a smile playing around her lips.

I'm not big on surprises, but I humored her. "Is it bigger than a bread box?"

"Not yet."

"Not yet? Oh, my God, *you're* pregnant."

"Don't be silly." Phoebe put her hands on her belly, which was as flat as mine was round. "Guess again."

"Umm, I don't know. Is it in the house?"

"No."

"No? Is it out in your car?"

"Nope. It's on the front porch."

"Why, is it too heavy for you to carry into the house?"

"Just go get it," Phoebe said, steering me by the shoulders. I opened the front door, and there on the porch sat the cutest, sweetest, tiniest, most adorable black-and-white, blue-eyed puppy you ever saw. I scooped him up and actually started bawling, which I immediately blamed on my hormones, but I don't think I fooled Phoebe one bit.

"He's a Harlequin Great Dane," Phoebe told me once I'd managed to calm down long enough to carry the puppy inside, where he promptly peed on the living room floor.

"A Great Dane?" I was shocked all over again. "Phoebe, he's going to weigh over a hundred pounds."

"I know," Phoebe said, grinning like this was the best news she'd ever heard. "I figured the bigger the dog, the more you'd know how much I love you."

So there we were, two girls, a kid, and a dog. Well, the kid wasn't there yet but soon would be. Phoebe cleared out all the junk that was collecting dust in our second bedroom, painted it yellow, and filled it with all kinds of baby stuff: a crib with an animal mobile hanging over it, a changing table with a poster of a lamb on the wall next to it, a trunk of toys, a shelf of books, a bureau filled with miniature clothes. I didn't help much; I was too busy training Spot, our overgrown puppy, to sit, stay, come, and most importantly, not crap on the carpet. And besides, I thought Phoebe would feel more a part of things if she was in charge of getting the house ready for little Miracle Growth, as she had dubbed our offspring. We still hadn't decided on a name (and since I was the one to pick out our dog's less-than-original moniker, Phoebe was a little worried), so Phoebe called the baby all sorts of things. Tiny Dancer, Small Potatoes, Buried Treasure, Tweetie Pie. I didn't call the kid much of anything; despite the hard and fast evidence of my growing abdomen, I was still half in denial that something alive and soon to be kicking was growing inside me.

One night when I was just starting my second trimester, Phoebe came home with several books of baby names. I moved over to make room for her next to me on the couch and wrestled with Spot over his chew toy while Phoebe studied page after page. Phoebe had let out a long sigh of relief when I got to my fourth month, since, according to the endless books she'd read on the subject, the first trimester is an absolute minefield of dangers. In fact, many mothers-to-be don't even tell anyone they're pregnant until they've made it to their twelfth week. But now that I was safely out of the woods, we were free to spread the word. We were also free to bond with the kid, though Phoebe had wasted no time on that, becoming completely attached the second I'd told her. As for me, well, that was another story. The little monster, which is how I thought of the creature inside me, was nothing but trouble, causing me heartburn, indigestion, exhaustion, headaches, and a set of extremely ugly varicose veins behind my left knee. Who could bond with such a bad seed? I tried to keep my complaints to myself, but I was hardly successful. Phoebe thought if the beast had a name, I'd soften up a bit.

"I think we should pick a name that'll work for a boy or a girl," Phoebe said, looking up from her reading, "so we can start using it right away." (Phoebe was adamant about not knowing the child's sex until the day I gave birth.) "And besides," Phoebe, ever the progressive, added, "what if our kid grows up to be transgendered?"

I had to say, I'd never thought of that, but since Phoebe brought it up I let her run some names by me: Pat. Chris. Dana. I wasn't crazy about any of them.

"Too bad Robin's already taken," I said as Phoebe pored over the books in her lap.

"Robin..." Phoebe repeated, thumbing through the R's. "Hey,

did you know your name, in addition to being a bird, means 'shining fame'?"

"Oh, so this isn't a pregnant glow?" I pointed to my face and sat up clumsily, trying to negotiate my blooming belly. "Drop it," I said to Spot, who had just brought me his favorite toy. "Hey, I've got it." I tossed the slimy tennis ball across the carpet and turned back to Phoebe. "Let's give the kid a bird name too. Like Phoebe. Or Robin."

"OK," Phoebe laughed. "How about Red-Winged Blackbird? Or Yellow-Bellied Sapsucker?"

"No, Phoebe, I'm serious." I don't know why I suddenly cared so much all of a sudden, but I did. "Let's see." I stroked Spot's head absently and stared out the window, as if some feathered friend would fly by with the answer in its beak. "Let's go through the alphabet. Albatross. Bluebird. Cardinal…"

"Dodo…"

I ignored her. "What about Dove? Or Finch? Grackle?" Phoebe rolled her eyes, but I continued. "Heron, Ibis, Jay…hey, Jay's not bad. What do you think?"

"Eh."

"OK, let's see. I can't think of anything that starts with K, can you?" Phoebe shook her head. "All right, let's skip it for now. Lark, Magpie…"

"Lark. I kind of like that," Phoebe said, surprising me. "You know, happy as a lark." She looked it up in her baby books but, not finding it, got up to get a dictionary. Spot leapt onto the now vacant left side of the couch and snuggled beside me.

"Listen to this, Robin." Phoebe was so excited she didn't even yell at Spot to get off the sofa. "Lark," she read out loud. "One: a merry, carefree adventure. Two: innocent or good-natured mischief. Three: to have fun, frolic, romp. I think it's perfect."

"I don't know." I pretended to frown. "I was starting to like Dodo."

"You dodo." Phoebe grabbed a pillow off the couch and bonked me over the head with it. I retaliated, and a rousing pillow fight ensued, followed by a fun-filled frolicking romp. Phoebe was definitely happy as a lark that day and for many days afterward. I, on the other hand, was up, down, and sideways. My moods, like most pregnant women's, were all over the map, but for the most part I guess I could say I was content. Phoebe was happy, and that's why I was doing this, right? In a few months it would be over, my baby would have her baby, and I'd have my life back. At least that was the plan. And then, right when I was hitting the home stretch, the trouble began.

It was early evening and I was home alone—Phoebe was working extra hours, figuring we'd need the dough. I had just come in from taking Spot for his walk. Or rather, I had just come in from having Spot, who could easily be mistaken for a Holstein cow at this point, take me for a walk. It was pretty hard to tell just who the alpha dog was between the two of us. Phoebe had insisted, after talking to someone who knew someone who knew someone whose shoulder had been dislocated when her dog pulled too hard on its leash, that I take Spot to dog obedience school. And my big kahuna of a puppy (eighty-five pounds and counting) had done me proud. But sometimes lessons were tossed out the window when, for example, a squirrel crossed our path, like one had done right at the end of the street earlier. Spot had given me a run for my money, but with my extra weight behind me I'd managed to rein him back.

Spot was panting on the cool kitchen floor, and I was sprawled on the living room couch. Though spring had just ended a few weeks before, the temperature was already inching its way toward the ninety-degree mark. I sure wasn't looking forward to spending my last month big as a house during the—excuse me, Spot—dog days of summer. Especially since my furnace had gone haywire over the past few weeks and my temperature was usually somewhere between roasting and boiling. It was especially hard for me at night, when I couldn't get comfortable anyway, having always slept on my stomach, which was impossible now. So between having to sleep on my side and sweating like a pig even with just a sheet covering Phoebe and me, I was one unhappy camper. Add to that my perpetual backache, frequent farting, and urge to pee every two seconds, and it was no wonder I was getting grumpier by the minute.

The previous night I had just about had it, because on top of all the lovely symptoms I've already described I was hit with some wicked stomach cramps, accompanied by a stinking bout of diarrhea that just about killed me. After I dragged my blimp of a body off the toilet and managed to clean myself up, I went to find Phoebe, who was in the baby's room sitting in our brand new rocker, content as can be.

"Listen," I snarled at her, "when Lark finally does arrive, you can have him."

"Or her." Phoebe got up and offered me the rocker.

"Whatever." I wasn't in a politically correct mood. "Listen, when all this is over I'll have carried Lark around for nine whole months, so I say you carry Lark around for the next nine."

"Fine by me," Phoebe said, opening her arms. "I'd take him now if I could."

"Or her," I said, and Phoebe smiled.

I wished I could give Lark to Phoebe this very minute, but Phoebe was still working and Lark was still tucked in tight. Or so I thought. As I lay there, too lazy to get up and pour myself some iced tea, I felt some fluid leak down my thigh. *Oh, shit,* I thought, *did I pee on the couch? What kind of role-modeling is this for Spot?* I got up to head into the bathroom yet again, but the fluid stopped. So I lay back down, but it started up again.

"I'm fucking leaking," I said aloud, and then, since I was so befuddled with hormones, my next thought was, *Phoebe's going to kill me if I ruin these pants.* If you think you have a hard time buying clothes, try being a pregnant butch. Luckily, Phoebe is a whiz with a needle and thread and made me a closetful of drawstring trousers. It took me a full five minutes to stop worrying about my pants and start worrying about the baby. Had my water broke? It couldn't have; it was at least a month too early. I got up slowly and went into the bedroom, where Phoebe had about a million books on pregnancy. Shit, there it was. Signs of premature labor: cramps with or without diarrhea—check. Lower back pain—check. Rupture of membranes—check, check, check. Every time I stood up, the fluid stopped pouring out of me, but when I lay down again, the floodgates opened. Was I in labor or wasn't I? Only my doctor would know for sure.

Before I phoned the doctor, I called Phoebe at work. "But it's too early," she said, like she was telling me something I didn't already know.

"Just come home," I told her, keeping my voice as neutral as possible. Then I called my doctor, who said: Go directly to the hospital. Do not pass go. Do not collect two hundred dollars. *C'mon, Phoebe, move it,* I prayed silently as I waited for her to pull into the driveway. Spot, sensing something was up, came into the bedroom and rested his great head on the mattress beside me.

"Spot, I think I'm going to have a baby," I said, stroking him. "The real thing. Not like Dodo." My sweet puppy's ears tilted forward at the name of the doll Phoebe had brought home for us to cuddle with in order for Spot to get used to the idea of having an infant in the house. "This is the real thing, Spot. Lark is going to laugh and cry and walk and talk...I hope." Suddenly the thought that it was too late to turn back, coupled with the terror that there might be something wrong with the baby, hit me like a sucker punch. What if Lark wasn't all right? But how could that be? My doctor said I was healthy as a horse. I'd done everything by the book: completely stopped drinking, ate the so-healthy-they-made-me-even-more-nauseous meals Phoebe had cooked for me, even took a pregnant women's exercise class. I didn't smoke (Phoebe wouldn't even let me enter a room in which someone was puffing away), I left the kitchen when the microwave was on, and the biggest problem I'd had besides the nausea, headaches, varicose veins, and deadly gas was constant and wicked heartburn. I'd gotten regular checkups, and the amniocentesis had come out perfectly normal. *If I fuck this up, Phoebe will kill me* ran through my mind as the other mother of my child finally ran through the door.

"Robin, what's going on?" she asked, but there was no time to explain. The backache I'd had all morning was getting worse and spreading to my abdomen. I felt like I was going to either lay the biggest fart of the century or soil myself with diarrhea just like a baby—just like our baby—surely would do time and time again, as soon as said *bambino* was safely in our arms. Right? Right? I kept begging Phoebe for reassurance as we sped toward the hospital.

"Of course everything's fine," Phoebe said, not daring to take her eyes off the road as she pushed the pedal to the metal. "Just relax, Robin." *Yeah, right.*

If you're like me, you can't stand the sight of blood, so I'll spare you the gory details and give you just the facts: I was in labor, and our daughter Lark was born prematurely. Turned out I had an "incompetent cervix," which is not a harsh judgment on my inept plumbing but an actual medical term. My doctor didn't pick up on it because it's hard to diagnosis until after a woman has already had a miscarriage or gone through premature labor. In other words, hindsight is 20-20. What happens, basically, is that your cervix opens before it's supposed to and your fluid leaks out. But if you stand up, the baby's head moves down to cover the opening and stop it. Like a little plug.

Phoebe said Lark was just in a big old hurry to come out into the world and meet us. And of course our child would be precocious and do everything ahead of schedule. Including race out into the world. I thought Lark was probably just sick and tired of being inside her bumpy, grumpy, non-lovey-dovey blob of a birth mother. *If only I had been kinder to her,* I thought, as I lay there in bed trying to gather my strength (I'd been in labor for sixteen hours). Would it have killed me to sing to her, talk to her, or at least stop complaining every time she gave me a good swift kick in the ribs? Lark wasn't an idiot. She wanted to make her great escape and meet the mommy who crooned to her night after night, holding one fist up to her ear and speaking into my protruding belly button like it was the mouthpiece of an old-fashioned telephone. "Hello, little Lark," Phoebe would say in a voice chock-full of love. "How's my sweet baby today?" she'd ask, turning her head so her ear lay flat against my belly, listening for a reply. Who wouldn't be in a rush to lay eyes on the woman who belonged to that sweet, gentle voice?

The nurse had whisked Lark out of the delivery room right away and brought her to wherever they bring preemies, barely pausing long enough to tell us she was a girl. They had to do all kinds of things to her: make sure her temperature and her glucose were stable, check for respiratory distress, anemia, infection, things like that. Frankly, I only half-listened to what Phoebe was telling me. All I wanted to do was sleep.

After I rested for a few…minutes? hours?—hospital time has a mind of its own—the nurse came in and said we could go and see Lark, but I told Phoebe to go ahead. I was too tired. Which wasn't entirely true, but I wanted to give the two of them a chance to bond. After all, I still wasn't sure I wanted to be a parent. That hadn't changed, despite everything I'd gone through. I thought of myself as Lark's birth mother, but instead of giving her up for adoption I was giving her up to Phoebe, who decided that if I was Lark's birth mother she was Lark's "earth mother."

I must have drifted back to sleep because the next thing I knew Phoebe was shaking me awake, her mouth curved into a huge smile, though tears were raining down her face. "Robin, she's so amazing," Phoebe said, taking both my hands and squeezing them. *Who?* I thought for a groggy moment, but then I remembered where I was. "She's really, really tiny, but she has all her fingers and toes, and the nurse says she thinks she's going to be fine."

"But there's a chance she won't be," I said, in an odd, flat tone.

"Only a *slight* chance, Robin. She's pretty strong, small as she is, and I'm sure she's stubborn too, especially if she takes after you. She just has to gain some weight," Phoebe said, laughing, "just like this roommate I had when I was at the eating disorder clinic—Belinda, her name was—she probably didn't weigh much more than little Lark weighs right now, but she pulled out of it—"

"Phoebe, you're babbling." I held my hand up to stop the words that were pouring out of her mouth.

"Oh. Sorry." Phoebe stopped abruptly but then started up again. "I'm just so happy, Robin. Aren't you happy? Happy as a lark. Happy as a clam. Happy as a pig in shit. Happy as a—"

"Phoebe," I cut her off again.

"What's the matter?"

"I'm tired. I didn't get any sleep last night, remember?"

"I know. I didn't either."

"Hey." Suddenly I had a brilliant idea. "Can you get me something to drink?"

"Sure. How about some apple juice?"

"Whatever."

"I'll be right back. Don't go anywhere." Phoebe dashed out and by the time she got back I had closed my eyes again. I wasn't really asleep, and I felt bad, but the truth was, her giddy euphoria was getting on my nerves. Maybe I had an instant case of post-partum depression, or maybe I'm just a callous son of a bitch, but I was feeling about as maternal as Spot's soggy, chewed-up tennis ball. Call me a cad, but at that moment I had no desire to see Lark at all. What I really wanted to do was get up, get dressed, go home, and take Spot for a walk around the block. I had given Phoebe what she wanted, hadn't I? Now it was time for what I wanted: I wanted my life back.

What's so special about a baby anyway? I wondered as I lay there pretending to doze. Every baby just grew up to become a person, and tell me the truth: How many people do you know who are really and truly special? Every asshole who cuts you off in traffic, every rude bastard who bumps into you on the street and doesn't say excuse me, every bored-stiff, gum-snapping, don't-do-me-any-favors teenage salesclerk who ignores you at the mall—all of them started out being somebody's baby. So what's the big deal?

Phoebe should have known to leave well enough alone, but she was too excited. "Wake up, Mommy," she whispered, poking my arm with a cold bottle of juice.

"Don't call me Mommy," I said with as much emotion as the day so long ago when Phoebe scolded me for calling her "baby." I still didn't know what Lark was going to call me, but it sure wasn't going to be Mommy. A mommy with a buzz cut? Give me a break.

"The doctor says you can go home tomorrow, but Lark has to stay here until she gains weight." Phoebe's chin trembled, but she held on and didn't cry. "But we can see her every day and talk to her, sing to her..."

"How's Spot?" By the clock on the opposite wall, I saw that it was way past my boy's suppertime.

"Spot?" Phoebe said his name like a foreign word she couldn't quite wrap her mouth around. "Fine, I guess."

"What do you mean, you guess?"

"Robin, you just had a baby, for God's sake. Spot is a dog. An animal. I'm sure he's fine."

"He'd better be," I growled. All of a sudden it was too much of an effort to hide my grouchiness.

"C'mon, Robin. Let's go up and see Lark." Phoebe pulled back the sheet covering me, but I pulled it back.

"Leave me alone," I snapped, turning over on my side.

"What's the matter with you?" Phoebe asked, but since I didn't know I couldn't answer her. I just wanted her and Lark and everyone else in the world to go away.

But Phoebe, of course, wasn't going anywhere. "What's the matter with you?" she asked again. "Don't you even want to see your own child?"

"Phoebe, what's the big rush? We'll be seeing her every day for the rest of our lives."

"Oh, my God." Her voice dropped to a whisper. "You are acting really weird, Robin. You don't even want to see her? What kind of mother are you?"

"First of all, I'm not a mother, I'm a parent." I reminded her of what we had agreed upon. "And second of all, lots of mothers aren't interested in their babies. Some give them up for adoption. Some leave them in bus stations. Some flush them down the toilet. Some…"

Phoebe stared at me, shocked. "I don't even know you anymore," she said, leaving my room to go back to the nursery again.

"…abandon their daughter and don't speak to her again unless they mistake her for her brother," I said to myself. Christ, did I have to be thinking about my mother now on top of everything else I was going through?

I was sitting up, staring glumly out the darkened window, when Phoebe came back. "The doctor said it's normal for some new mothers—parents—to respond with distance to a baby in distress." She sounded like a textbook.

"So I'm normal." I crossed my arms and glared at her. "Don't try to change me."

"I'm going home." Phoebe bent down to kiss my stubborn mouth. "I'll be back first thing in the morning. Do you want me to bring you anything?"

Spot, I thought, but even I couldn't be cruel enough to say that. So I stayed quiet and Phoebe left me alone.

But wouldn't you know it, the night nurse didn't. "Nurse Nellie here," announced a big teddy bear of a man who looked forty (and I'm sure he'd say fabulous) as he breezed into the room. "And how's Mommy doing?" he asked, grabbing the chart at the foot of my bed.

"Christ, we *are* everywhere." I shook my head. "I'm not Mommy," I informed my new lady in waiting, whose nametag read "Lee."

"Well, you sure ain't Daddy." Lee pointed to the front of my hospital gown, which had two round, wet stains on it.

"What the hell?"

"You're leaking, Elsie. We're going to have to get you a breast pump."

"A what? Christ," I said again. "I thought my job was over."

"Your job is just beginning, honey." Lee shook down a thermometer and motioned for me to sit up. "You've signed on for the rest of your life, missy. No weekends off. No holidays. No paid vacations. You're in it for the long haul, pal. Especially with a girl. So, who does she look like, you or Papa?"

"There is no Papa," I told him. "My girlfriend and I used 'man in a can.'" When Lee just looked at me blankly, I explained. "You know. A sperm donor."

"Eek!" Lee put his hand over his heart and then tsk-tsked.

"What a waste. Oh, well. So, does the baby look like you?"

"I don't know."

"I guess it's too early to tell, huh? Especially with a preemie."

"No, it's not that. I haven't seen her yet."

"What?" Lee gasped and put his hand over his heart again. "Are you crazy, girlfriend? Get out of that bed. C'mon, now, you're getting up."

"But it's nighttime," I whimpered, like a sleepy little girl. "And don't you have to take my temperature?"

Lee stuck his thermometer in my mouth and pulled it out two seconds later. "Perfectly normal," he pronounced, without even glancing at it. "And it doesn't matter if it's day or night. Babies don't know the difference. All they know is asleep and awake. So, c'mon."

"All right. I might as well get it over with."

"What?" This time Lee clasped both hands up to his chest. "Are you trying to give me a heart attack? What kind of mother are you?"

For the third time that day I said, loudly and clearly, "I am not a mother. I am a parent."

But that only made Lee laugh. "Hey, you know what they say: If it looks like a duck and walks like a duck and quacks like a duck..." When I didn't respond, Lee enlightened me. "Listen, you can call yourself Old Father Time for all I care and it still won't matter—the baby's going to treat you like her mother. Especially when you give her some of that." He nodded to the front of my soggy gown.

"The baby has a mother," I told Lee, who handed me some terry cloth slippers. "Her name is Phoebe."

"Auburn hair, blue eyes, hubba-hubba-hubba?" Lee moved his hands through the air outlining the shape of an exaggerated hourglass figure.

"Yep."

"Ooh, Mama. Oops, sorry," Lee cringed as I glared at him. "I saw her when I first started my shift. Wow. That's some chick you got there."

"Don't I know it," I mumbled. "If it wasn't for that chick, I wouldn't be here in the first place."

"OK, OK. Time for a chat." Now that he had finally gotten me sitting up, Lee pushed me back down against my pillow. "I was the star pupil in my psych class, and you are one classic case, baby. Now, tell me what's going on for real. I won't even charge you my usual eighty-five bucks an hour."

I sighed and told Lee everything. Took it from the top and went right down the line: how Phoebe and I met and fell in love, her insemination trials and tribulations, the article I'd read that changed our lives, Spot, my mother... I'm sure it was way more than he wanted to know, but Lee was great. He spent so much time with me, I'm sure he could have lost his job, but as he said, "If we don't take care of the family, who the hell will?" I'm sure Lee had some sad tale of his own to tell—I could see it in his eyes—but for now I was center stage. Until I was done. Then he stepped into the spotlight.

"OK, Robin Redbreast, listen up. This is a multiple-choice test. Are you: (a) feeling guilty you disappointed Phoebe by delivering an underweight baby ahead of schedule who might have some problems; (b) afraid Lark isn't going to make it so you don't want to get too attached until you know for sure; (c) afraid Phoebe will love Lark more than she loves you; (d) afraid Lark will love Phoebe more than she'll love you; (e) afraid Spot will love Lark more than he loves you; (f) you can stop me any time here—afraid that..."

"OK, stop." My head was spinning as Lee's words whirled through my mind.

"Seriously," Lee nodded encouragement, "which one is it?"

"None of the above," I said, then told him the truth. "I'm afraid Lark is going to grow up to hate me."

Lee leaned against the bed and folded his arms. "Why?"

"Because the apple does not fall far from the tree," I said. "Why wouldn't she hate me? I hate *my* mother." To my horror, as the soon as the words were out my eyes filled and I began to cry.

"I don't think you hate your mother," Lee said gently. He turned away for a minute, giving me time to compose myself. I was grateful he understood us butches and our pride.

"From everything you've told me," Lee continued, "I think you love your mother. That's the bitch of it, isn't it? If we could only hate them—"

"I knew it." I interrupted him. "Tell."

"Yeah, yeah, so what else is new?" Lee shrugged his shoulders like he really didn't care, but I knew he did. "Another queer kicked out by his immoral majority parents. Blah, blah, blah. Big deal."

"Damn right. Big fucking deal."

"Yeah, whatever. Anyway, as I was saying, it would be so easy if we could hate them. But we don't. We fucking love them. Despite everything. Don't we?"

It was hard to admit it, but I had to. "Yes. We do."

"Well, then, if we love our parents after all they've done to us, how can you think Lark will hate you when you haven't even had a chance to fuck her up yet?"

"Even though I really didn't want her and only did it for Phoebe?" My voice caught around Phoebe's name and cracked as though it would break.

"First of all, Lark doesn't know that." Lee handed me a tissue. "And second of all, you didn't not want *her*, personally. She wasn't real to you. She was just an idea, a concept. But as soon as you see her, you're going to fall in love with her. Trust me."

"But what if I don't? What if I'm really as heartless as my own mother?" My pride flew out the window and I began sobbing in earnest now. "What if I can't love her? What if she turns out to be a terrible daughter, just like me?"

Lee lifted my hand in his great big paw and squeezed it. "There are no terrible daughters. Of either gender," he said softly. "There are only terrible mothers."

"That's what Spot's teacher said the first day of class," I told him, still holding his hand. "He said, 'There are no bad dogs. There are only bad dog owners.'"

"Exactly," said Lee. "And the good news is, you were trained by the best. You know exactly what kind of mother you don't want to be like."

"Yeah, but the problem is I also don't know what kind of mother I *do* want to be like."

"You'll figure it out. What's that saying? 'Mothers are the invention of necessity'?"

"I think it's 'Necessity is the mother of invention.'"

"Whatever."

I smiled and Lee did too. I had a feeling we were going to be friends. "Hey," I looked into his eyes, "maybe Lark will need an uncle."

"Maybe," he said. "But I don't know if I'm man enough for the job. I think I'd be better as her fairy godmother."

I laughed. "I think she has enough mothers as it is," I said, surprising myself.

"Sounds like you're ready now." Lee let go of my hand. "Do you want me to come with you?"

"No, I think I want to go it alone," I said, getting to my feet.

"Ah, the stoic butch. Now I know you'll be all right."

I nodded, left the room, and headed down the hall before Lee had a chance to point me in the right direction of the nursery. But I flew to it like a homing pigeon, my breath and steps both quickening as soon as I turned the correct corner.

I stood outside at first, gathering my courage as I peeked through the window. There were several babies there, all sound asleep, but I knew Lark instantly. I don't know how I knew her, but I did. Mother's intuition maybe, or maybe something else. *She's already tamed me,* I thought as I stepped inside and tiptoed up to where she lay on her back, to study her hands, her feet, her face, her tiny, closed eyes. She was no bigger than a puppy, but still, even with her eyes shut, it was clear she was the most beautiful girl in the world. I couldn't wait for her to wake up, and when she did the nurse led me to a rocking chair and showed me how to hold her. I still had her on my lap the next morning when Phoebe entered the nursery, stopped dead in her tracks, and then ran toward us, laughing and crying, her arms open wide.

Mary Vazquez

About the Author

Lesléa Newman is an award-winning author and editor whose 35 books include *Girls Will Be Girls, Out of the Closet and Nothing to Wear, The Femme Mystique, The Little Butch Book, Still Life With Buddy, My Lover Is a Woman: Contemporary Lesbian Love Poems, Pillow Talk: Lesbian Stories Between the Covers* (Volumes 1 and 2), and *Heather Has Two Mommies.* Her literary awards include fellowships from the Massachusetts Artists Foundation and the National Endowment for the Arts, a fiction-writing grant from the Money for Women/Barbara Deming Memorial Fund Inc., and two Pushcart Prize nominations. In addition, she was named second-place finalist in the Raymond Carver Short Story competition, and six of her books have been Lambda Literary Award finalists. A native New Yorker, she now makes her home in western Massachusetts. Visit her Web site at www.lesleanewman.com.